RASPUTIN'S LEGACY

LEE JACKSON

SEVERN RIVER
PUBLISHING

Severn River Publishing
www.SevernRiverBooks.com

This is a work of fiction. Names, characters, businesses, places, events and incidents are either the products of the author's imagination or used in a fictitious manner. Any resemblance to actual persons, living or dead, or actual events is purely coincidental.

ISBN: 978-1-64875-570-5 (Paperback)

PRAISE FOR RASPUTIN'S LEGACY

"Pure Gold! Atcho grabs you at the beginning, and won't let go."

— CARMINE ZOZZORA, PRODUCER OF DIE HARD
WITH A VENGEANCE AND COLOR OF NIGHT

"With this page-turning thriller, Lee connects the brooding mystic Rasputin to the Cold War, traces his dark influence into the present, and makes it relevant to today's churning world events. Stunning!"

— BILL THOMPSON, EDITOR OF STEPHEN KING'S
CARRIE AND JOHN GRISHAM'S THE FIRM

"Clearly one of the best books of historical fiction I have ever read. Extremely entertaining and educational at the same time."

— LIEUTENANT-GENERAL RICK LYNCH (RETIRED),
FORMER COMMANDING GENERAL, 3RD INFANTRY
DIVISION DURING THE SURGE IN IRAQ

"Wow! The story is gripping and plausible, the warning real. A must read."

— JOE GALLOWAY, NYT BESTSELLING AUTHOR OF WE
WERE SOLDIERS ONCE...AND YOUNG (ADAPTED TO A
MEL GIBSON MOVIE) AND WE ARE SOLDIERS STILL

"Riveting! Lee Jackson takes you on a thrilling ride through the intrigue of the Soviet Union as it raced toward its final days. Feel the fight of those reaching for freedom against the chaos brought on by Rasputin. Couldn't put it down."

— KRIS "TANTO" PARONTO, HERO OF BENGHAZI,
BESTSELLING AUTHOR OF THE RANGER WAY

ALSO BY LEE JACKSON

The Reluctant Assassin Series

The Reluctant Assassin

Rasputin's Legacy

Vortex: Berlin

Fahrenheit Kuwait

Target: New York

The After Dunkirk Series

After Dunkirk

Eagles Over Britain

Turning the Storm

The Giant Awakens

Riding the Tempest

Driving the Tide

Never miss a new release! Sign up to receive exclusive updates from author Lee Jackson.

severnriverbooks.com

Irene Fisk
The best teacher who ever lived.

Barbara Jackson
My wife and the other best teacher who ever lived.

Carmine Zozzora
My very patient and unexpected mentor in writing this book.

MAJOR CHARACTERS

ATCHO (Eduardo Xiquez Rodriguez de Arciniega)

Colonel General Borya: Yermolov, aka Govorov, aka Paul Clary

Grigori Yefimovich Rasputin: Legendary Russian Mystic

Sofia Stahl: Atcho's Fiancée

Burly: Retired CIA Officer

Anthony (Tony) Collins: Investigative Reporter

Tom Jakes: Newspaper Editor

Rafael Arteaga: Atcho's Long-Time Friend

Nestor Murin: Chairman of the KGB

Colonel Dmitri Drygin: KGB Officer

Major Ivan Chekov: KGB Officer

Jeloudov: Soviet Ambassador to Cuba

Aleksey: Former Rasputin Servant

Marcel: Aleksey's Grandson

Francine: Marcel's Wife

Millie Brown: Intelligence Analyst at US Embassy in Bern, Switzerland

Vassily Aznabaev: Soviet Ambassador to France

Colonel General Kutuzov: Regional Army Commanding General in Siberia

Lieutenant General Fierko: Commanding General of KGB Border Troops

Marat: Russian Tour Guide

Father Matfey: Priest at the Nevsky Cathedral in Novosibirsk

Lieutenant Colonel Zhukov: Soviet Pilot

Zane McFadden: CIA Station Chief in Moscow

PROLOGUE

30 December 1916 – St. Petersburg, Russia

On that freezing winter night, Grigori Yefimovich Rasputin came to what much of the Russian nobility regarded as his just end: he was murdered. A Russian nightmare had ended. The world's nightmare had just begun.

November 1988 – A village outside of Paris, France

The heavy smell of fish soup assaulted the CIA officer's nostrils. It came from two booths away. He had come into the tavern for a quiet drink before calling it a day, and had not expected to see the dark visage that scrutinized his own from that booth as he took his seat. He sucked in his breath, and quietly cursed himself for showing a rookie's surprise.

The man knew he had been recognized. He appeared to be the central figure among men sitting around him, and the CIA officer recognized most of them. They belonged to a loose sect of zealots who revered a shadowy figure from Russia's past, the mystic called Rasputin.

Sitting next to him was another smaller man the CIA officer did not know. He was older, but his bespectacled face was strikingly like the central figure, as though they could be related. That could be worrisome.

The presence of this group in the tavern with the sinister man in the booth seemed incongruous. The men had always seemed harmless, monitored only because of their ties to the former Imperial Russian royal family. And yet here they were, with him.

The CIA officer knew the last man well. He was KGB. Short, blond, and muscular. The two had shadowed each other for years across operations involving competing national interests in Paris. Now the Soviet operative stared at the American with a doleful, almost regretful expression.

The officer knew he had only minutes to report the existence of a man believed to be dead for over a year. The implications were unfathomable. He set his drink on the table, rose, and walked though the tavern. Even as he reached the exit he saw movement from the corner of his eye, and knew the blond KGB officer followed him.

1

December 1988 – Washington, DC

Atcho pulled his 9mm Glock from his belt and threw his full weight against his oak town house door. Pain shot through his shoulder as the door crashed in, and he heard an anguished cry from the dark interior.

He pulled back, and drove harder. The door slammed forward, propelling someone against the inner wall. Atcho drew back and drove again, and again. He heard a muffled groan.

Crouching low, he stepped inside and pointed his pistol into the shadows, listening for signs of an additional intruder. He heard none. The door swung shut, but did not catch. He chambered a round. The sharp *kerchink* of steel on steel resounded.

A dark figure hurtled through the shadows. Atcho fired. He heard a gasp, and then fell back as a fist caught his throat and knocked him against furniture. He gulped for air. The intruder clutched his hair, pulled his head up, and slammed a fist into his chin.

Atcho's temple pounded into the floor. He struggled to roll, but the man's legs had his arms pinned. Atcho tried to raise his pistol, but his assailant rose, kicked it from his hand, and ran through the dark living room and out the back door.

Atcho found his gun, and followed. When he arrived in the backyard, it was empty. He went into the alley and checked both ways, stopping to listen. Nothing.

He walked back into his living room. The front door swung open and another figure stood silhouetted in the porch light. Atcho raised his pistol.

"Don't shoot!" a voice called. "It's me, Burly."

Atcho loosened his grip on his gun only slightly. A light over the entrance flicked on, illuminating his big bald friend.

"What the hell?" Atcho groused. "I almost shot you." He cleared his pistol and replaced it in its holster.

Burly stepped into the room, a retired CIA officer in his late fifties whose athletic body had softened with plenty of Irish ale and probably only intermittent exercise. He glanced about, noting the displaced furniture. "What happened?"

Atcho told him. Burly examined the front door. "Whoever it was had to be professional," he said. "There are no marks on the lock and he knew the layout of your apartment."

"He's not all that professional," Atcho growled. "He didn't have a lookout, and I surprised him." He looked at Burly curiously. "What are you doing here?"

Burly ignored the question. He crossed the room and leaned over a scarlet blotch on the floor. "You hit him," he said. He followed a trail of small blood spots through the kitchen. "He's not hurt bad. You must have grazed him." He settled onto a plain beige couch and took in Atcho's dark complexion and the silver strands streaking his otherwise jet-black hair. Atcho was a few years younger than Burly, and even in a suit, he looked a superb athlete. "Are you going to call the police?"

"I'll file a report."

Burly looked around at the meager furnishings. "Sofia has her work cut out for her. When's the wedding?"

"Next month. I'm a little busy. Will you tell me why you're here?"

Burly arched his brows. "I'm a courier this time." His voice intoned reluctance. "I have a message for you." He leaned back, but did not alter his gaze. "An invitation."

"An invitation. You're retired."

"Yeah, I'm retired. The higher powers thought you might be more, uh," he searched for a word, "amenable, if I approached you."

Atcho showed his impatience. "I don't have time for chitchat."

"I know." Burly held up his palms in a placating gesture. "Ronald Reagan requests your presence with me, in New York."

"The president? Why? Why not here in DC?"

"Mikhail Gorbachev is there to address the United Nations. Reagan will be there to say goodbye before leaving office. It's the last time they'll be together officially. They're both grateful about what we did last year, and want to say so."

"The president wants to see us to say thank you—again? And Gorbachev too." He stood. "Why wouldn't he have a staff member arrange a meeting? Why send you?"

Burly looked nonplussed. "You need to go with me to New York. Sorry to call in a favor, but you need to do this. Get the cops over here and file a burglary report. I'll handle them. Then we both need to be on an early morning flight to New York."

* * *

They first flew to Denver. They had a layover for several hours before departing to New York City, with plenty of time to reflect. Atcho barely thought about the burglary; he kept nothing of value in his town house. But he was amused and irritated at the circuitous route that Burly had insisted they take to New York. *Too much cloak and dagger.*

Thoughts of his impending marriage brought images of Sofia to mind, and he smiled. She was a widow twelve years younger than he, and had worked for State Department Intelligence since before her marriage to her late husband.

He recalled when they had first met in the swelter of Havana. He, a just released political prisoner, gaunt, half-starved, unkempt, smelly. She, beautiful, elegant, kind. The twists of fortune that had brought them together, separated them, and then returned them to each other, were surreal; yet here they were, preparing to commit to a life together, *if only the world will leave us alone to live our lives.*

His thoughts returned to his current trip. *Maybe Reagan and Gorbachev just want to avoid the press.* By the time he landed, angst was just a dull sensation in the pit of his stomach.

2

When Atcho and Burly arrived at the Long Island estate where the two heads of state would meet, Secret Service agents ushered them into the mansion's library. Moments later, they heard a commotion outside the door. Burly opened it. A Secret Service agent blocked his passage, but did not obstruct his view. Atcho noticed that the two seemed to exchange glances. He joined Burly in the doorframe.

In the grand foyer beyond them, a throng of senior White House staffers, media luminaries, and camera crews were about to move past them like a wave of suited humanity. Ahead of them, President Ronald Reagan and Soviet Communist Party General Secretary Mikhail Gorbachev walked together, apparently trying to confer above the din.

The president always impressed Atcho. He had heard rumors of waning lucidity, and searched for signs, but today, Reagan seemed in full control. No handlers hovered nearby.

Just as the two men drew even with the library door, they both stopped and gazed about the foyer while Reagan pointed out various architectural pieces of interest. Then he looked in Atcho's direction, made eye contact, and nudged Gorbachev. The general secretary also made eye contact. They did the same with Burly.

Atcho stared back at them, fascinated by Gorbachev's elongated birthmark over his left eye. He recalled how it had appeared through the scope of a high-powered rifle. Then both men moved on, and Reagan commenced once again to draw Gorbachev's attention to points of interest.

The Secret Service agent moved in front of Atcho and Burly and closed the door, leaving them inside. Atcho turned on Burly. "That's it," he murmured. "You dragged me up here for that?"

Burly pulled him by the shoulder to a seating area, and they both sat down.

"What's going on?" Atcho demanded. "What does Reagan want?" He was not prepared for what Burly told him.

"Govorov's alive!" Atcho leaped from his chair and glared at Burly. "How is that possible? I buried a knife in his chest in Havana last year. Where is he? I'll finish the job."

Burly eyed him somberly. "Well, to start with," he said, and his reluctance was obvious. "His real name isn't Govorov. That was an alias he used for what KGB operatives called the 'Atcho Project.'" He left that to sink in.

Atcho's head jerked up. "Nice to get special attention," he said sarcastically. "What's his real name?"

"Officially, in Soviet intelligence circles, he is Borya Yermolov."

Atcho shook his head. Yermolov, the erstwhile Govorov, had masterminded a plot to assassinate General Secretary Gorbachev a year earlier. Atcho had stopped him in bloody hand-to-hand combat on a military base outside of Havana.

"We thought you'd killed him too," Burly went on. "So did the Soviets. We don't know where he is." He told Atcho that the Cuban Army had rushed Soviet General Yermolov to a hospital, and had worked overtime to save him. "You punctured his lung, but the knife glanced off a rib and missed his heart. He was comatose for a while." Burly spread his hands in a gesture of futility. "The Soviet Embassy reported him dead."

"And Moscow believed it?" Atcho groaned. "How could he escape Cuba without the KGB or the CIA knowing? Castro wouldn't jeopardize the billions of rubles the Soviets send him."

"Not overtly." Burly broke into a wry smile. "It's no secret he isn't fond of the general secretary's reforms. As long as he could keep Soviet aid flowing, Castro would help Yermolov."

Atcho paced. "I suppose they want me to go after him." He stared at the floor. "I just had my first full year of living normally. I'm not going back into a spook's life." He continued staring as he ruminated. "Yermolov won't come after me. He's too pragmatic for revenge. He has a plan and he's implementing it." He glanced at Burly. "Why would I look for trouble?"

"You just said you'd finish the job."

"I know what I said." Atcho's eyes glinted. "Tell me where he is, and I'll go after him. But I'm not going to spend months in shadows trying to find him. Get someone else to smoke him out."

"Got it," Burly rejoined. "Think of this. If the assassination had succeeded, the conspirators would be in power right now. Yermolov could be occupying a senior position in the KGB or on the Politburo."

"Not my problem. Reagan is the guy who called the Soviet Union an evil empire. Now he wants me to help save that government?" He walked across the room to a window, and stared past the scenery into nowhere. "The Soviet Union helped a dictator kill Cuba." He whirled around to face Burly. "You know what those people did to me personally—to my family." Burly watched him. Fury lined Atcho's face. "Give me one reason why I should care what happens to the Soviets."

Burly stood and put a hand on his shoulder. "I know, buddy. If you refuse, no one will blame you. But picture Yermolov's finger on the nuclear launch button. How safe would anyone be, including your family?"

Atcho stared at him. "They think he can do that? How? He can't have much of an organization."

Burly sighed. Before he could answer, Atcho cut in again. "Reagan and Gorbachev are together on this. Why can't the KGB go after him, or the CIA?"

"It's complicated. Those two agencies must be kept out. The idea is to head him off at the pass. Will you sit down and listen?"

Atcho crossed to the couch. "Fine. Let's hear it—only because you're my friend."

Burly exhaled, relieved. Before he could speak, Atcho interjected again. "There's no way the CIA won't pick up on this. Or the KGB. It's too explosive."

"You 're right. A CIA officer saw Yermolov last month in Paris. The officer was killed shortly after he filed his report."

"Killed?"

"Executed. We don't know who did the hit, but it was a professional job. No witnesses." He settled back in his chair. "For your information, the director of the CIA is in the loop. He's not happy about the way the president wants to handle this, but he'll live with it. We don't know who inside the KGB might support Yermolov."

Atcho mulled. "You keep talking about 'we.' Where do you fit?"

The big man exhaled. "I'll be your case officer."

Atcho looked startled. "I haven't accepted the mission. They assume a lot. I'm done with that life."

"That's why they brought me out of retirement.".

Atcho nodded as understanding seeped in. "They're leaning on our friendship. You're okay with that?"

"I made every argument you've given me, because I *am* your friend. I know where you've been. I'd tell them to go fly a kite if the stakes were not so high—but Atcho, they are." He let that sink in.

"I'll work from an office in the basement of the White House," Burly went on. He described the reporting structure, including daily briefings to the national security adviser, attended by the director of the CIA when so desired. "He'll provide support as necessary, on a close-hold basis." He nudged Atcho. "One other thing. If needed, I have direct access to the president."

Atcho stretched, and rubbed his eyes as weariness set in. "I need to think." He ambled over to one of the windows and looked out. It overlooked a grand driveway. Reagan and Gorbachev were shaking hands, and then both moved off to their respective limousines.

Atcho watched as their motorcades disappeared along the tree-lined driveway. He sensed the end of an era that had been survived. The future felt fraught with peril.

He remembered that after their rough-and-tumble summit at Reykjavik, an astonished world watched relations flourish between the two heads of state. Both men were charismatic and defended their national philosophies, yet they had forged a personal friendship that reduced tensions dominating relations between their countries.

Atcho recalled when the president stood in front of the Brandenburg Gate in Berlin and demanded, "Mr. Gorbachev, tear down this wall!" The wall still stood, but restrictions on personal freedoms had eased. East-West travel increased. Poland seemed on the verge of reasserting independence. Soviet states exercised greater autonomy.

Calm had settled over the Western hemisphere. Atcho felt it to be false. He perceived calamitous tensions. In Central and South America, civil wars ignited and abated with unsettling frequency. In the Soviet Union, satellite states clamored for independence. In the Mideast, a war that had raged between Iraq and Iran ended, with no finality. *Sooner or later, violence will touch our homes.*

3

At his house in Washington, DC early the next morning, Atcho exited the taxi that brought him from the airport after his flight from New York. Burly had taken a separate taxi home. They agreed to meet the next day. Right now, Atcho wanted time to be alone and think.

As he mounted the stairs at his front door, a man he did not recognize approached, and spoke quietly to him. "Mr. Xiquez?" Atcho turned to him.

"Mr. Xiquez, my name is Tony Collins. May I speak with you?"

Atcho was irritated. "Can it wait? I've been traveling. If you're selling something, no dice."

The man smiled. "This is no sales call." He pulled a business card from his pocket showing that he was a reporter for the *Washington Herald*. "I won't keep you long."

Atcho examined the card. He knew of Collins, a well-known investigative journalist; and searching his memory, he recalled having seen Collins on television a few times regarding some pressing issues, though none currently came to mind. He reminded Atcho of the TV character Columbo, down to his wrinkled overcoat, although with considerably less hair, and he wore horn-rimmed glasses.

After a moment, Atcho looked up. "Are you here about the burglary?

Nothing was taken. The police are handling it. I know probably less than you do."

"No." Collins was puzzled and surprised. "I haven't heard anything about a burglary. What can you tell me?"

"There's not much to tell. I walked in on him, but he got away. Probably a kid." Atcho dismissed the subject. "If it's not the burglary, did I do something wrong? Your reports are not usually about real estate investors, unless there's corruption."

"No," Collins reassured. "Nothing like that. I just have a few questions."

Atcho regarded him through tired eyes. "Come in. I'll make coffee. But this had better be important." Collins chuckled, and followed Atcho into the kitchen.

After filling the coffeemaker, Atcho sat at the breakfast table across from the reporter. "So, what do you want to know?"

"I saw the president honor you at the State of the Union Address last year," Collins began. "That was intriguing."

Atcho waved away the comment and studied Collins as the newspaperman took a dog-eared notebook and a Bic pen from his overcoat pocket.

He fumbled through his notes. "Let me tell you what I know about spotty pieces of information that seem to tie together, but I'm not sure how. Maybe you could help?"

"I'll try."

"Thanks. Last year, during Gorbachev's visit to the US, he was greeting the crowd along Pennsylvania Avenue when a car backfired."

Atcho tensed, but otherwise showed no expression. He saw that Collins watched him closely. "I remember. It caused a stir."

"As far as the public knew, that's all there was to it," Collins went on. "But on the same day, a man was found in a building down the street. He had been shot and killed. The bullet was fired from across the street."

"I never heard about that," Atcho lied. "That's interesting."

"I thought so too. But news of the body was kept from the public. I only learned of it recently through a confidential source. The guy is reliable, but couldn't provide corroboration."

Atcho was relieved, but only slightly. He sighed. "Get to the point. What does all this have to do with me?"

Collins held his steady gaze. "You own that building."

Atcho's eyes did not shift. "I own many buildings, including one on Pennsylvania Avenue. I'm in the real estate business. If a body was found as you say, who owns the building where the weapon was fired seems irrelevant."

"I thought so too. And the media reported the backfire as coincidental to being in front of your building. Frankly, I think the story was planted. How else would the media have made those connections? Anyway, on that very day you were sought for questioning about irregular real estate transactions."

"That's right. The police admitted a mistake." He shifted irritably. "You told me this interview isn't about real estate. You'd better have another reason for coming to my house early in the morning, or you can leave." His demeanor resembled that of a German shepherd giving warning.

Collins chuckled and leaned back in his chair. "You're as direct as they say. Believe me, this is not about real estate."

Atcho looked less than mollified.

"I remember that all-points bulletin about you," Collins continued. "In fact, except for one other event, I wouldn't have considered a possible link between the backfire and the search for you." He looked at his notes again. "Around eleven o'clock that night, a Cuban MiG flew into Andrews Air Force Base under fighter escort. It was there only long enough to refuel, and then took off again. Then, a helicopter from Andrews flew to the White House."

"That's interesting," Atcho rejoined, "but it falls in the realm of little green Martians. What does any of this have to do with me?"

Collins enunciated slowly. "My source tells me you were the sole passenger on the MiG and the helicopter."

Atcho's neck stiffened. He fought to remain deadpan. "Mr. Collins, you're going to be disappointed. First you have me shooting someone in downtown Washington; then you have me flying in from a hostile country a few hours later."

"I didn't say you'd shot anyone," Collins replied. "Did you?"

Atcho fought down an angry retort, and sat studying Collins in silence. At last he leaned forward in his chair and smiled. "I'm a businessman trying to make a living." He stood and indicated the door. "I'm sorry you won't have time for coffee."

Collins stood with an air of being accustomed to seeing interviews terminated abruptly. "One more question, sir." He handed Atcho a photograph. "I took this yesterday. It's not very clear, but that's you."

He waited while Atcho studied the photo. It showed him outside the Long Island estate. "Why were you at the estate where the president and the general secretary met yesterday? I was there, with the press. I saw the exchange of glances between you, Reagan, and Gorbachev."

Once again, Atcho struggled against a hostile impulse. He set his jaw, and pointed. "The door is that way."

"Got it." The reporter smiled ingratiatingly. "I'll check with the police about that burglary for you."

* * *

Atcho's mind worked furiously as he reviewed events. *Who else saw me on Long Island?*

He reached a discomforting conclusion. *Yermolov might already expect me.*

He called Burly. They had been fast friends since working together deep in the swamps of Cuba, while preparing for the US invasion at the Bay of Pigs. Although Burly had retired four years ago, he had taken personal risks last year to help bring Yermolov down.

Burly answered the phone. "I thought we were going to talk again tomorrow."

Atcho told him about his conversation with Collins. "I thought he was here about the burglary. I spilled that news. Turns out he thinks there was an assassination plot last year, and that I might have been involved in it."

"Not good," Burly groaned. "If he senses a story, he's like a bulldog on an ankle. He's a good guy, though. He's spiked stories that could hurt national interests. Can you come over?"

4

An hour later Atcho sat in Burly's living room.

"How can Yermolov expect to threaten Gorbachev?" Atcho asked. "Give me the details."

Burly furrowed his brow. "Have you studied the KGB?"

Atcho shook his head. "Not beyond what I did for them."

Burly nodded. "It answers to no one. It's kept in check by how much the national political leader dominates the KGB chief."

"You mean Gorbachev and whoever honchos the KGB now?"

"Yeah. The KGB boss is an oily guy, Nestor Murin. He has a solid lock on the KGB. He probably opposes Gorbachev's policies, the ones that set off the conspiracy last year. They translated to less KGB power. Murin would never be happy with that."

"I know the KGB has its own army. Is that threatened by the reforms?"

Burly nodded. "It's more than a million men strong, including armor and artillery, even an air force. It dominates the Party through its secret police." He cleared his throat. "If Yermolov had control of the KGB, he would make Stalin look like a little boy in short pants."

Atcho looked at him steadily. "You think he could do that?"

Burly shrugged. "Maybe as a successor to Murin. Remember, he spied for the Soviets for nearly three decades. He was big in the nuclear arms reduction talks." He paused. "The factions against the general secretary would welcome him with open arms."

"Why can't we sic the CIA on him?"

Burly shook his head. "Gorbachev asked Reagan for help to find Yermolov. Getting a US intelligence agency to operate in his own country would be treason."

"Why can't they put together a team from both the KGB and the CIA? Handpick 'em."

"Remember, officially our countries are enemies."

"But Reagan and Gorbachev are buds. This is a special case."

Burly took his time to reply. "Gorbachev doesn't know who in the KGB might help Yermolov. An individual both he and Reagan trust has to go after him."

"You mean me."

Burly nodded. He reached across and grasped Atcho by the shoulder. "You're the number-one guy on a very short list that they both trust." He gave Atcho a sidelong look. "Frankly, you're the only one on the list."

Atcho glanced around the room while he absorbed what Burly had said. "The threat is real," Burly continued. "We can't let Yermolov take over the second-most powerful country in the world."

"A coup?" Atcho's head jerked up. "That's farfetched, even with *his* past, maybe because of it. He's been in the US for most of his career. He couldn't have set up the networks he'd need."

Burly shrugged. "He has all the credentials. If the KGB likes him, he doesn't need much else. With what he knows, if all he does is get into the KGB or the nuclear establishment, he could wreak havoc."

Awareness dawned in Atcho's eyes. He spoke low and slow as his thought developed. "If I get caught, there won't be any cavalry riding to the rescue. That's why Reagan brought me to New York—to impress on me how crucial the mission is, with complete deniability."

Burly thrust his hands deep into his pockets. "That's right. You never spoke to either of them. They will both disavow you." He studied Atcho's face as if to discern whether he fully understood.

Atcho's eyes narrowed. "Got it. Has Yermolov made contact inside the Soviet Union?"

"Don't know. A good bet is that he has. He'll move cautiously. The CIA guy in Paris was monitoring a group with a lot of money. They might provide Yermolov safe haven until he's built a base of support inside the Soviet Union, and then finance his return."

"What's their skin in the game?"

Burly seemed reluctant to go into depth. "C'mon," Atcho urged. "I need to know this stuff."

The big man spoke deliberately. "Elections are coming up in the Soviet Union in four months. They're the first that resemble free elections since the Russian Revolution. Any disruption of voting could set up a return to a Stalin-like dictatorship, and you know what that could mean for US-Soviet relations."

"None of that explains why a group in Paris would help Yermolov."

Burly arched his eyebrows. He sat back as if reluctant to proceed. "We've known each other a long time, buddy. Stay with me. What I'm going to tell you is way out there."

"Get on with it."

Burly leaned toward Atcho. "Do you know anything about the fall of the tsar, or a Russian mystic called Rasputin?"

"I've heard of that Rasputin guy; and I know that the tsar's family was executed. What does that have to do with now?"

Burly told him, in detail. Atcho listened, stunned. "Yermolov," he whispered. "I suppose they want me to make sure he stays dead." As he spoke, visions swirled in his head, of unspeakably small torture boxes in dank, dark dungeons; of an impossible escape attempt under the unforgiving glare of an accursed full moon; of coerced training in a non-existent camp outside of Moscow; of years lost while separated from his beloved daughter. *Would I risk that again?*

Burly exhaled slowly. "I'm your friend. Believe that, even if I'm the guy sending you into harm's way." His reluctance to say more was palpable. "Reagan wants him alive."

Atcho's disbelief showed. "You can't be serious. Reagan wants me to bring Yermolov back to Washington?"

Burly shrugged. "We need to know the damage he's done, and we can't allow him to pass more military secrets to the Soviets. But if you can't catch him, kill him. Your call."

Atcho closed his eyes and leaned his head back. "Does Gorbachev know about that part of the mission?"

"No."

Atcho sat back in his chair, deep in thought. After some moments, he lifted his head and looked at Burly. "Anything on the burglary at my house?"

"Yeah." Burly was somber. He reached into his pocket, pulled out several small objects, and held them in his open palm. "The cops think it was a burglary, but my guys did a sweep of your apartment. Whoever it was planted these bugs there."

Atcho stared at the listening devices. "So, someone is already on to this mission," he said slowly.

"Maybe. The cops don't know about the bugs. I'll get them to downplay the burglary. Maybe that'll keep Collins from going down that rabbit hole."

Atcho stood. He felt fatigue seeping into his bones. "We can talk about this again tomorrow. I'll give you my answer then."

5

After leaving Atcho's town house, Collins stopped by the police station. Finding the officer who answered the call and made the report took a while. As Atcho had indicated, there was not much to tell.

"We don't know who the burglar was, and he got away." The officer laughed. "The resident had to travel, so some retired CIA guy handled things for him." That piqued Collins' curiosity, but just then, the officer's phone rang. While he listened to his caller, he looked up at the reporter sharply, and when he hung up, he was in a hurry to be rid of Collins. "Sorry, I gotta go."

Collins wanted to find out more about this retired CIA officer, so he called Atcho's office. His secretary told him that Atcho was at the library. That surprised Collins. He had thought Atcho might have stayed home to rest, but go to the library? Collins drove over and found Atcho engrossed in a book.

"Mr. Xiquez, how nice to see you again."

Atcho looked up and squinted against the light coming through the window behind the reporter. It took a second to recognize him. When he did, he slammed the book he had been reading down on the table.

Collins explained how he came to know his whereabouts. "I hope you don't mind." He leaned over to see the cover of the book.

Atcho was not pleased. "I'll have to give my secretary better instructions. You and I concluded our business this morning."

"I had another question." Collins sat down across from him, and picked up the book. It was a biography of Rasputin.

"That's an intriguing character," he remarked, setting it back down.

"Your question?" Atcho growled.

"I was wondering why you flew to Denver to go to New York. That seems a long way round the bend."

Atcho reacted angrily. "That's really none of your business."

"But you did go to New York."

Realizing his tacit admission, Atcho stared at Collins and started to rise.

"One more question," the reporter said. "What can you tell me about the retired CIA officer who took care of your burglary with the cops?"

Atcho almost bolted to his feet. Then, he leaned back and scrutinized the journalist. He felt fatigue settling in. "I did some checking on you. Your reputation is admirable." He spoke with reluctance. "I have a proposition."

"You checked me out?" Collins was startled. Then he looked skeptical. "You have a proposition?"

"Yes." Atcho's voice acquired an insistent note. "Postpone your investigation for five months. In return I'll give you an exclusive interview about a fascinating story."

Collins rubbed his eyes. "We're both tired from too much travel."

Atcho considered him, puzzled.

Collins contemplated how best to state what was on his mind. "Did you ever watch *High Noon*?"

Atcho stared at him, and then started to rise dismissively.

"No, wait," Collins entreated him. "I asked because you remind me of Gary Cooper's character in that movie. Strong, moral, restrained, and carrying the world on your shoulders. Yet, like him, you walk every step with the potential to unleash holy hell, any instant."

"What's your point?" Atcho asked irritably.

"Your credentials. They're incredible. West Point, Airborne Ranger, Cuban anti-Castro fighter," Collins recited. "Now, a real estate mogul and honored by the president." He paused in thought, and started to continue.

Atcho interrupted him. "How is that relevant?"

"Just an observation," Collins rejoined. He remained silent a moment, and then fixed a steady gaze on Atcho. "Something happened on Pennsylvania Avenue during Gorbachev's visit," he said, "and you're involved."

They watched each other.

Atcho broke the silence. "Where does that leave us?" he growled, anger flaring beneath the surface. "What do you think happened on Pennsylvania Avenue?"

Collins did not have a ready answer. He ran his fingers over the cover of Rasputin's biography. "I don't know, but I decide which stories I publish and when, and to be blunt, your proposal doesn't offer much."

He glanced at the book about Rasputin. Atcho's intense interest in it so soon after travel, when he was obviously very tired, seemed strange. Collins tucked the observation into the back of his mind. "Here's a counteroffer," he said. "If you tell me now how those events tie together—the building where the shot was fired, the MiG, your trip to New York –and if I judge there to be a national security risk, I'll hold on to the story until a better time."

Atcho glared at him.

"You can throw in the facts of that burglary," Collins pursued, "and tell me about the CIA guy."

Atcho slid his chair back. "You live in a fantasy world," he spat out. "I thought you might be interested in a factual story. Apparently, I was wrong." He grasped the book and stood.

Collins rose from his seat. "I have a job to do." He squinted at Atcho. "There's a story swirling around you. I'm going to find out what it is."

Atcho turned on his heel, leaving Collins standing alone. He went to the checkout counter, and signed out the Rasputin biography.

Collins watched as Atcho made his way to the street and hailed a cab. Then he went to the card catalog to get the specifics of the Rasputin book.

* * *

Atcho gave the taxi driver his home address. He craved sleep, but was angry that he had been seen on Long Island, and that he had confirmed for Collins that he was a principal in an important story.

He recalled how Burly had described the reporter: a bulldog. *And now with a fresh bone under his nose.* He tapped the driver on the shoulder and redirected him to Burly's house.

6

Burly was reading in his study when Atcho arrived. "What's up?" He gestured to a seat.

Holding nothing back, Atcho told Burly of his second meeting with "that reporter," including the new fact that Collins knew of a retired CIA officer "taking care of the burglary." The old intelligence pro listened intently until Atcho was finished, then sat quietly. At last, slowly, he raised his eyebrows. "You sure attract the tough ones. What do you think Collins has on his mind?"

"He'll investigate. That's what he does. I must consider worst case. He thinks there was an assassination attempt and that I might be one of the shooters. He won't back off, especially now that he thinks there's a CIA officer involved."

"Retired."

"That won't matter to Collins."

"How do you plan on handling it?"

"I haven't had time to put ideas together. I hoped you'd have some."

"Does that mean you're taking the mission?"

"Don't make a big deal out of it. Let's get on with it."

"Right. We have to step up our timetable and get you out of Collins' line of sight. He won't let go."

They agreed that Paris was the place to start. That was where Yermolov was seen and the location of the group that Burly suspected of financing him. Burly committed to coordinating arrangements and having the required documents for Atcho to travel early the next morning.

"You'll need an alias."

Atcho nodded. "And someone who knows his way around Russia, someone who can get me in and back out. I was thinking Ivan. Do you know where he is?"

Burly's eyes widened. "Ivan? He's KGB."

"I don't know anyone else who can get the job done."

"He's probably still here in Washington. I'll check it out. How do you expect to make this work?"

"Call Rafael Arteaga in Miami." He explained his idea.

Burly looked skeptical. "You think Rafael can pull that off?"

"He's been our go-to guy for a long time." He reminded Burly what the former resistance fighter had done at the Battle of the Bay of Pigs and how he had set up security around Atcho's family under the noses of the KGB and the Secret Service last year.

Burly protested. "You're proposing something that can't be done."

"Agreed," Atcho snapped, "and neither can this mission. If anyone can grab Ivan, it's Rafael. Then you'll send Ivan to me."

After several iterations of back and forth, Burly acceded. "I'll have things ready so you can leave in the morning, including someone to double for you on a flight to Austin. Collins will be watching. One other thing, you'll stay in a safe house in Paris with secure commo gear there. Make sure you talk to me only over that equipment. Here's the number to use." He handed Atcho a slip of paper with the address of the safe house.

After hashing through details, they drove to Sofia's house. "What are you going to tell her? She's still in the intelligence game, and I'm not her only contact. If I stonewall, she'll know something's up."

Atcho agreed. "There's a tech company in Austin that I've thought of buying. It produces a highly classified power source. The defense industry is crazy about the technology. I'll have to get involved up to my eyeballs to come up to speed technologically, including going there for due diligence. That could give me an alibi."

"That's interesting," Burly said. "What can you say about the company?"

"Not much. I had to sign my life away with nondisclosure agreements. The technology is still experimental. They only have two products. One is a power source. That's the moneymaker. It has the same applications as batteries, but is more reliable, costs less, and pound for pound, is a lot more powerful."

"That's huge," Burly said. "Sounds great, especially since Defense already wants it. What's the other product?"

"It's a limited use byproduct. It's a nuke exterminator. We call it the NukeX. If it works, it's incredible. The power source heats the NukeX thousands of degrees instantly, and it concentrates the heat through special alloys onto a target several inches below its base. Those alloys, how they concentrate the heat, and how the power source works are the nubs of their proprietary secret technology."

Burly's curiosity was piqued. "What's it used for?"

"You put it on the casing of a nuclear device, and it'll melt the parts needed to start the reaction to explode the bomb. It's supposed to do that without setting it off, even if it's been activated."

Burly was incredulous. "Nuclear missiles move fast. How do you get it on there?"

The corners of Atcho's mouth turned up slightly. "It's like the idea of a laser aimed at a missile, but there's been concern about small nuclear devices coming into the country in briefcases. If a bomb squad can get to the bomb in time, the NukeX is supposed to stop it from going off without opening it and cutting wires."

"Wow! That's amazing. How does it work?"

Atcho mulled how best to explain. "Think of a match. You strike it, and it immediately heats to somewhere around twenty-two hundred degrees Fahrenheit. Essentially, the NukeX strikes an electronic match and then maintains and focuses the heat at that high temperature through those alloys into the nuclear device, until you switch it off. It's easy to use, just a small handheld device that you slap on the bomb over the trigger mechanism, and hold it there. You push a button, and it melts the system enough to make it useless."

Burly thought about that. "Sounds plausible," he mused. "Anyway, it should give you an alibi to get out of town."

Atcho looked grim. "I know that Sofia came to you for help in the Yermolov thing last year when we all thought he was Govorov. Keep her out of this. Thankfully, she's an intelligence analyst, and not a field officer."

Burly looked at him sharply, but only nodded.

They shook hands in front of Sofia's house. As Burly's car disappeared around the corner, Atcho wondered if he would ever see his big friend again.

* * *

Late that afternoon, Atcho watched through Sofia's living room window as she parked her car and proceeded up the walkway. Dread mingled with the pleasure of seeing her.

Sofia spotted him, and her green eyes sparkled over a brilliant smile. She stepped up her pace. Her shoulder-length brown hair bounced around her finely sculpted face.

Atcho met her on the porch. "My Yale-educated beauty," he quipped as they embraced.

Sofia gave him a sidelong glance. "That was a strange greeting. What a surprise. I thought you'd be resting. How was your trip?"

Atcho chided himself for allowing anxiety to seep in. "It was a bust," he said, doing his best to be upbeat. "I was thinking that your background might be helpful in a new project, that's why the greeting. I talked with some people about that power source company in Austin. It's shaping up like a real opportunity."

Sofia stared at him momentarily, but said nothing.

"I'm flying out tomorrow to take a first look," he continued.

"So soon?" she asked, her face surprised.

"Yeah. The technology is complex, and several companies want it. If I don't get on it, I won't have a chance."

"But you're in the real estate business."

"I know. I've wanted to diversify out. My contacts in the defense industry make this a good entry point. The company is still small enough for me to absorb, but it will take a lot of time and study."

Sofia gazed at him quizzically, and then seemed to shake off her thoughts. "Let's make dinner." She took Atcho's hand and led him through tastefully appointed rooms to the kitchen. While they cooked, she studied him.

They dined by candlelight, and then sipped Château Margaux in front of the fireplace. Dim lights and the soft strains of a Cuban bolero warmed the romantic atmosphere.

"You're tense," Sofia interrupted the quiet. "What's wrong?"

He smiled. "I'm tired, and I'm concerned about this transaction. I might bite off more than I can chew." He almost mentioned the burglary, but thought better of it.

"How long will you be gone?"

Atcho breathed deeply. "I don't know, a few weeks at least. It'll probably take several trips."

Sofia sat erect. Her eyes searched his. "That'll push right up against our wedding."

Atcho nodded, dismayed. "We might have to postpone."

Sofia was silent. She studied his face. "Tell me what's going on." Her normally musical voice flattened to matter-of-fact.

"It's a complicated transaction," Atcho protested. "I've never been involved in one this big and with such advanced technology. I need to stay on top of it."

She searched his expression. "That makes no sense. You can't take off a day for your wedding? The honeymoon can wait."

Atcho shook his head.

Sofia continued to study him. Then she sat back abruptly. "Do you know who you're talking to?" When he began to object, she held up a hand. "Darling, I know you, your past, your attitudes, and what you can do. I saw your look when I came through the door. Something else is going on."

Atcho tried to hold her steady gaze, but felt himself faltering.

"There are only two times that something kept us apart," Sofia said slowly, "and both times you had similar attitudes." Her eyes opened wide. "It's Govorov again, isn't it?" She sat back. "That's it! I thought he was dead."

She doesn't know about Govorov's real name. When Atcho did not respond, she pulled back into silence. "You're not going to tell me anything, are you?"

she asked after a time. When Atcho still did not respond, she softened, but her face was resolute. She reached forward and stroked his face. "I'll be okay," she said. "Can I see you to the airport?"

"I'm afraid not," Atcho muttered, unnerved by her calmness.

Sofia leaned into him. For several minutes, neither spoke. Then Sofia straightened. She wiped moisture from one eye. "I'll take care of canceling the wedding arrangements. We can reset later. Let's not talk about this anymore now."

At dawn, Atcho rose and showered. When he was dressed, he went into the kitchen. Sofia was already there in a white terrycloth robe. Dark circles ringed her eyes. She stood and wrapped her arms around Atcho's neck. He felt her controlled sobs against his chest.

"I'm sorry," she said. "I promised myself I wouldn't do this."

A car honked. "That's my cab," Atcho said hoarsely.

"Where's your luggage?"

Atcho hesitated. "I'll pick it up on the way."

She looked askance, and then embraced him again. "Be careful," she whispered. "Come back to me safely."

"This is just a business transaction." He was gruff. He kissed her, and walked down to the car Burly had sent. Settling into the rear, he looked back at the town house. Sofia stood in the window. She waved to him, and then disappeared into the interior.

* * *

Two hours later, Atcho sank into a seat on a plane bound for New York. Prior to takeoff, he had changed his appearance in a VIP lounge. He walked out in time to see a double of himself move through the boarding gate of a plane bound for Austin, and watched in amusement as Collins followed, ticket in hand.

Atcho would change disguises and planes in New York. There, he boarded his flight to Paris. As the jet raced into the skies, he closed his eyes. *How did I get in the middle of this again?* His thoughts turned to Sofia. She had been too self-possessed for a woman who thought her world might be coming apart. He tried to sleep, but current pressures and past nightmares of his childhood home in flames and the stench of burning flesh roiled together to jar him awake every time he dozed. Paris seemed an eternity away.

* * *

At roughly the time that Atcho's plane took off across the Atlantic, Collins disembarked in Austin. Careful to recede into the crowd, he trailed the man he thought was Atcho through the broad corridors into the main lobby. To his confusion, the man did not seem hurried.

Fifteen minutes later, Collins cursed under his breath. When the man he thought was Atcho did not come out of a restroom and he found it empty, he knew he had been duped. He took the notebook from his pocket and reviewed his scribbling. Minutes later, his annoyance receded.

He called his editor, Tom Jakes, and explained what had just happened. "I wasn't even sure that was Atcho on Long Island," he told Jakes. "And those bits of information I gave him seemed farfetched. But he's trying to ditch me. And he's got very professional help." He chuckled.

"What do you think is going on?" Jakes asked.

"Something happened in DC when Gorbachev visited last time. The story got past the press. There's a feel of cover-up, and now there's this retired CIA guy involved."

"Do you suspect Atcho of trying to kill Gorbachev?"

"Or trying to cover up an attempt? I don't know. If Atcho were the assassin, why would he be at the estate with Reagan and Gorbachev? Doesn't add up."

A thought crossed Collins' mind. He explained his encounter with Atcho in the library the day before. "Find that author," he said, referring to Rasputin's biography. "Have someone read that book. I want to know about any references that might have current significance."

Two hours later, Jakes called back. "We located the author," he said, "but she was uncooperative. Someone else already inquired and must have spooked her. We'll keep working on it."

"Fine," he replied. "I'm coming back to Washington."

7

After Sofia saw Atcho's taxi drive off, she poured a cup of coffee and sipped it, staring absently. After some moments, she reached into her robe pocket and pulled out a crinkled piece of paper. She flattened it and gazed at the words, written in her own handwriting.

Dear Atcho,
Something isn't right. The other two times I saw you act as if the world were coming apart, Govorov was involved. I think he is again. I'm going to find out. You won't be alone again. All my love,
Sofia.

Intending for him to open the note while in flight, she had written it in a moment of emotion just before Atcho entered the kitchen. She had thrust it into her pocket as he walked through the door. *No use adding to his problems. It could get him killed.* She shredded it in the garbage disposal.

She called Burly. "What's going on? This is Sofia."

"What?" He sounded sleepy.

"Why did Atcho really go on that business trip to Austin?"

"I don't—"

"Don't tell me you don't know, and don't play games. This has something to do with Govorov again."

Burly exhaled. "This isn't a secure line."

"Fine," Sofia snapped. "I'll be at your place in twenty minutes."

Burly met her at the door. "Calm down. Atcho is on a business trip. I'm sure of it."

"Since when did he inform you of his business arrangements?" She shoved past him into his living room, turning to face him. She had changed clothes, but was still disheveled. "I know Atcho—his moods. I know when he's facing a business problem and when he's facing something overwhelming." Her eyes sharpened. "Incidentally, why would we need a secure line to talk about Atcho's business?"

Burly stared at her, speechless.

She stared back. "Here's what I've figured out. I don't know where Atcho went two days ago, but he didn't stay in Denver and he has no transactions there. I know his business. I checked. Furthermore, he had the same attitude that he had while that crap with Govorov was going on. Call it women's intuition with a heavy dose of intelligence experience." She stood feet apart, glaring. "Are you going to tell me what I need to know?"

Burly let the reference to Yermolov as Govorov go by. To do otherwise was to give credence to Sofia's theory. He shook his head. "I can't. You know that."

"Ah, so there is something." She saw that Burly looked flummoxed. "Now you hear me," she went on. "You tell whoever needs to know, that Atcho is not going to be out there alone this time. He rotted in prison for nineteen years, and operated by himself for another ten. We have no right to ask him to do more." Fury sparked in her eyes, and her cheeks flushed. She started toward the door.

"Where are you going?"

"To find answers. Obviously, I'm not going to get any here." She stopped. When she turned, emotion had disappeared, replaced by the poker face of a professional. "Atcho came home from somewhere with those same old fears, and that was right after Reagan and Gorbachev met in New York. He's probably the only guy that both trust. He knows Govorov.

Somehow all that ties together. If I'm right, you're the guy he'd come to. Am I close?"

Burly only stared.

"Will you at least tell me who's running the op?" Again, silence. She left.

* * *

Sofia listened to her phone ring at the same time that Collins tracked a decoy in Austin and Atcho flew over the Atlantic. She did not answer it. She had returned to her house, cleaned up, packed a few things, and was on her way out the door.

She paused to hear if a message would be left on her answering machine. There was, and she recognized Burly's voice. *That cinches it.* She walked out without answering. Minutes later, she drove onto a freeway bound for the suburbs.

Within two hours, Sofia had parked in a private rental garage and purchased a used automobile with cash. She registered the vehicle using an alias backed by an out-of-state driver's license. In her purse, she carried documents and major credit cards to further support that alias, and others.

Then she headed for a safe house in Alexandria. It was currently unoccupied; she had checked. She could stay there only long enough to make phone calls.

8

Eight men gathered around a table in the back room of a tavern in a village outside of Paris. On the table in front of them was a large serving bowl with fish soup. The heavy smell permeated the room. They spoke in hushed tones.

"Can you do it?" one asked. He directed his query to a slight man who sat at their center.

"It's already done," the man replied. "I made a few calls. Soviet security is incredibly weak on its nuclear stockpiles these days, and the black market is active. I'm not saying it was easy, but I managed to get enough of what I needed to do the job."

The men peered at him wide-eyed, almost fearful. "How soon can you have it ready?" one asked.

"I've been working on the design for months," he replied, "and I constructed the bomb over the last few weeks. All I needed was the nuclear material, and now that I have it, I'll finish within three days."

The room was deathly quiet as each man contemplated the implications. Then they murmured among themselves. "Is this something we should be doing?" one asked.

"Of course it is," another responded harshly. "The Soviets have ground us under their jackboots for seven decades. This is a chance to bring them down, and we'll probably never get another one."

"Or we could start a nuclear war that will kill everyone," another retorted.

"It won't come to that," the bomb-maker interjected. "This is a very small bomb, and the intent is to use it for blackmail."

"You say that," another broke in, "but both superpowers are ready to strike back. If Moscow thinks the US is involved, it's all over. And how much do you know about this distant cousin of yours, this Yermolov? Just a few months ago you didn't even know he existed."

"That's not quite true," the old man replied. "Rasputin left several illegitimate children around. We had heard rumors of Yermolov, but until he appeared, we had no means of confirming his existence. He provided impressive documentation."

"You know Aleksey won't go for this," another chimed in. "He's not an active follower of Rasputin despite having served him, and he owns the cabins and cars that Yermolov and his men are using."

"Then we'll just have to make sure Aleksey doesn't know," the bomb-maker replied. His voice took on a bitter note. "Look, we're all here because we were driven from our homes by this Soviet monstrosity. I saw Stalin's goons kill my parents in the Ukraine. We've lived our entire lives in exile because Germany sent Lenin to Moscow to keep Russia out of World War I. This is the first and maybe only chance we'll ever have to strike back, and I'm not going to pass it up."

"You're a nuclear physicist," another broke in. "How certain are you that this thing won't go off accidentally?"

"It could," came the grim reply. "None of Yermolov's men will know of its existence. It has some fail-safe mechanisms to prevent disarming it once it's set. That's so Yermolov can activate it remotely. But if someone finds it..." He shrugged. "I'll give it to Yermolov as soon as I finish it."

* * *

"Sir, you'd better see this."

Noting the urgency in his voice, Burly crossed his thrown-together headquarters in the basement of the White House. Computers and communications equipment lined the walls, and a team of people sat at monitors. His home phone had been forwarded.

The man who had spoken handed Burly several pages. "We just got this from NSA, the section that monitors commo between the Soviets and western Europe," he said. "A few days ago, they started catching telephone conversations between Paris and an area near a Soviet nuclear weapons depot. Look at this." He indicated highlighted text on the page.

Burly scanned through the pages. When he looked up, the blood had drained from his face. "Call the national security adviser," he ordered as he headed for the door. "Tell him I'm on my way." When he arrived, he barged directly into the adviser's office. "Sir," he said, "Yermolov might already have a nuclear bomb."

9

As soon as Atcho had cleared customs in Paris, he took a taxi to the safe house as Burly had instructed, and called him on the secure line. "I'm here. Did you speak to Sofia?"

"She came to see me right after you left," Burly replied. "She didn't believe the Austin transaction. She didn't answer my messages. She's on her own."

Atcho noticed an unusual level of tension in Burly's voice. "To do what?" he replied. "She doesn't know what I'm doing."

"She figures things out."

"What's to figure out?"

When Burly responded, his voice was quiet, his tone flat. "She works for us."

Dread seized Atcho's stomach. "You mean the CIA?"

"Yes."

Silence.

"Atcho, did you hear me?"

"How long have you known?"

"Since we worked together last year."

Atcho felt deadly calm. "Why wasn't I told?"

"You would have been informed before the wedding. Until then, there was no need for you to know. Now there is."

Atcho's head snapped back, his jaw set in a hard line. His mind flashed to the tender embraces of the night before. He felt betrayed by the woman he loved and by a respected friend, but this was no time for recriminations. "Is she an analyst or an operator?"

"She's a high-level analyst."

"So, she isn't trained for fieldwork."

"That's not accurate. She was an operator years ago. But…"

"No buts!" Atcho interrupted angrily. "She could get herself killed! Tell the president she has to be stopped, or I'm done."

"Listen to me," Burly butted in. "You need to know that Sofia was a top field officer. She can take care of herself, but we'll find her."

"Obviously, you know her better than I do." Atcho's fury was barely contained. "I need to think." He stood with his head pressed against the back of the booth. "What about Rafael and Ivan?" His mind raced while Burly told him that Rafael was closing in on the KGB officer. The Russian worked out of a shipping front-company for the KGB north of DC. Ivan should be in Paris within a week.

"What about the author of that Rasputin biography?"

"We called her and asked a few questions, but she wasn't much help. She feels obligated to protect the privacy of that group. We tracked down its location in Paris." He gave Atcho the address.

"Any news on Yermolov?"

There was none. "The president's not happy with the way things turned out. We had hoped to gather resources and do better planning before we launched."

"Got it," Atcho snapped. "You tell him I'll stay on the job for one week. If Sofia isn't found in that time, I'm coming home. I'll be in touch." He hung up without waiting for a response.

He tried to sleep, but his mind was plagued by the ironies of his changed life. Four days had passed since Burly showed up in his apartment with the president's message. Now, he was thousands of miles across the Atlantic, leading a shadowy existence and pursuing an enemy thought long dead. And the woman he would have married in less than a month was a stranger.

He felt the familiar pricking of nerves in his arms and legs, but finally dozed, his mind flayed by memories of happier times, and then danger and treachery. He dreamed of the thrill of galloping through sugarcane fields as a boy with his father on their prize horses. Then, almost immediately, his mind descended into the torment of his wife's death during childbirth; of the sight of his parents being consumed in fire only feet from him; of the haunting laughter of the man he had known as Govorov stealing away his little daughter; of the final humiliation, the defeat and his capture at the Bay of Pigs and subsequent cruel imprisonment. After each remembered horror, he awakened with a start, and moisture streamed down his face. He was alone again.

Then, fully awake, he thought of Collins, wondering if he would uncover additional information, or find support for what he thought he already knew. *What if he finds something solid to galvanize his activity; or worse yet, he decides to publish?* He hoped his decoy in Austin had worked.

Early the next afternoon, Atcho hailed a taxi and directed it to the address Burly had supplied. Scattered clouds hung in the sky.

When the driver indicated that they approached the destination, Atcho told him to drive past. He alighted two blocks farther on. With leaves swirling on the sidewalk and the cold December wind biting through his jacket, he circled the neighborhood on foot. He drew closer until he was across the street from the house. Several park benches lined the curb. Atcho sat down to observe.

The house was five hundred meters down a residential street from a commercial intersection. It was square and surrounded by a high fence with two gates: a driveway, and a pedestrian entry. Far from appearing sinister, the house blended into the peaceful neighborhood.

Atcho watched for half an hour. He had read enough of Rasputin's biography to be fascinated by the notion of a Christian cult that revered the memory of a sex-crazed mystic. Having expected a dark building with high walls and cowled, chanting fanatics, he found this peaceful setting disconcerting.

A car entered the driveway and parked. A young couple got out and carried bags of groceries into the house. A moment later they reappeared, followed by a toddler pushing a toy truck.

Atcho wondered if he had been given the correct address. He waited a few more minutes, then made his way back to the hotel.

"That is the place," Burly informed him on their next call. He told Atcho that the group was very private about its religious beliefs, but otherwise its members were normal in every way. "They might not even know what Yermolov is up to."

"Anything on Sofia?"

Burly sighed. "The president agrees that if Sofia can't be found, you should terminate the mission. They'll have to go another route."

"Doesn't the CIA or the State Department know where she is?"

"She took a leave of absence from the State Department, and no one at the Agency knows where she's gone. Reagan called the director into the Oval Office." He paused. "She totally vanished. She might be a little rusty, but she knows what she's doing."

"Tell the president I'll be on the next plane to Washington."

"Wait!" Burly exclaimed. "He ordered a full covert search. They have to do that; she has top clearances. When they find her, the director will bring her straight to the president. He sends a personal request that you stay on the job at least until the search is well underway. Then you won't need to repeat preparations."

Atcho mulled the situation. "All right, but speaking of wasted time, I'm twiddling my thumbs. I need Ivan."

"We're working on it. Ivan's accident will occur in three days."

"Fine. I'll keep watching the house."

"Before you go." Burly sounded reluctant, but urgent. "There's another issue. You need to meet with a courier. He'll contact you at the safe house."

Atcho felt suddenly wary. "What's that about?"

"I can't say. He'll explain."

"I've had it with spook games," Atcho blurted. "We talk about everything on secure lines? How will I even know him?"

"You'll have to trust me." Burly was clearly annoyed. "He'll know you. He'll ask about who you lost shortly after you and I first met."

Atcho's chest caught. He knew Burly referred to Juan, his childhood hero, family sugar-plantation foreman, and later his best friend and deputy in the fight against Castro. "All right," he said quietly. "I'll expect to hear from him."

After he hung up, he reflected on Juan. He had been a noble, good man who had worked for Atcho's family for many years. When the family plantation had been burned down, Juan had entered the flaming mansion and carried an unconscious Atcho to safety on his broad shoulders. He was too late to save Atcho's parents.

Grief stricken on recovering consciousness, Atcho's only desire was to take his four-year-old motherless daughter, and escape to America. Juan convinced him of his duty to stay and use his superior military training to try to help win his country back from Castro and communism.

In the heat of battle at the Bay of Pigs, Atcho and Juan had been separated, and Juan was killed. Years later, Yermolov had taunted Atcho with Juan's death, and had laughed about it.

Atcho had never spoken to anyone about Juan, except Burly. If the courier knew the details, he would certainly be the man sent by Burly.

For the next three days, Atcho moved about the neighborhood. In the evenings, he re-read the biography, *Rasputin: The Power-Crazed Mystic.* Combined with the gloominess of the weather, it kept his spirits at a low ebb. Nevertheless, he was amazed at how Rasputin gained raw power in the tsar's court. An incredible story of tragedy and corruption unfolded with each page.

Rasputin rose to influence within the Romanov family due to his extraordinary ability to resuscitate the hemophiliac heir to the throne. The tsar, a weak personality heavily influenced by his wife, regarded Rasputin's advice as divine. The mystic exercised his power with caution, seeing the royal family through countless political crises.

His influence, however, was not enough to save the family from forces gathering to eliminate it. After six years, disaffected aristocrats worried about the dictatorial influence Rasputin exerted over the tsar and thus Russia, murdered the notorious mystic. They were too late to save the throne. Lenin was already on his way to Moscow.

Atcho read on. Near the end of the book was mention of Rasputin's followers in Paris. *I hope Collins doesn't read this.*

10

KGB Major Ivan Chekov pulled his car into the gravel parking lot of Chewys Bar on a back road north of DC. It was his sanctuary for maintaining sanity. His Soviet bosses knew of his frequent visits; he had not tried to hide them. He met no one there, made no observations, and took no notes. He just went there for light conversation and relaxation. His perfect Midwestern accent earned him acceptance among the regulars with no more disruption than normal pleasantries exchanged between friends.

As a midlevel field operator, Ivan was under constant watch, as was normal for Soviet intelligence officers. Even in his apartment he could not feel alone with his thoughts.

At Chewys, he could think of home, and pretend he was free. That he could take such liberties was a testament to the high regard his superiors held for his political reliability, buttressed by the holy hell that would be visited on his family should he defect.

The cozy furnishings and atmosphere were exactly the quality that had kept Ivan coming back. He stopped at the bar to order a beer, and made his way to his regular table at the rear, greeting familiar faces as he went.

A smattering of people he had not seen before were spread about the room. He gave them quick scrutiny. *Just don't be paranoid,* he chided himself as he took his seat and continued his observations. Satisfied that he could set aside concern for a time, he reached into his jacket pocket and pulled out one of Louis L'Amour's novels from *The Sacketts* series.

He enjoyed books about the "Old West." He read them when assigned to the US as a means of picking up small talk and colloquialisms. From them, he learned of the rugged individualism that permeated American history. The idea that people could determine their own lives was contrary to his education.

He sat back and contemplated the notion, and sighed. *If only I could bring Lara and Kirill here.* But he knew that could never happen.

His mind went to last year and his involvement with the Atcho-Yermolov matter. That had been distasteful. Caught between two factions within his directorate, he had heard of a possible assassination operation, but had had no idea that it had been directed at General Secretary Gorbachev.

Only a year before, he had reached a level of clearance that allowed him to know that a Soviet mole resided deep within the US military establishment. He had been as shocked as anyone to learn that the mole had been General Yermolov in the guise of Lieutenant-General Paul Clary of the US Air Force.

As Clary, Yermolov had risen to become one of the foremost nuclear armaments experts in the US. His depth of knowledge had been counted upon during negotiations with the Soviet Union for Reagan's Strategic Arms Reduction Talks.

By a twist of fate, Ivan had been paired with a Cuban he knew as Atcho to chase down the rogue general after the failed assassination attempt. It had culminated in Atcho's stabbing the fugitive general in the chest during hand-to-hand combat on a sultry moonlit airstrip just outside of Havana. *And here we go again.* Ivan grimaced.

He took a sip of his beer, and found his place in *The Sacketts*. He tried to become engrossed in the story. Concentration became difficult.

He felt tension rise as thoughts intruded about the phone call he had received a week earlier, after midnight. As was his habit, Ivan had stayed up late reading news stories related to his intelligence cases to gain context. He had barely dozed off when the phone rang.

"Major Chekov. This is General Yermolov. Do you remember me?"

Shocked, Ivan sat up on the edge of the bed. His muscles tensed. "You were reported dead."

The general laughed. "I assure you I am very much alive." He used the long-practiced northeastern accent of Paul Clary. His disembodied voice mocked while it commanded. He gave Ivan very explicit instructions. "I need you to keep tabs on Atcho, and report to me all of his activity." Lest there be any reluctance to comply, he left a parting taunt: "I'll have my men look in on Lara and Kirill to make sure they are safe." He gave Ivan a telephone number for keeping in contact. It looked like it might be from Paris or the surrounding area.

When he hung up, Ivan sat in a cold sweat. He dared not refuse to comply. Yermolov's threat to his family was plain and deadly.

The next day, Ivan made quiet inquiries about Atcho. That evening, while Ivan placed listening devices in Atcho's apartment, his heart pounded when Atcho came home earlier than expected. Fortunately, Atcho's shot had just grazed his shoulder. The only information Ivan had gained in the interim was that Atcho had boarded a plane for Denver the morning after their encounter. He had returned to DC overnight, and then left for Austin without returning.

Now Ivan sat in Chewys, nursing his beer. Frustration rising, he tucked his book back in his coat pocket and prepared to leave.

Two other men were paying their tabs ahead of him. He waited, and then took care of his own. As he stepped through the door, a strong hand grabbed his shoulder and jerked him outside. He whirled and prepared to fight. Another set of arms encircled him and forced a cloth with a sweet-smelling substance over his nose.

Ivan blacked out. The two men who had been ahead of him looped his arms over their shoulders and dragged him into the night.

* * *

The old nuclear physicist peered at his handiwork under the lamplight in his workshop. It appeared to be a small rocket, barely eighteen inches long, but minus fins or any guidance system. He picked it up and placed it diagonally in a briefcase. It fit snugly among packing material and an external control panel.

Satisfied, he placed a carefully prepared cover of sheet metal over it, on which the shape of the rocket had been etched for easy orientation. He connected some wires, secured the control panel and a digital timer, and pressed a test button.

Five minutes later, he placed a call. "It's functional," he said when the phone was answered. "Tell me when to deliver it."

11

During the three days that Atcho surveilled the "Rasputin group" house, he noticed a pattern. The young couple carried a steaming stewpot through their front door to put in the trunk of their car. Then they drove off.

On the third night, he called Burly. "Nothing much to report," he said. "All I've seen is a young couple taking something somewhere in a stewpot, but they seem to do it every day. I'll follow them tomorrow. By the way, I haven't heard from your courier."

"He'll be there the day after tomorrow. He's picking up a piece of equipment for you, and had to wait until it was ready." Burly would provide no other details.

The next morning, Atcho rented a car to continue his surveillance. When the couple went through their regular routine, he waited. As they started down the street, he followed.

They drove through back streets of Paris until they neared the edge of the city. Then they maneuvered onto Paris' beltway, crossed a bridge to the opposite side of the River Seine, and proceeded into the countryside.

Thick traffic assured Atcho that he drove undetected. The couple entered a town, turned off the main road, and stopped in front of a tavern. Atcho parked nearby. Moments later, a man approached the couple's car, spoke through their window, and indicated a blue sedan.

Within minutes, the couple transferred the stewpot to the second car, and it pulled away.

Noting which way the second car turned onto the main road, Atcho waited until both were out of sight, then pursued. A mile farther on, he saw the blue sedan, and hung back far enough to remain unnoticed. It continued out of town a few miles, turned abruptly onto a dirt road that crossed a wide field, climbed a steep slope, and entered a forest on the hilltop.

Atcho cursed. There was no way he could follow unobserved. Since he was completely unfamiliar with the terrain, waiting until dark was no solution. And if Yermolov or his men were there, security would be airtight, and probably included night-vision devices.

The sun sank on the horizon. Atcho would have to wait at least until tomorrow. Dismayed, he drove back to Paris.

Late that night he called Burly.

"We have Ivan," Burly said. "We'll keep him sedated."

"What will the Soviets know?"

"Nothing. They'll see personal items from a burned-out car with a corpse no one can identify. County officials have the body. It's a John Doe from a local morgue. The teeth are under tight security."

"I guess that's good. Won't the missing teeth raise suspicions?"

"Yeah, they will. But that's a calculated risk. Hopefully, by the time they become an issue, you'll be done."

"Right." Atcho let his tone carry his skepticism. "Get Ivan here as quickly as possible."

"He'll be there tomorrow afternoon. I'm sending him on the Concorde. That's the fastest way. Took string-pulling to work."

"Fine. What about Sofia?"

Burly responded with reluctance. "She's still loose. We think we know where she's been, but that's not much help."

Atcho's voice was tinged with ice. "Tell the president I'll stay five more days. If Sofia isn't found by then, I'm coming home."

"I hear you loud and clear," Burly's tone became cautious, "but has there been any progress?"

"I might have found something significant, but I'm not sure." He relayed the information about the young couple delivering the stewpot to the blue car, and the hilltop in the countryside. "If you recall, in that book about Rasputin, it mentions that his followers revere his fish soup concoction. I've smelled whiffs of fish soup when they carry that pot out."

Burley made a dubious noise. "Sounds a little far-fetched, but if you get a positive sighting on Yermolov, I can order a raid to go in there and get him. The French will cooperate, but it'll be tricky. No one wants the French countryside to turn into a combat zone again."

"I'll try," Atcho replied. "My guess is that after that sighting by the CIA guy, Yermolov's keeping his head down."

Burly grunted his agreement.

"When's your courier coming?" Atcho asked.

"He's still scheduled to be there tomorrow night."

"And you can't tell me anything about it?"

Burly's silence answered the question. They hung up.

Late the next afternoon, Atcho went to the airport. He located the gate through which passengers exited customs, and sat to wait. Soon he heard an announcement that the flight had arrived.

Minutes later, people streamed through the portal. As the crowd thinned, Atcho saw Ivan pushed out on a wheelchair by an airport service aide. He wore the clothing Burly had specified, and he appeared listless.

Behind the aide, two men walked together in conversation. One was very attentive to Ivan and appeared to be his escort. Atcho looked closer, and was pleasantly surprised to see Rafael Arteaga, Atcho's Bay of Pigs comrade and the man who had arranged Ivan's disappearance. Atcho was about to rise to greet them when he glanced at the other man with Rafael—and froze. The man was Tony Collins.

Dumbfounded, Atcho watched as the attendant moved Ivan beside a row of seats in the passenger lounge. Collins sat next to Ivan while Rafael looked around.

Atcho wondered how long they had been together. He hoped that the journalist had been a coincidental helping hand to bring Ivan off the plane, and nothing more. He wanted to be rid of the man, and quickly.

He went to a phone booth, called the operator, and conversed in low tones. Then he returned to his seat. Moments later, a female voice announced over the public-address system, "Mr. Anthony Collins, please call the operator for a message."

Atcho watched Collins go to respond to the page at a courtesy phone across the lobby. Then he crossed rapidly to where Rafael stood. Seizing his arm, he murmured, "Let's go!"

Startled, Rafael stared at him. Then, recognizing Atcho and sensing his urgency, he gathered their bags. Atcho pushed the wheelchair, and they headed into the crowd. Not until they were in the rented car speeding into the city did Atcho relax. Then he looked across at Rafael.

"What a surprise seeing you. That was close. Do you know who that was helping you?"

Rafael shook his head. "I had trouble getting Ivan into the wheelchair. That man offered to assist. I didn't get his name."

"He's a reporter. I'll tell you all about him." Ivan sprawled lifelessly on the backseat. "What did they drug him with?"

Rafael shrugged. "I injected him with some stuff Burly gave me." He grinned. "You have the pleasure of speaking with Dr. Lazaro Diaz, oncologist extraordinaire." He deepened his voice in mock seriousness. "I traveled all this way to provide my patient with specialized care." He looked curious. "What's going on? Burly wouldn't tell me much. I agreed to do the job because you asked."

"Thanks." Atcho glanced at his friend. Rafael approached mid-fifties and looked fit, with a deep tan and silver hair.

"You're always trouble for me." Rafael grinned. "You drive a tank into my position with everyone in Cuba shooting at you, then you get me involved in an assassination. When are you going to let me just run my real estate business?"

Atcho filled him in.

12

Collins was puzzled. The message from the operator on the courtesy phone instructed him to call his editor in DC. Having done so, he was informed that no one from his office had called. He returned to his seat and was dismayed to find his bags unattended. Neither of the men he had helped off the airplane were in sight.

He gazed about, perplexed. Whoever had placed the courtesy summons knew that he would be in the airport. Furthermore, he had not been gone from his luggage long. Why would a man who had exhibited courtesy abandon the luggage of someone who had helped him?

The thought crossed his mind that Atcho might be involved in a deliberate diversion, but that seemed too much of a stretch. Collins knew nothing of Atcho's travel, and was sure Atcho had forgotten about him. Collins had come to Paris on a long-shot notion of finding a link between Atcho and the Rasputin group, but the odds of encountering him here in the airport were remote.

He sat a few more minutes reflecting on his efforts to interview Rasputin's biographer since last speaking with Atcho. The only item in the book Collins' researcher thought might be relevant was a reference to a religious sect in Paris. The story interested him only as something marginally connected to Atcho. He pursued it simply to leave no stone unturned.

After he had returned to Washington from Austin, Collins had read through the chapter. He was skeptical, and called the author. She was courteous but firm in her insistence that she would provide no information beyond that contained in her book.

"I wrote about Rasputin, not the group," she said. "Those are good people. I mentioned them peripherally. I didn't want anyone bothering them. Why so much sudden interest?"

She told Collins the same thing his editor had said, that someone else had called asking questions on the same morning that he had flown to Austin.

"How about if I fly out there?" Collins asked. "We want to do a human-interest article on Rasputin."

The author was having no part of Collins' curiosity, and turned defensive. "It'll be a useless trip, but I can't stop you."

In a mild effort at charm and intimidation, he flew to California and presented himself at her door. She refused him entrance. He turned on all his persuasive ability. Nothing swayed her.

He might have ended the Rasputin investigation there but for a car parked in shadows down the street from the author's house. It seemed peculiarly placed, away from any driveway and under trees providing heavy shade. Two men sat in the front. When Collins drove by to take a closer look, they slouched low in their seats. His curiosity was piqued. *A surveillance team?*

He called the *Washington Herald* bureau chief in Paris, explained what he wanted and was promised cooperation. Yesterday, when he arrived back in Washington, DC, he received a reply.

Although little was known about the religious group, it was based in Paris, and an address was available. He thought a quick trip there might resolve that loose end. Either he would find a more direct link to Atcho, or that part of the story would fizzle.

He booked the earliest flight to Paris aboard the Concorde. He had been seated near an invalid under the care of an oncologist traveling to Paris for specialized treatment, and was happy to help move the patient off the jet. Now he wondered, *What doctor travels with his patient?*

13

At the time that Collins arrived in Paris, Sofia was ensconced in a farmhouse in northern Virginia's rolling hills, with rent prepaid in cash for two months. She had altered her appearance, and her hair now fell in frizzy, artificially gray-streaked strands.

As her efforts to learn of Atcho's whereabouts failed, initial concern turned to anger, and then fear for him. A call to Burly had been disheartening. A day after confronting him in his apartment, she called him from a phone in a bar far out in the country. When they spoke, he was evasive, and his questions were subtly targeted to discover her location.

In frustration, she hung up and called other associates. None had useful information, but all invited her to lunch or dinner, or wanted to know her whereabouts. Obviously, she was being sought. *What did you expect? You're a senior intelligence supervisor.*

Sofia had found her own refuge along a country road near Washington. Somberly, she contemplated the way she would probably spend Christmas —much different than she had planned.

She curled up on a hard sofa before a meager fire, her hands wrapped around a mug of brackish coffee, and stared out a bare window at a bleak sky. Her throat constricted; her eyes brimmed.

"Where are you, Atcho?" she whispered. Her mind drifted to the events that had brought her to this place.

Sofia had been barely out of high school when first approached by the CIA. She had been accepted into Yale on a linguistic and music-dance scholarship. Her father had been a diplomat, assigned to various embassies around the world, so she had been neither surprised nor put off by the recruitment.

She had become vaguely aware of the notion of CIA "agents" at the embassies; and as a teenager, she had even tried to figure out who they might be among people she knew. She never did identify one.

Sofia had been a superb athlete, good at any sport she tried. Her favorite was ice-skating. In all her father's assignments in northern countries, skating rinks had been close by. In the southern regions they had been scarce, so she had taken up ballet.

In matters of culture, she gravitated to classical styles. An aspect of her job she loved was the opportunity to enjoy classical music, art, and architecture around the world.

The CIA offered to pay the difference between what scholarships would cover and the total outlay for her tuition. Since linguistics and music-dance covered much ground, her cost of education was high and the difference significant. With such an academic load, outside work was not feasible, so the CIA offer had presented another attractive element: on graduation, she would immediately enter a paying profession for which her obligation was to serve with the CIA for a specified time. No student loans.

As Sofia advanced through college, she received CIA guidance on shaping her courses of study. From her dance and skating training, she had developed strong legs. Her recruiters urged her to take up martial arts as well, and to her surprise she found that she enjoyed them immensely, and that she was also good at them.

During her junior year, she began winning tournaments. She also intensified her language studies so that she became conversational in French, Spanish, and Russian. In the years since, she attended defense-sponsored language schools, and became fluent enough to speak without an accent.

While attending basic CIA courses after graduation, Sofia's natural charm and language skills and her long exposure to the diplomatic community caught the eyes of her superiors. When finally assigned to the field, she found herself embedded with the State Department in foreign embassies. Her father had been pleased because she appeared to follow in his footsteps.

Now, as she sipped her coffee, a painful memory intruded: a zipped bag enshrouding the body of her slain husband. He had been a CIA case officer whose expertise had been the Middle East. When they married, she had cut her activity with the CIA to that of an analyst.

The burial was closed-casket. He had been severely mauled. Even with her high-level clearances, Sofia never received a credible report about what happened. The ordeal left her feeling broken.

Now she felt again the agony of her loss and the fury from not knowing what happened. Outwardly, she had maintained her professional composure. Inwardly she had seethed as she worked her way through embassies around the world and resumed an active role as a CIA field officer. Then, she met Atcho.

She remembered how hopeful he had seemed when she first saw him at the Swiss Embassy in Havana, where he had just been released from nineteen years in prison. That was in 1981. He was still wearing dirty, smelly prison clothes, had a growth of beard and unkempt hair, and was very thin. Sofia was there to help process political prisoners released under a program negotiated with Castro by the Carter Administration.

Moments after greeting him, Atcho had been emotionally crushed while speaking over the phone with his now-grown daughter in upstate New York, and finding that not only had she thought him dead all these years, but she wanted no part of him. His sister had raised her. All these years, she had thought that he deserted her. His anguish was palpable, and Sofia was moved.

Despite his pain and appearance, Atcho had maintained an air of dignity that had captivated Sofia. When later that day, he had disappeared back into Castro's dungeons, she could not keep him out of her mind. Many years later, he had surfaced, in all places, as Ronald Reagan's guest of honor at the State of the Union Address. She had been invited to a reception after the address, as someone who had interacted with Atcho at the Swiss

Embassy, and there the two re-met. He was then a successful real estate tycoon, and she was officially a senior intelligence supervisor at the State Department. Their romance sparked.

It was she, Sofia, who had alerted Burly that something was wrong in the way that Atcho acted; that he seemed distanced from his daughter by forces outside of himself; that despite his obvious longing to be close to his daughter, he made no move to reconcile; and that he seemed to deliberately alienate all who came close, including Sofia herself. Weeks later, she learned the truth: that Atcho had been coerced to be a sleeper agent for the Soviet KGB, and had been used to attempt to assassinate Mikhail Gorbachev.

Suddenly angry in her farmhouse room in Virginia, Sofia sat up on the couch. "This will not happen again," she murmured, grim-faced. "I will not lose another husband." She reached over and picked up the receiver of a rotary telephone setting on a side table. She dialed a number and listened as the call went through. Burly answered.

"This is Sofia." She heard his sudden intake of air. "Listen and don't talk. I'll move when we're done. You won't find me."

"Sofia—"

"I said listen. I'm in no mood to be placated, lied to, misled, or any of the other things that our employer does so well. I want straight answers, and I want them now."

Burly sighed. "What do you want?"

"I'll tell you what I know. You fill in the gaps. Atcho is on mission. I'm certain of that."

"Sofia, this isn't a secure line."

"I know. Look, Atcho is not involved in a transaction in Austin or anywhere else. I checked. He talked with those people at the power source company, but he's not there now. So, I still think it's the thing from last year. I did inquiries at home base, and I'm positive that headquarters is not involved." She left it to Burly to read between the lines.

He remained quiet.

"Atcho's not a professional operator," Sofia went on, "and you sent him against a killer." Controlled rage tinged her voice. "You brave guys can't even give him much support."

"I can't say anything," Burly said. "You need to come back in." His tone grew stern. "People want to speak with you."

"Which tells me I'm on the right track. Tell 'people' to stop trying to find me. Now."

"Please come in. You'll only make things worse."

"You know I won't. I know this." As she spoke, her voice broke. She took a deep breath. "My fiancé is putting his life in danger for the rest of us again. I'm trained. I'll figure out what to do."

"You haven't been in the field in years."

"I can take care of myself. Will you help or not?"

Burly sighed audibly. "There's not a lot I can do. He's already mad at both of us for not telling him where you work."

Sofia shook off dismay tinged with guilt. "He'll cope. You can help. I don't know how, but you do."

Burly was quiet. Then he spoke, low and slow. "All right. I'll give you what I can. Get to a library. Find a biography about Rasputin."

"Rasputin? Was he even real?"

"Do you want my help or not? Get the book." He gave her the name of the author and the title. "After you've read it, give me a call."

"Got it. Thanks."

"Sure," he replied gruffly. "I want you to think about something. I'm a good friend to both of you. I always will be."

Sofia's tone softened. "I know, and I love you for it. I can't leave Atcho out there alone again."

"He's resourceful. That's why he's effective."

"I know," she whispered.

As soon as Sofia hung up, Burly turned to the other men in the room. "Did you get a trace?" One shook his head in dismay.

"She's in Virginia, but that covers a lot of ground."

"All right. Contact local authorities statewide. Have them notify libraries to alert police to anyone requesting any book on Rasputin. Do the same for bookstores. Tell them to be on the lookout for any lone woman." The men stared at him skeptically. "I know, I know. She could look like anything. But it's all I've got."

* * *

Twenty-four hours later, Sofia sat in the Bibliothèque de Saint-Michel in Montreal. She expected that Burly would expand and intensify the search, but she would probably have some time before he reached beyond US borders.

She was deathly tired. She had managed a little sleep on the airplane, but having found the biography Burly had named, she struggled to comprehend what she was reading. The narrative fascinated, but the twists and turns of Rasputin's life and the heights of power he ascended seemed too darkly humorous to be true. She read rapidly, trying not to miss anything, but when she had finished, she was bewildered. *Why did Burly want me to read this?*

She started at the beginning again and read slowly, deliberately. Her eyelids felt heavy. Her body ached. Then near the end, she found reference to a group of Rasputin followers in Paris. There were no specifics about where in Paris they were located, but Sofia was certain this was the link she needed. Fifteen minutes later she was in a taxi headed back to the airport. Her spirits lifted.

14

Four thousand miles away, Atcho and Rafael left Ivan lying on a bed in the safe house, and then went into the sitting room. "How did you manage the accident?" Atcho asked.

"Simple. Burly located Ivan working out of a Soviet trade company north of Washington. He has a favorite bar, Chewys." Rafael explained how the operation had been pulled off. "We put a dead guy from the local morgue in Ivan's car. One of my men drove it off a back road into a ditch and made sure it would burn. Burly had it reported as a DUI fatality. The whole thing took a few minutes."

"Who's we?"

Rafael grinned. "Who do you think? Our guys from Brigade 2506."

Atcho smiled at the reference to the brigade of Cuban refugees that had landed at the Bay of Pigs more than twenty years ago. It was for them that he, Burly, Juan and their band of compatriots had prepared the beaches to assist the invading force that was supposed to have been supported by the United States. Among the brigade's fighters had been Rafael. It was the veterans of Brigade 2506 who had kept Atcho's family safe during last year's encounter with Yermolov.

"Why did Burly send you?"

"He couldn't send Ivan alone, and you needed him right away. I volunteered. I knew you needed help over here, and Burly isn't providing much."

Atcho regarded Rafael with the warmth of old friends. "Thanks. He's providing what he can, but do you know how dangerous this is?"

Rafael laughed. "Are you serious? After I kidnapped a KGB officer and brought him across the ocean on a public airplane?"

Atcho felt sheepish. "Silly question."

"What's your plan?"

Atcho grimaced. "I don't have one. We need to find out where Yermolov is and what his plan is. Then we can figure out what to do."

* * *

Late that night, Atcho called Burly. "Your courier didn't show."

"I know," Burly grunted. "There's been a delay in getting the piece of equipment you'll need."

"Can you give me a hint?"

"No."

15

At the time that Atcho and Rafael settled Ivan into the safe house, Borya Yermolov watched a blue sedan laboring up a gravel road on a hilltop twenty miles east of Paris. It ended where he stood, in front of a hunting cabin. He was tall and erect, and the cold wind moaning through towering pines lashed against still-sensitive scar tissue, a reminder of his last encounter with Atcho.

Aside from eyes that burned with ferocity over a protruding jaw, Yermolov's face was expressionless. Despite his red plaid shirt and brown corduroy trousers over rugged leather boots, he had the look of a human weapon—more of a honed killing machine than a man.

"More fish soup?" he snapped, indicating the car.

"Yes, General." They spoke in Russian.

"That stuff is going to be the death of me. Dispose of it as usual."

As Yermolov spoke, another man took the stewpot from the sedan now parked in front of the cabin. Yermolov's expression changed momentarily to amused distaste. It hardened as the driver of the car approached him, carrying the pot.

Yermolov glared at the man, who changed course and took it around to the back of the cabin. Moments later he heard liquid poured onto the ground. A breeze carried the acrid smell of fish.

The rogue Soviet general saw the soup as a security risk. He doubted that the couple that brought it to the town thought their actions carried real import. Their parents were members of the faithful who attached religious significance to eating the horrible concoction. But he had had to humor the older ones while establishing his base. They still had valuable contributions to make. He tolerated their overtures, but with increasing revulsion.

His mouth formed a lascivious grin as he recalled the origin of the superstitious reverence for Rasputin's favorite dish. The mystic had hosted bawdy feasts in his apartment for the aristocracy of St. Petersburg. No invited minister dared refuse.

A gambit Rasputin used was to have his servant prepare a huge bowl of fish soup. While he circled the room eating chunks of bread dipped into the bowl down to his knuckles, his eyes penetrated to the core of his guests. Then he selected a particularly attractive wife of a noble supplicant. While his eyes silenced protest, he stood in front of her and pressed a shapeless mass of dripping, smelly bread into her mouth. As greasy liquid ran down her exquisitely tailored dress, and while her hapless husband watched transfixed, Rasputin wiped his hand across her breasts and down into the folds between her thighs.

Yermolov knew that despite Rasputin's scorn for nobility, he respected his limits and was kind to servants and peasants. His mysticism combined with national prominence created his charisma. His followers worshipped his affectations. Fish soup became to them what holy water was to Catholics, and reverence for it passed through the generations among followers, including the group Yermolov had met with in the tavern.

Returning his thoughts to the present, Yermolov crossed the clearing to the main cabin. As he entered, six men snapped erect around a conference table. All wore civilian garb.

"Be seated," Yermolov said. "Before we begin, let's resolve what to do about that fish soup." Several staff members chuckled.

He chided them. "I enjoy humor, but someone might become curious and follow those people out here. We can no longer tolerate the security risk." He leaned toward a clean-shaven man seated to his left. "Adjutant, take care of it, but use finesse. We don't want to upset our hosts. Now, let's hear the intelligence report."

A blond man seated near the center rose. "There's nothing worrisome to report. Since eliminating the CIA officer in Paris last month, there's no indication that he reported seeing you. We've heard rumors of your existence, but our sources at CIA and KGB say they are being handled as unsubstantiated reports."

Yermolov raised an eyebrow. "Wouldn't those rumors indicate that the CIA officer's report got through?"

"Maybe. Or maybe someone else saw you. We haven't detected a big effort to find you."

Yermolov thought a moment. "Has either Reagan or Gorbachev been informed of these 'unsubstantiated reports'?"

"Both, and they both ordered low-key inquiries. Neither the CIA nor the KGB is committing many resources."

Yermolov was silent, thinking. Then he waved his hand. "Go on."

The intelligence officer continued. "There is one situation we have to monitor. We've had a team keeping surveillance on the author who wrote your grandfather's biography. That was done purely as a precaution in case someone got curious as we continue to progress." Yermolov nodded his approval. "Several days ago," the intelligence officer went on, "a man showed up at her door. She wouldn't let him in. He was persistent, so when he left, our team followed him. He took a flight to Washington. Another surveillance team watched him there. He turned out to be a reporter for the *Washington Herald*."

"Did you learn his name?"

"Yes, sir. Anthony Collins."

Yermolov jerked forward in his chair. "Tony Collins?"

"Do you know him?"

"I met him a few times. He interviewed me once. He's a well-known investigative reporter. What story is he tracking?"

The officer shrugged. "We don't know. He was in Austin about a week ago, and in New York when Gorbachev and Reagan met, but so far we've found no connecting link."

"Believe me, there is one. Monitor him and keep me informed. Anything else?"

"Just one. We lost an officer, Major Ivan Chekov."

Before the officer could continue, he was astonished to see Yermolov almost launch himself across the table, his eyes bulging. "Chekov? Lost?"

"He was killed outside Washington two nights ago. His death is being pegged as a drunk-driving accident, but authorities are closemouthed about it. His body was badly burned." The intelligence officer ceased talking and stared apprehensively at the general.

Yermolov remained still, his brow furrowed. At last he looked up. "Fine. Operations, how are preparations coming?"

Another man stood. "On schedule. Through Rasputin's followers here we have contact with members of their sect in Novosibirsk. Plans for your reception are well underway."

Yermolov nodded. "Any solid penetrations yet?"

"Definitely. We'll fly from here to Romania and then to Novosibirsk. KGB Border Troops will provide security there and facilitate further plans."

"Good." Next Yermolov listened to reports from his personnel officer on new recruits, and from his logistics officer on the status of finances and equipment. When they were finished, he looked around at the full staff.

"Gentlemen," he said, feigning the paternalistic air of General Paul Clary, "things are progressing nicely, but there are several areas that concern me.

"First is this report that there are no active searches to find me, by either side. That goes against logic and good security. I nearly succeeded in having the general secretary killed, and I had access to the most sensitive US nuclear secrets. Both countries should be doing anything and everything to find me, at least until they're satisfied that reports of my sighting are only rumor.

"Then there's this incident with Collins. Unless there's a major story, he is far too influential to be spending time on dead-end leads or background articles on Rasputin, and the timing is too coincidental.

"Finally, Chekov's disappearance." He glowered at the men, and by degrees he shed his air of amiability. His staff officers stirred uneasily, but kept their eyes fixed on him.

His tone turned sarcastic. "Major Ivan Chekov was the field officer the

KGB sent to capture me." He stared into nothingness while his right hand massaged the scars on his chest. "Was he identified by his teeth?"

The intelligence officer's face blanched. "We didn't ask."

Yermolov slammed his fist on the table. "You didn't ask? If he can't be positively identified by his teeth, don't you think that would be suspicious?" He glared into the wide eyes of his staff officers. "Listen to me! We're being complacent, patting ourselves on the back for success before we've even started." He watched to make sure his words had the desired impact. "We don't wait for things to happen. We seize initiative. And we don't leave security to chance."

He glared around the room. "Our enemies are gathering. We'd better find out who and where they are." He moved from his chair, strode to the door, and stopped. "I want a report tomorrow that ties these details together. Executive Officer, take charge." His eyes seemed to bore through the man. "And stop deliveries of that fish soup. Now!"

* * *

Late that night, Yermolov drove into the town at the foot of the hill. He went alone, something unusual for him; the security risk was high.

He stopped in the tavern. As he entered, he remembered the CIA officer he had seen there a month ago, and wondered idly if the man had managed to get his report through.

The retired nuclear physicist with whom he shared a striking resemblance waited for him in the same booth they had sat in that night. Yermolov recalled that some members had remarked that the two had a common grandfather: Rasputin.

"Well," Yermolov had told him, "we share many reasons to ensure the success of our cause." The old man had nodded his agreement.

Now, Yermolov and his alleged distant cousin spoke in hushed tones, and as they parted, the man handed him the briefcase he had prepared so carefully.

"It's simple to arm, but be careful of the fail-safe," he told Yermolov. "The instructions and the remote control are included."

"Are you sure no one outside the group knows about this?" Yermolov asked. The old man nodded.

On returning to his cabin, Yermolov inspected the contents, drawing his hand across the rough etching on the inner metal sheet that covered the bomb. Then he examined the control panel and studied the printed instructions that accompanied it. Satisfied, he closed the briefcase, and secured it inside a wall locker.

16

The morning after their arrival, Rafael looked at Ivan stretched across the safe house bed, sound asleep. "What do we do with him?"

"I don't know yet," Atcho replied. "I haven't thought it all the way through. He needs to get me in and out of the Soviet Union. Keep him drugged a while longer. I have to be out for a few hours."

"What will you tell him when he wakes up?"

"The truth. We worked together last year. He said he hoped we could do it again." Atcho grimaced. "And here we are."

"What if he doesn't cooperate?"

"We've got options. We could turn him loose, but he won't like the idea of reappearing to the Soviets after what looks like faking his own death. It looks like he tried to defect. We might be able to use that as leverage. Or we could let the US Embassy sort it out. I don't have time for complexity."

Rafael scrutinized him. "Are you all right, Atcho? You look like you're losing sleep."

Atcho rubbed his eyes. He had wondered several times during the night about the news that Burly's courier would bring. "Just figuring out how to pull this off." He looked at his watch wearily. "I'd better get going. I'll get back as fast as I can."

Forty-five minutes later, he sat in his car observing the house. At the regular time, he saw the young couple carry the steaming pot out to their car. Just then, the blue sedan he had seen the day before pulled up to the driveway. A man alighted from the passenger side and approached the couple. They seemed to know him, and even displayed deference.

The man spoke with them a short while, and then started back to his vehicle. The couple went to their trunk and removed the steaming pot. Even at this distance, Atcho caught a whiff of malodorous fish soup.

An elderly woman entered through the pedestrian gate. She was stooped, and she pulled her coat tightly about her against the cold. Across one shoulder she slung a book bag.

She seemed to ask for directions. The couple pointed this way and that, and the woman glanced about in concert with their gestures. At one point, the young man pointed in Atcho's direction, and the old woman looked directly at his car.

Atcho thought she stared at him, but discarded the notion. He doubted she could see inside the car from the driveway. He had parked in shadows with the sun reflecting off the windshield.

The man walking toward the blue sedan turned once to wave at the young couple, but they were absorbed in conversation with the elderly woman. He got into the sedan, and it pulled away.

Atcho waited a few seconds, then followed. As he passed in front of the house, the elderly lady stared as if trying to see inside the car. He had no time to discern that she was Sofia, in disguise. He drove on down the street after the blue sedan.

The sidewalks were empty, but ahead was an intersection that joined the commercial area with the neighborhood. Crowds moved in the crosswalk. When there was a break, the blue sedan turned right.

Following behind two hundred feet, Atcho eased up to the intersection and waited while pedestrians cleared the crosswalk. To his left, he saw a man turn the corner to enter the residential street in the direction Atcho had just come.

The man had an easy gait, but seemed rushed. He wore a dark fedora and pulled a trench coat tightly around him. His collar was up, so Atcho could not see his face.

Atcho glanced back at the intersection. Pedestrians were still in the crosswalk. He scanned back to his left.

The man in the trench coat arrested his attention. He had halted on the corner, and stared at Atcho. He started toward the car.

Atcho took in the man's build. He recognized the horn-rimmed glasses and rounded chin protruding over the collar. He sucked in his breath, checked the intersection again, and drove behind the remaining pedestrians. Then he slid over one lane to put other cars between him and the man on the corner.

That man was Collins.

* * *

Atcho hung back in traffic as he followed the blue sedan. His mind whirled with the events of the past few days. He dismissed thoughts of Collins to concentrate on more immediate concerns. He had no clear plan for how to use Ivan. For that matter, he had not even ascertained if Ivan could get him into the Soviet Union and back out.

Ivan had been the senior KGB officer working with Atcho in pursuit of Yermolov last year. He was quick and agile, and he commanded authority. While pursuing the rogue general, he had directed subordinates to seize a private jet on quick order, and he had posted KGB subordinates at bus terminals, train stations and airports around DC to prevent Yermolov from escaping. *But does that mean he knows how to get me safely across the border and back?*

* * *

In the blue sedan, Colonel Dmitri Drygin had his driver check the mirror for the car that had appeared to follow them. It was not in sight.

Drygin was in his mid-thirties, shorter than average, but with a powerful physique, blond medium-length hair, and cold blue eyes over an elegant smirk. He held the tenuous position of executive officer to General Yermolov. He knew that bringing unwanted attention to their group and headquarters could end his livelihood abruptly, maybe fatally.

Drygin had gone personally to stop the fish soup delivery. It had been provided by their landlord, Aleksey, the only one of Rasputin's servants still alive. Drygin had contacted him while Yermolov was still in Cuba, and had nurtured good relations that he did not want disrupted. They had been too valuable.

"Yermolov is a direct descendant of the mystic," he had told Aleksey. He said they would provide proof.

Now as he rode back to headquarters, he recalled Yermolov's order regarding the CIA officer in the tavern last month: "Remove him."

Drygin had been reluctant to kill the officer. The two had developed an odd mutual respect as competent professional peers. But the hit was necessary. The man had recognized Yermolov and would sound alarm. Failure to carry out the execution would have invited Drygin's own termination. One shot through the temple had done the job.

Drygin reflected on a twisting career with the KGB. He recalled his unnerving days as deep-cover liaison between Yermolov in the role of General Clary and the renegade KGB faction during the assassination attempt. All his skill had been tested to bring the general out of Cuba and establish relations with Rasputin followers in Paris. That action was necessary because the group provided untraceable funds and a haven for Yermolov during planning and while gathering forces. Drygin had accomplished those things without drawing suspicion from Gorbachev's regime.

"Sir." His driver interrupted his thoughts. "That car you told me to watch caught up and moved behind us a few vehicles back."

Drygin glanced through the rear window. "Keep at traffic speed and make a few unnecessary turns. We'll see if it's coincidence."

He had not been concerned that the car was tailing him. However, he had noticed that the elderly woman who showed up at Aleksey's house had stared at it, and that it fell in behind them as soon as Drygin's vehicle pulled away.

* * *

Three cars behind, Atcho's thoughts turned to Sofia. The last time he had spoken with Burly, her whereabouts were still unknown. His admiration rose grudgingly. He was still angry, but he worried that no one was at her back.

The blue sedan took a right. He pursued. The street sloped down, exposing a country vista in the distance. A two-lane road cut across from the left. Atcho recognized the turnoff where he had seen the blue sedan leave the main road and drive into a forest yesterday. If it were going there, he could see it from this observation point.

The sedan entered an intersection and turned left. Atcho followed. It made another left. When it came to the main road again, it turned right. *They've seen me.*

Instead of pursuing, Atcho returned to the observation point. Minutes later, he saw the sedan drive along the two-lane road to the turnoff. It stopped. A few minutes passed, then it turned onto the gravel road and drove uphill into the forest.

17

A short while later at Yermolov's headquarters, his staff assembled for the daily briefing. Before it started, the general turned to Drygin. "Will we be receiving any more of that fish soup?"

"No. I took care of that. Our benefactors are happy to cooperate."

"Good. Anything new on Major Ivan Chekov?"

"No. The situation is the same as yesterday. His remains are burned beyond recognition. The teeth are gone. His personal effects were with the car: his ring, his watch, his wallet and identification. There was nothing to positively identify him. The State Department is facilitating moving the remains to Moscow."

"His teeth are gone," Yermolov said, his voice thick with sarcasm. He started talking through his fingers as though thinking out loud. "Things are not adding up. I spoke with Chekov shortly before he disappeared. He wouldn't defy me."

He turned to Drygin. "Can we put surveillance on his wife and son? I want to know about anyone they talk to, the nature of phone calls, where they go, et cetera. And don't lose them."

"We can use KGB assets in their hometown," Drygin replied. "I'll take care of it."

Yermolov acknowledged with no emotion. He continued his reflection.

"Any sign that either government is trying to find me?" He addressed his question to the intelligence officer.

"None," the man replied, "but there is an interesting search going on through the FBI. A State Department employee vanished, and she was reportedly a covert officer of the CIA."

"Interesting. Any reason to believe she's connected with us?"

"Just one, but it might be significant. She is the fiancée of the man you call Atcho."

"Atcho's fiancée?" Yermolov leaned forward, startled. "I met her once at my house in Washington. We had a barbecue. She came with Atcho." He reflected momentarily. "Sofia Stahl. Beautiful woman. CIA? I didn't know. When did she disappear?"

Yermolov's men regarded him in awe. "As well as we can piece things together," the intelligence officer said, "Atcho visited her one night last week. He left for the airport the next morning, and flew to Austin, Texas. Shortly after that she left her apartment and has not been seen since." He gave the full rundown of what they had learned. "We can't confirm the information."

Yermolov tucked the report into his mind. "What about Atcho? He must be concerned."

"He has not returned to DC since he flew to Austin. We don't know where he is now. We tried to track him in Austin, but found no sign of him."

Yermolov's eyes flashed. "So, he's missing too?"

No one spoke.

Yermolov's face grew angry. "Anything else?"

"Yes, sir. Just one. I don't know the significance, but we received word that the reporter, Collins, flew to Paris yesterday. We don't have him under surveillance, and we don't know what story he's on."

"Find out," Yermolov snapped. "When are we moving to Novosibirsk?"

"On your order, General," Drygin cut in, interrupting the operations officer. He regarded Yermolov with cool detachment. "Our operators in Novosibirsk contacted the Rasputin followers. They're prepared to support.

"Section V of the KGB will secure our transportation. In addition, the KGB's commander of Border Troops, Lieutenant-General Fierko, will be at your immediate disposal when we arrive, but formal command must continue with him until you are in control."

"Excellent!" Yermolov exclaimed. His annoyance subsided.

"One more thing," Drygin continued. "When we are there, the KGB will pave the way into the nuclear control apparatus."

With an image of the locked-up briefcase in his mind, Yermolov nodded in satisfaction. He also took note of Drygin's steady demeanor, and recalled Drygin's actions during the lead-up to the assassination attempt, and then bringing Yermolov out of Cuba. *His competence is remarkable, maybe even that of an eventual rival.*

He was gratified to hear of Section V's participation, the part of the KGB responsible for assassinations. Its director would not commit to an effort so far outside his charter unless he was serious.

The logistics officer stood to give his report. He briefed that a small Soviet cargo plane would meet them at a private airstrip and fly them east to a Soviet air base in Romania. A cargo jet with regularly scheduled flights would then fly them into Novosibirsk.

"Good," Yermolov responded. "Personnel?"

"Going well, sir. We've been able to reach your former colleagues from your operation last year."

"You mean my co-conspirators in the assassination attempt," Yermolov retorted. "Go on."

The personnel officer shifted his feet. "Several are still in prison, but their guards are sympathetic. The units that had cooperated in the operation are still intact. Once you are in control, getting release of their former commanders will be easy. Those units should be immediately reliable."

"Do we know which units they are?"

Drygin spoke up again. "They're all KGB. They oversee the army units rigorously. We should realize minimum bloodshed, possibly only among senior officers who resist."

Yermolov contemplated that. "How will this look to the populace?"

"Transparent," Drygin replied. "Gorbachev came out of obscurity, so the public is already conditioned to accept an unknown leader.

"When the Soviet people comprehend your entire background, a propaganda blitz will solidify your position. We'll stage a ceremony where Gorbachev resigns in your favor."

"Good plan." Yermolov appeared mollified from his previous irritation. "Let's not get ahead of ourselves though. We need to step through each phase deliberately." He looked around the room. "Anything else?"

The staff was silent. Drygin gestured that he had more to say. Once again, Yermolov took note of his steady eyes.

"We don't want to be afraid of shadows," Drygin said, "but we're in the intelligence business. Piecing details together is what we do."

Something in Drygin's manner caused Yermolov's stomach to take an anxious jolt. "What is it?"

"I spoke with Aleksey's son and daughter-in-law, Marcel and Francine," Drygin began. "As I was leaving, an elderly woman walked up." He explained the interactions. "While they were talking, she spotted a car parked down the street and showed keen interest in it. She continued talking, but as we drove away, the car followed us."

He explained the maneuvers they had executed. "The car did not pursue back onto the main road."

"Who was the woman?"

"I don't know. She was not someone that Marcel or Francine were acquainted with."

Yermolov sat deep in thought. When he spoke again, his eyes were half-closed. "Let's go over what we know. Neither Reagan nor Gorbachev is overtly mounting a search, not even a covert one with intelligence assets. That's not normal.

"Next, a surveillance team in California sees Tony Collins at the house of the author of Rasputin's biography linking the group of followers here in Paris.

"Then we learned that Chekov was killed in an accident, but there's no proof of his death. And Collins comes to Paris."

Yermolov tapped his fingers on the table while he contemplated. "If I were Reagan or Gorbachev, I'd keep a search as quiet as possible. I'd choose a man we both trusted, who had already captured me once. That's Atcho."

Yermolov closed his eyes as he pieced together data bits. "Meanwhile, Atcho and Ms. Stahl both vanished, and she's CIA."

He lingered in thought. When he spoke again, he was calm but his voice was icy. "Executive Officer." He spoke directly to Drygin. "Accelerate our plans. I want to be off this hill within two days.

"Circulate Atcho's and Ms. Stahl's pictures and issue an alert, but don't use a lot of resources to search for them. We don't want them to be picked up by the wrong people."

He stood abruptly, and his staff sprang to its feet. He turned to Drygin, his eyes burning with intensity. "Get back to Aleksey's house, and find out who that woman is. Bring her to me. Do it now."

18

Sofia had watched the car go by behind the blue sedan. It caught her attention because it was in shadows, with the sun reflecting off its windshield, in perfect position to observe the house. She also took note of its departure, simultaneous with the blue sedan.

Finding this house had not been difficult. From the information in the Rasputin biography, an attendant at a tourist bureau had helped narrow down to this neighborhood. A few inquiries with residents had brought her to this address. She hoped to learn something to lead her to Atcho or indicate Yermolov's intentions, but she still had no idea why Burly directed her to Rasputin's followers.

"Have you lived here long?" she asked the young couple. "I've been researching the area for a possible book." She spoke with a southern French accent.

"Come inside where we can talk," the woman said. "This is my husband, Marcel, and I am Francine. We both grew up in this neighborhood."

The smell of fish from the stewpot assaulted Sofia's nostrils. "What is that?"

Marcel and Francine laughed. "Fish soup. We've been taking it out to some people every day for several weeks," Francine said. "The man in the blue car came to tell us we didn't need to do it anymore. What a relief."

Marcel left on errands. Francine picked up the stewpot and led Sofia into the house. It was a simple concrete structure, painted light beige and surrounded by a well-kept but dormant garden. *Doesn't seem threatening.* They settled into the kitchen.

"Why were you taking that soup out to them?"

"It's a religious tradition started by Rasputin, the mystic who served Tsar Nicholas."

"Seriously? The last Russian tsar?" Sofia remembered the soup stories from the Rasputin biography, but feigned ignorance on the matter. "Why would that man want you bringing it out all the time?"

"I don't know. He came by a few weeks ago to visit Marcel's Grandfather Aleksey. When he left, Grandfather told us to take it to him. It was Rasputin's favorite, and some people in our religion revere it like holy water. Grandfather was Rasputin's servant and made the recipe for him."

Sofia stared. "Marcel's grandfather was around when Rasputin was alive? And he's in this house now?"

"Certainly. He's almost ninety, but very much alive. Maybe the soup keeps him healthy." She laughed again.

A very old man shuffled in. He leaned on a cane and peered at Sofia with intelligent eyes. Francine guided him to an empty chair and introduced him. "This is Marcel's grandfather."

Sofia rose to greet him. "I feel like I'm in the presence of history," she said. "Francine told me that you knew Rasputin?"

The old man looked at her with a jovial grin. "Rah rah Rasputin," he said, and coughing laughter shook his body. "Call me Aleksey. What are you doing here?"

"I'm a writer. I'm thinking of doing a book on Rasputin and his effect on the Russian Orthodox Church. What I haven't figured out is why there is such reverence for him."

Aleksey replied with disgust befitting someone who had lived through too many global traumatic events. "He should not be revered. He was an evil man. I was there when he was murdered and when this Soviet monstrosity began." He forced a smile. "Never helps to dwell on the past."

Surprised at his vehemence, Sofia asked, "How did Rasputin's death and the fall of the tsar happen?"

Aleksey waved a hand. "When Germany sent Lenin into Russia they created a whirlwind." Outrage still boiled. "They started a civil war in Russia to stop the threat against Germany, but they created hell for the whole world. Lenin promised the people everything. He delivered slavery." He shook his head. "No different than any tyrant. They come in unknown, rise to power on the backs of people, and then lower the boom."

"How did Rasputin bring that about?"

"He was close to the tsarevna. That's how he exercised power." He made the statement as if it were self-explanatory.

Sofia pressed him. "How did that work?"

Aleksey sighed. "The tsar was a weak personality. He did whatever his wife told him. She did whatever Rasputin instructed. He mainly exercised influence by recommending ministerial appointments, and making them stick. Then, he'd dictate to the ministers. If they opposed him, he'd get them fired, or worse.

"The aristocracy hated Rasputin because of his power and the way he publicly humiliated them. They were afraid he would destroy the country. They murdered him to save Russia, but they were too late. Lenin was already on his way."

"So why would people revere Rasputin?" Sofia felt pressed for time. *What does any of this have to do with here and now?*

She listened intently as Aleksey told of the history and legend surrounding Rasputin and the fall of the Russian monarchy. He seemed practiced in telling it and enjoyed doing so, but she heard no helpful information. She hesitated before asking her next question. "Can you tell me about the night he was murdered?"

Aleksey nodded somberly. "That was a strange day, and a horrible night," he began in a voice hoarse with age. He told a surreal story of aristocrats who lured Rasputin to a sumptuous palace on the promise of a dalliance with the beautiful wife of a pliable prince. When the mystic didn't die from poisoning, they shot him, and stuffed his body through a hole in the ice of River Neva.

As the afternoon wore on, Sofia felt despair weighing in. Although intriguing, all she had gained was a secondhand account of the murder. Her spirits sank. On impulse, she asked, "Does anyone really worship Rasputin?"

Aleksey chuckled. He jabbed a finger at her. "A lot of refugees that escaped Russia were poor people that Rasputin had helped. They were grateful to his memory. I guess since they're mainly members of the Russian Orthodox Church, you could call them a sect. But to say they worship him? That's not for me to say."

Sofia glanced at her watch. She was shocked to see that nearly three hours had passed. "I've taken up so much of your time," she said. Her spirits had sunk to dismal. "I'd better go." *I still don't know how any of this relates to Atcho or Govorov.*

They ambled toward the front door. Daylight waned outside the window, throwing a pall over the room. Sofia had a sudden thought. "May I ask one more question? You said others had recently inquired about Rasputin. What do you think is suddenly driving such interest?"

Aleksey shook his head. "I don't know. A man came here weeks ago. He thinks I'm the leader of this supposed sect. He insisted his group members are devout Rasputin followers. He wanted to pay us to deliver the soup." He chuckled. "I don't think he really liked the soup. He just wanted to get close to us."

"Do you mean the man who was here today?" Francine interrupted. "He came to tell us to stop deliveries. He said his group knows it's an imposition."

"Good," Aleksey said. "That was a burden on you and Marcel."

"The man in the blue car?" Sofia interjected. "Is he the one who came by weeks ago? Why would he want to get close to you?"

"He wanted help contacting Rasputin followers in Novosibirsk," Aleksey replied. "There are a lot of Russian Orthodox members there, some who revered Rasputin." He stood still as though capturing a thought. "He told me something strange when he first came. It seemed so far-fetched, I dismissed it."

Sofia looked at him quizzically. "What was that?"

Aleksey searched his memory before responding. "He wanted funding and a place for a large group to stay for a few weeks. We were happy to consider his request, and we let them use some hunting cabins we have outside of Paris, and some cars."

"Did he say what the funds were for?"

"Yes. They want to return a member of the tsar's family to Russia. He said this man was also Rasputin's grandson."

Sofia's breath caught, and a sense of foreboding spread through her mind and gut. *That's it! Govorov thinks he's a Romanov and Rasputin's grandson.* Her survival instinct kicked into high gear. The man in the blue car must have noticed her.

Taking pains not to be rude, Sofia said her goodbyes and hurried away under waning sunlight. A recessed section of the wall lining the street was already in shadows, deepened by the column of trees along the sidewalk. Seeing no one, she stepped into it.

When she emerged two minutes later, she was shapely, wore stylish slacks, a smart jacket, and a red wig. The trappings of an elderly lady were now in her book bag.

Her heart pounded as she headed toward the commercial center. Despite her changed appearance, she was still the only pedestrian on the street that she could see. If that blue sedan approached now, the occupants would surely scrutinize her, or worse.

Screeching tires rounding the corner at the commercial intersection broke the quiet. The blue sedan swerved to the curb in front of her. She glanced at it, projecting nonchalance. The sun had dipped below the horizon, and only streetlights broke the darkness.

Two men stepped out of the car. The nearest one called to her. She ignored him and increased her pace. She heard footsteps behind her. A heavy hand grabbed her shoulder.

Sofia seized it just below the wrist. While forcing it up with all her strength, she dropped her full weight, and heard the wrist crack. The man cried out in pain.

Sofia rolled away and jumped to her feet. Her right leg swung in an arc that caught his chin and sent him sprawling.

The second man moved in. Sofia had time only to note that he was not a large man but very muscular, and even in this light, his cold blue eyes bored through her.

She pivoted in the opposite direction, striking the man's groin. He groaned and grabbed himself. Sofia spun full circle and faced him. Painfully immobilized, he glared at her in the lamplight.

Sofia lowered her head and rushed in. She leaped into the air and brought her right foot forward to strike under his chin. He crumpled backward. Sofia ran as hard as she could.

19

Yermolov tapped the table in the conference room. He felt an invisible ring tightening around him. He had expected that Reagan and Gorbachev might cooperate to pursue him. That made sense.

If regular intelligence resources had been used to track him, the actions of operatives sent against him would be predictable. That was particularly true on the Soviet side, where Yermolov had served the KGB clandestinely for decades.

But Atcho was an intelligence amateur, moving on instinct—unpredictable—and highly effective. He was now sure to be trusted by Reagan and Gorbachev, and he knew and had stopped Yermolov before. He was an obvious choice.

Yermolov rubbed his scars. That quality of doing something entirely unexpected on a large scale and in plain sight made Atcho dangerous. He recalled that Atcho had killed a backup sniper and escaped in broad daylight in the presence of thousands, including Gorbachev's personal security and the US Secret Service.

Still, Yermolov planned to expend no resources searching for him. Movement to Novosibirsk was only two days away. There, if Atcho became an irritant, he would let the KGB deal with him.

Drygin entered, his face implacable.

"Did you find the woman?" Yermolov asked.

"No. She had left by the time we arrived." He did not mention that his groin still ached where Sofia had kicked him. He was chagrinned that he had gone looking for an old woman and had gotten beat up by a girl. He had only wanted to ask if she had seen the lady. He did not mention that medics had treated his driver for a fractured wrist.

"Do they have any idea who the woman was or where she lives?"

"No. I spoke with Aleksey's grandson, Marcel. He said she was a nice woman writing a book. She wanted to know about Rasputin."

Yermolov thought a moment. "All this interest in Rasputin. It's come up quickly. Can you trust Aleksey's group?"

"They're harmless. Whether the woman was a danger wouldn't enter their minds. It's not a matter of trust. We've told them nothing. We've been able to move around invisibly because of them." He reminded Yermolov that the group had contributed money and the use of the cars and the cabins. "They serve us well."

Yermolov searched Drygin's face. "You're fond of them."

The cool blue eyes met his scrutiny. "I'm pragmatic. Aleksey is an old man who settled in a good place. His position with Rasputin turned him into a quiet legend. That helped us. We should take care to maintain a show of respect."

"In other words, you didn't press them."

"Correct. I saw nothing to be gained, and sensed no threat."

"I hope you're right." Yermolov shifted in his seat. He made a mental switch to another subject. "It's time to move. Atcho is coming for us. I feel it. Our advantage lies in staying ahead of him. When is the soonest we can transfer to Romania?"

"On your order."

"Give it. I want to be gone by tomorrow afternoon."

20

Although alone, Collins grumbled out loud. He was in a nondescript office that served as the Paris bureau for the *Washington Herald*. Night had settled and the staff had vacated hours earlier. The heat had been turned down. Cold permeated the room.

He felt dismay as he reviewed events. Most startling was his encounter with Atcho on the street corner. He had taken a taxi to the vicinity of the address his editor had supplied, and had hoped to find members of the Rasputin religious sect there.

He had exited the cab several blocks before his destination, and continued on foot. When he saw Atcho appear in a car right in front of him at the intersection of the exact street he sought, he was amazed. Days had passed since they had first met in DC. He saw Atcho now before Atcho saw him, and the reaction amused Collins. He watched the car speed off, and grinned behind his collar. "I'm catching up to you, Atcho."

He turned into the residential area. After a few hundred meters, a gate to one of the houses stood open. A young man and woman and an elderly lady conversed at the rear of a car.

Before Collins could reach them, the young woman picked up a cooking pot from the ground, and all three entered the house. He pulled a crinkled slip of paper from his pocket and checked the address written there against the street number posted on the gate. This was the house he sought.

"So, Atcho," he murmured. "No way you were on this street by coincidence. You're tied to Rasputin somehow. Maybe that *was* you paging me at the airport."

He strolled to a park bench down the street. It was the same one where Atcho had sat to watch the house four days earlier.

He stayed there for hours. Occasionally, he got up and moved to other benches located along the street. Shadows lengthened. Just as early evening turned into the half-light of dusk, he heard the garden gate opening. The elderly lady stepped through and hurried toward the commercial thoroughfare, away from him.

He kept his seat. He wanted to speak with her, but approaching on a darkening street could be misconstrued, so he lingered behind, intending to catch up in the commercial area.

Then, as the lady continued along the sidewalk, her stride seemed to lengthen. Collins started after her, being careful to keep a distance. Her stride increased into one showing younger vitality.

Behind Collins, the sun dipped below the horizon. Shadows formed under the columns of trees between the street and the wall. Ahead was a recessed section already in darkness. As he watched from half a block away, the woman glanced around and stepped into it.

After barely two minutes, a seemingly much younger woman emerged. She was shapely and stylish, and she walked with the energy that the elderly lady had exhibited just before entering the shadows. Her hair was now red.

Collins' pulse quickened and he started after her again. When he was at the recession in the wall, he stepped in momentarily, saw that it was empty, and hurried after her. He had no idea then that this was Sofia.

A blue sedan rounded the corner. The smell of hot rubber accompanied the screech of tires as the sedan pulled to a stop by Sofia. Two men leaped out and accosted her. Then a flurry of action happened so fast that Collins barely took it in. The two men fell to the ground, one after the other, and Sofia took off in a dead run.

The men writhed. Collins stayed behind a tree. Far down the block, Sofia disappeared around the corner.

The men staggered to their feet and talked at the front of the car. One of them nursed an injured wrist while the other limped. They looked up and down the street and shook their heads. Then, they climbed into the car and continued down the street.

Collins considered retracing his steps to the Rasputin house, thinking perhaps he could speak with one of the occupants. Darkness descended to full night. He stayed in shadows cast by amber streetlights, waiting until the blue sedan passed. He intended to stay there until it disappeared, but when it was two blocks farther on, it swerved left again, and parked.

He sucked in his breath. The car had stopped in front of the Rasputin house.

He quickened his pace, careful to stay hidden. The passenger emerged and disappeared inside the gate. Before Collins could close the distance, the man came back to the car, got in, and sped off.

Collins raised his hands to his face and shook his head in frustration. *I'm always a step behind.*

Setting his jaw, he reached the garden gate, turned in, and pushed the doorbell. When the door opened, a young man stood in front of him. He was tall and thin, and seemed affable.

"Do you speak English?" Collins asked after the young man greeted him.

The man rolled his eyes, but responded courteously. "A little. Can I help you?"

"I hope so. I was looking for a colleague, a woman. I was supposed to meet her in this neighborhood, but I can't locate her." He gave Sofia's disguised description.

"Ah yes, the writer. She wanted to know about Rasputin. You're a colleague?"

She told them she's writing about Rasputin. I can go with that. "I'm her editor."

"She left here a few minutes ago," Marcel said. "She was going to her hotel."

Collins was crestfallen. "She forgot to give me the name of the hotel. Did she mention it?"

"She might have told my wife. Come in. My name is Marcel."

"Thank you."

Marcel closed the door and called out to his wife. Soon, a young woman appeared. "I am Francine," she said in English. Her husband filled her in. "I'm so sorry you missed her. There was another man here a few minutes ago asking about her."

Although startled, Collins maintained a steady composure. "Did she mention that she was expecting anyone?"

Francine looked at Marcel, who shook his head. "Maybe she wanted to interview him," Francine said. "He claims to know a descendant of Rasputin." She chatted on, but Collins noticed that Marcel stiffened as she provided more information. Behind them came sounds of shuffling footsteps. Then a very old man approached.

"Ah, Grandfather," Francine called to him. "Here is someone else interested in Rasputin." She turned to Collins. "My husband's grandfather was Rasputin's servant," she said proudly.

Startled again, Collins found himself staring. Despite Francine's enthusiasm, the old man seemed displeased. He regarded Collins through tired eyes. "I've talked about Rasputin too much today," he rasped. "I'm going to bed." He shuffled back down the hall.

Next to him, Marcel fidgeted, and moved closer to the front door. "Please, Mr. ...?"

"Collins." As soon as he responded, Collins regretted giving his real name. *But who knows me over here—besides Atcho?*

"Mr. Collins, you see that my grandfather is very tired. I'm sorry to be rude—" Marcel took his arm and exerted enough pressure to move him toward the door. "He has talked enough for one day."

* * *

A few minutes later, the phone rang in Colonel Drygin's room at the temporary headquarters compound. He picked up on the third ring. "Drygin."

"This is Marcel, Aleksey's grandson."

"I didn't expect to hear from you so soon." They spoke in Russian.

"I know, but when you gave me this number tonight, you said to let you know if anyone else came asking about Rasputin."

"And...?"

"Right after you left an American came by. He claimed to be the editor for the writer who was here. The odd thing was that he spoke no French, and she was fluent. I don't even know if she speaks English. I assumed she was French."

"What did he want?"

"He was looking for the woman, and he gave an accurate description. He said that he was supposed to meet her in this neighborhood, but that she had forgotten to give him the address. His name was Collins."

"Collins?" Drygin's tone sharpened. "Are you sure?"

"I'm positive. He didn't say where he was going."

After hanging up, Drygin walked down the hall to Yermolov's room and reported his conversation. Yermolov's words were few, and terse. "Get everyone packing. Now! We leave tomorrow morning."

21

As soon as Atcho saw the blue sedan disappear into the forest, he returned to the safe house. He arrived during the time that Aleksey described to Sofia the details of Rasputin's murder.

Rafael guessed that Ivan was expert in weaponry and hand-to-hand combat. He was sure he could give Ivan a good fight, but the Russian was younger, and probably better trained. With that in mind, Rafael had bound him.

Ivan woke up shortly after Atcho's return. Finding his arms and legs tied, his eyes flashed anger. He recognized Atcho.

"Help me get him up," Atcho said. He crossed the room, put an arm behind Ivan's back, and brought him to a sitting position. Rafael helped untie him, and supported him to a wingback chair.

"Where am I?" Ivan asked, his voice deep and raspy. "What am I doing here?" Despite several days' growth of beard, he resembled a serious and lethal version of the comedian Bob Newhart, complete with balding head.

"We need your help," Atcho replied.

Ivan smirked. "This is the way you ask for it?"

"Remember how your people coerced me all those years?" Atcho retorted. "Hear me out."

Ivan nodded sardonically. "The things men do to each other. Go ahead."

"You remember Govorov, also known as Yermolov?"

On hearing the name, blood drained from Ivan's face.

"Are you all right?" Atcho came to his aid.

Ivan waved him away. "Drugs wearing off. Go on."

Atcho summarized events. Recalling their joint mission to Cuba and his meeting with Reagan and Gorbachev, he finished by briefing plans to seek out the religious sect in Paris. He gestured toward Rafael. "We fought together at the Bay of Pigs. He organized security for my daughter, her husband and his extended family against Yermolov last year. They were scattered across the county, so it was no easy deal."

Ivan regarded Rafael. "Impressive! Things could have been a lot messier." He left the matter at that. "Continue."

"I need you to get me across the Soviet border and back."

Ivan looked startled. "That's it? That's all you want from me?"

Now Atcho was surprised. "There might be other ways you could help, but that's why I brought you in."

"Brought me in," Ivan repeated, his voice heavy with sarcasm. "Do you know that I have a family?"

Atcho looked bewildered. "What? No. I didn't think—"

"Exactly, you didn't think. The Soviet Union believes I'm dead. By now, my family has been informed. I had a career. Now, I have no family, no career, and you ask for my help." His expression turned dark. "You took away my life so that I could get you across the border and back."

Atcho stared. In his haste to dodge Collins, he had not considered the ramifications to the KGB officer. "I'm sorry," he said. "I'm a businessman, not a spy. Can you get me into the Soviet Union and back out?"

Ivan bristled in disbelief, and then settled into deep thought. "I don't know." He saw Atcho's puzzled face. "I'm dead, remember? I can't call in favors. If I do, alarms will go off all over the place. You should have approached me before you had me killed."

"What would you have done? The CIA and KGB were supposed to be kept out. Tony Collins was at my heels."

Ivan jerked his head up. "Tony Collins? The newspaperman? What's he doing?"

Atcho filled him in, including his perception that he might suspect

Atcho of either being a conspirator or part of a cover-up in last year's assassination plan.

"The plot thickens," Ivan observed gloomily.

"I'm sure when all this is done, Gorbachev will restore you," Atcho replied.

"Yeah, I'm sure you're right." His sarcasm was thick. "What happens if we fail? We're three men with no organization. I'm effectively neutralized, and you didn't trust me enough to ask."

"I couldn't," Atcho retorted. "You're a spy in our country."

Ivan snorted his disgust. "You think I'm KGB because I like it?" He tossed his head. "Being 'brilliant' in the Soviet Union comes at a cost."

Atcho eyed him. "For all I know you might support Yermolov."

"Right!" Ivan retorted. He rose on wobbly legs and walked over to stare out the window. *Paris? Really?* But right there was the Arch of Triumph. A gray mist hung over the City of Lights. Temperatures had dropped.

Behind him, Rafael sprawled across one of the beds. Atcho sat in an armchair, his face showing strain. Ivan almost felt sorry for him.

Atcho watched Ivan. Coercing him past this point would be counterproductive. *If he doesn't cooperate I'll let the CIA handle him.*

Ivan left the window, stretched out on his bed, and closed his eyes. Visions of his family crossed his mind. His wife, Lara, was lovely. He smiled despite his dark mood. His job had allowed them to enjoy a lifestyle beyond that of most Soviets. The price was constant, unaccompanied travel to places around the planet, mostly to the US, doing things that made him less than proud.

He thought of his son, Kirill, fourteen years old and looking forward to the upcoming *futbol* season. He was the image of his father, although with a full head of hair, and he had the same natural intelligence. The two of them loved their time together, kicking a ball, hiking in the forests, playing chess... *Will I get my life back?*

Although he had felt Atcho's immense strength during the skirmish in the town house, he was sure he could overpower both Atcho and Rafael. His training restrained him. They were capable fighters. If he failed to subdue them both, the results could be tragic.

Does Yermolov know I'm 'dead'? Therein lay his dilemma. If he escaped, should he go to the KGB or to Yermolov? Neither alternative was good. In either case, he would fall under suspicion. Furthermore, if he escaped, he would be on his own with no ID, no money, no credit card, and no contacts. *I am alone.*

He saw Atcho studying him. "You screwed up my life."

"I don't see it that way."

"What if we don't succeed? What then?"

Atcho held his angry stare. On the other bed, Rafael stirred. He rolled onto his left side, looking back and forth between them.

"We'd better not fail," Atcho said.

"That's your plan? We'd better not fail?" Ivan snorted. "What do you think; that if Yermolov takes power he'll launch an attack? He's not stupid. He knows US launch protocols would have changed because of his escape, but they're still on a hair trigger. He'll move to consolidate power and lower tensions with the US."

Atcho's gaze bore into Ivan. "So, you think that if Yermolov calls the nuclear shots in the Soviet Union, that would be a good thing?"

Warnings buzzed in Ivan's head. *Careful. He's probing.* "No," he said slowly, "Yermolov's a survivor. He won't do something to get himself killed or invite an attack. He'll want to consolidate and establish legitimacy. He'll do that before making threats abroad."

Both men were quiet. Rafael looked on without saying a word.

Ivan spoke again, and his voice contained a wistful quality. "Russia is still a proud country. We have military, cultural, and educational achievements to rival anywhere in the world."

"Maybe, but you enslaved whole countries and called them the Soviet Union."

"My point is that your Ronald Reagan created the conditions for Yermolov to emerge. He said that our people suffer most under communism, but he nearly bankrupted us with that arms race. He drove the price of oil down to kill our production and dry up our financial reserves. Things will be worse for us."

"So, what is Yermolov going to do?" Atcho's voice was sharp as he asked the question.

Only at the last moment did Ivan stop an impulse to look around quickly at him. He shook his head. "I don't know. Maybe reverse diplomatic initiatives; eliminate *glasnost* and *perestroika*."

Both men were quiet. Rafael rolled back onto his stomach and closed his eyes.

"Tell me something, Ivan," Atcho said. "I'm curious."

"What?" His mental warnings blared. He had an idea where the next line of questions was going, and he was right.

"What happened in Havana last year, after I flew out?"

Ivan steeled himself to continue a consistent demeanor. He shrugged. "Fidel Castro had already gone away in his Jeep by the time you got in that MiG." He said that Yermolov had lain unconscious and bleeding. The Cuban soldiers thought he was dead, so they loaded him into the back of a pickup.

Ivan said he rode with the commander of the security detail, and they drove back to Cuban Army headquarters. When the soldiers went to unload Yermolov, he groaned.

"No one knew what to do," Ivan said. "Keep him alive? Let him die? The commander ordered first aid and went to inform his higher-ups. Apparently, the message went all the way to Castro, because orders came back quickly to do everything to save him."

Atcho took that in. "What did you do?"

"Me?" The buzz in Ivan's head warned. He shrugged. "I reported to my superiors. My orders were to keep an eye on Yermolov until our comrades at the Soviet Embassy could get the situation under control. As soon as Yermolov could be safely moved, he was taken by ambulance to the embassy clinic."

Atcho digested Ivan's response. On the other bed, Rafael lay quiet. Atcho was sure he listened to every word. "So, you were there for several days with Yermolov." He cast a steady gaze at Ivan.

Ivan held it. "Yes. At the time that I was relieved of my duties, he was in no shape to escape, and as you know, the embassy reported him dead."

"How did he get away?"

Ivan shook his head and relaxed imperceptibly. "I don't know," he said slowly. "You said that General Secretary Gorbachev contained word of Yermolov's escape. News had not seeped to the field at the time of my death." He grinned slightly and went on. "It's been more than a year since we captured the bastard. Obviously, he had high-level help. What will you do now?"

Atcho continued to study Ivan. Then he shook off his thoughts. He filled Ivan in on the connection between the Rasputin followers in Paris and the men he had observed on the hill outside the city. He related what he had observed about the couple with the steaming pot, the blue sedan, and its apparent destination. "The young couple seems harmless, but I'm sure the men in the blue sedan figured out I was following them. We need to get on that hill. We'll go there tomorrow."

Ivan looked up sharply. "You said you needed me to get you across the Soviet borders."

"I don't know when that will be or where we should cross. Do you think you can do it?"

"A dead man's options are limited." Ivan was still visibly angry. "The Soviet border is thousands of miles long. But a trained KGB officer can get most things done. Is that all you need?"

"No. Staging a coup in the Soviet Union by an outsider is crazy. It'll have to be done so quietly that most of the world will have no clue it's happening." Yermolov's new government would have to establish legitimacy quickly. That would require incredible cooperation across the Soviet government, especially between military, intelligence, and police elements. "I don't believe that Yermolov will attempt a coup until those assets are in place."

While he spoke, Ivan's face remained sphinxlike, impenetrable. "Are you sure a coup is in the plan?"

"Has to be. If he's not doing it, someone else is, and he's a player." Atcho pointed out that Yermolov was a wanted man in the Soviet Union. He could not participate in Gorbachev's government, so without a coup, there would be no reason for him to return there.

"He's got to be thinking of blackmail against the Soviet government," Atcho went on. "The most effective way would be to threaten a tactical nuclear strike, probably against Moscow."

Ivan looked askance. "You're heading into fantasyland."

"Maybe. Yermolov has no patience for political posturing. He'll go for a quick sweep where he controls the trigger. That points to a tactical nuke."

"So, what are you thinking?"

"We have to get close to him."

"What do you mean?"

"We have to locate him," Atcho replied. "We have to get inside his organization, and be ready to act when he makes his move."

22

Ivan tossed sleeplessly. His muscles still felt the effect of drugs, but his mind functioned in adrenaline-induced overdrive. *What will Yermolov do to Lara and Kirill if he finds out I've been absent for days?*

When Yermolov had been captured in Havana, Ivan had been left to clean up the international relations mess. His duty to watch over the general ended after Soviet officials moved him to their embassy's clinic. On his last day, Ivan was alone with Yermolov. Tubes protruded from the general's mouth, and his complexion was deathlike. The only indication that he lived was the slight rise and fall of his chest and the hiss of labored breathing.

Maintaining a cold countenance, Ivan looked at the general, remembering his maniacal laugh just before his violent arrest. *This is the great Soviet general and master spy?*

Yermolov stirred. His eyes moved, but they seemed unfocused. Then they rested on Ivan and scrutinized him. He gestured for Ivan to come to the side of the bed.

Ivan sat down next to the general's head. "What do you want?"

Yermolov opened his eyes further. His chest shook as though he had laughed. No sound emerged. "You don't like me." His voice was barely audible. "Are you the officer who captured me?"

"I am."

"Great job!" Yermolov's admiration seemed genuine.

"I can't take credit. I was glad to help."

Yermolov turned his head slightly to get a better view, but still could do no better than glance from the corners of his eyes. "Ah," he whispered. "You think I'm a traitor. Doesn't matter. I don't have strength to discuss." He was surprisingly aware for a man recently coming out of a coma. "Gorbachev will destroy the Soviet Union."

"Is that all, Yermolov? I have a plane to catch."

The rogue general's face tensed. "You don't render military courtesies?" He glared at Ivan. Then he relaxed, composed. "I'm glad I met the Soviet officer who captured me."

Ivan sat, impassive.

"I want to tell you this." Yermolov placed his hand over Ivan's arm. Even in his weakened state, he had a tough physique. As he spoke his next words, a heavy weight formed in Ivan's abdomen. "My great-grandfather was the last tsar of Russia," Yermolov hissed. His grip tightened. "My grandfather was Grigori Yefimovich Rasputin." He glared at Ivan. "My day will come. Be ready when I call."

He released his grip. Sinking into the pillows, he closed his eyes. "You are dismissed, Major Chekov. Go."

Stunned, Ivan stared at the man. Yermolov said nothing more.

Two days later, Ivan arrived in Washington. He never mentioned the conversation. It seemed bizarre, the ravings of a madman.

Now Ivan lay in his bed in Paris, his muscles tensed. For the moment, his best course was to bide his time and look for a chance to call the number Yermolov had given him that night in Virginia. He was sure it was in France and might even be close by. An opportunity to escape and link up with Yermolov might occur when Atcho took him to observe the forested hill. *I'll watch for it.*

On a trundle bed across the room, Atcho struggled with his own thoughts. Ivan's seeming familiarity with Yermolov's thinking was disconcerting. *How long were they together in Havana?* He did not see an alternative to Ivan. Having someone on hand to navigate the borders and inside the Soviet Union was crucial. If they could stop Yermolov from making the crossing they would avoid a lot of grief, but he doubted that Yermolov would wait long.

23

An hour after escaping her attackers near the Rasputin house, Sofia ducked into the consular services office at the American Embassy, using her regular passport to enter. Then, using her security credentials, she gained access to an office with a secure line. She bet with herself that Burly had not yet reached across the ocean through State Department channels. Nevertheless, she felt some angst as she entered and moved about the facility.

She dialed Burly's number. "It's me."

"Where are you?" He was plainly both pleased and annoyed to hear her. "How did you get on a secure line? Will you get your butt back here?"

"Not so fast. I have information you can use."

"You need to get back here. You're endangering a mission."

"Novosibirsk," Sofia retorted. "Govorov is headed to Novosibirsk. He's saying he's a Romanov and Rasputin's grandson."

"You keep fixating on Govorov." Burly sounded flustered. "If you're going to keep talking about him, you should know that his real name is Borya Yermolov."

Sofia took that in. She noted that Burly neither refuted nor showed surprise at her conclusion. "Let's not play games. Yermolov is the commonality between Gorbachev, Reagan, and Atcho. There's no other reason for both the general secretary and the president to call Atcho in. You know it, and I know it." She felt rising anger. "I'm mad, and losing patience."

Both were quiet, and then Burly said, "Let's say that you're in the ball-park. What's the scoop on Novosibirsk? How did you get it?"

Sofia disregarded the question. "Yermolov is going to Novosibirsk. Tell Atcho. Tell Reagan it's time to bring out the big guns."

When Burly spoke again, his voice was low and deliberate. "Sofia, come in. That's not a request. You've got to come in."

Sofia started to protest, but Burly kept talking. The quiet of the secure facility closed around her like a shroud.

"This could get bad," Burly went on. "You're not helping. Atcho sent a message to the president four days ago. He said that if you were not home within a week, he was off the job."

Sofia remained silent. She knew that Atcho would not be recalled, and he would not duck from completing such a crucial task.

"Sofia," Burly broke in again, "listen carefully. Do you know what a NukeX is?"

Suddenly jarred to greater awareness, Sofia's breath caught. "Yes," she replied hesitantly.

"Atcho is going to need one," Burly said bluntly.

Sofia's mind spun. "Do you mean..."

"I can't tell you more," Burly interrupted, "but you can see how nasty things are getting."

"Does Atcho know?"

"No. We had a courier set up to bring the device to him, but there was a delay in having it ready. We don't need you there causing more distraction. You've got to come in."

Sofia slumped against the back of her chair. She suddenly felt emotion-ally and physically spent. "Does Moscow know?"

"Yes."

Sofia looked vacantly around the bare office. "All right. I'll be there tomorrow night."

"Why so long?"

"It's a long drive."

As soon as she hung up, Burly whirled around. "Did you locate her?

She was on a secure line."

"I think she's in France," a man told him, "but it'll take a little time to confirm that."

"Call the embassy in Paris. Get them looking for her. If she read the book, that's where she would go. Did you get a tape of the conversation?"

"Yes."

"Analyze for background noise. We've got to know where she is."

* * *

With only minutes to spare, Sofia hurried aboard the train to Bern, Switzerland. The weight of Burly's news of the NukeX bore down. As the train began its journey through the night, sleep eluded her. She knew her actions might end her career, but now that was hardly a consideration. Her mind reeled with the implications of Burly's revelation: Atcho could be required to disarm a nuclear device.

She doubted that Burly expected to see her the next evening. He knew her too well to believe that she could be deterred. Having traced the call, he would try to determine her whereabouts. That should provide her enough time to pursue the next part of her loosely forming plan.

She arrived in Bern shortly after midnight, and spent the balance of the night in a small hotel. The next morning, she hailed a taxi. Her stomach tightened when it dropped her at her destination, the US Embassy. Her adrenaline rushed as she handed her passport and State Department ID to the civilian behind the glass-enclosed booth. He scanned it and compared her picture to her face. Satisfied, he returned them.

She breathed a sigh of relief. *Burly hasn't reached here yet.* The attendant showed her where to sign the guest log and gave her an unescorted visitor's badge.

The area reserved for intelligence analysis was always behind heavy doors with cypher locks, and included a steel-encased vault. Sofia remembered where it was from being assigned there several years ago. *I hope Millie still works there.*

She reached the third floor. A nondescript door with a sign stood at the end of the hall. This was the office she sought. She sucked in her breath. *If an order comes to arrest me, this is where they'll get it.*

A young Marine sitting at a table blocked the hall. "This is a restricted area, ma'am. May I see your ID?"

Sofia's throat caught. She showed her visitor's pass and pulled out her ID. The Marine examined both carefully, looked her over, and allowed her passage. "Thank you, ma'am."

Sofia exhaled. "Do you know if Millie still works here?"

"Millie Brown? Yes, ma'am, the place couldn't run without her. She's in the vault. I'll tell her you're here."

Moments later, a friendly voice called out. "Goodness gracious, Sofia, what are you doing here?" She turned and saw Millie, arms outstretched for a hug. "I am so glad to see you. I was thinking about you just the other day..."

Sofia had to laugh. This was vintage Millie: short, rotund, with dirty blonde hair, and nonstop talking. Millie was one of a handful of civilian intelligence specialists on staff to provide continuity between succeeding administrations. She might be friendly and exuberant, but she had gained the trust and confidence of the intelligence community by keen insights, not by missing things.

Sofia wanted to get right to the point of her visit, to acquire travel documents; but she could not appear hurried. Millie knew her way around. Embassy staff would respond to an unusual request because it was Millie who asked. Sofia was abusing their friendship to acquire what she needed. *What if Burly has already reached here?* She studied Millie's face, but saw no vestige of hidden concern.

* * *

Five hours later, Sofia slumped into a seat on the train to Geneva. Pangs of guilt intruded on her thoughts. *I owe Millie big time.* Outside, the magnificence of the Alps cloaked in fresh snow swept by. She slept. Inside her bag were the documents she needed, signed by the ambassador, allowing her travel to Moscow.

24

Collins paced. After Marcel had closed the door behind him at the Rasputin house, he mentally kicked himself for giving his real name.

He was still in the Paris offices of the *Washington Herald* thinking through the events of the past two days, and trying to make sense of them in the context of Atcho's movements. The office had closed for the day. He was alone with his thoughts.

He crossed to a window and stared at the snow blanketing the street. "How do I get in front of this story?" A whiteboard hung on the opposite wall with markers lying in a tray. "What do I know?" He wrote with a marker at the top of the board, and stared at the words, imploring them to speak. When nothing came, he made another entry and stood back. Nothing popped to mind. After more staring, he wrote furiously until completing his regurgitation of facts. Then he viewed what he had written:

NEW YORK: Reagan, Gorbachev, Atcho @ Long Island Estate
WASHINGTON, DC: Something happened on PA Ave last year, Atcho involved. Backfire/dead man
Atcho clammed up about meeting in NY.
Met in library. Rasputin book
AUSTIN: Atcho diversion

CALIFORNIA: Rasputin bio-author refuses to cooperate—saw surveillance team

PARIS:

- From lead in Rasputin book—helped sick man/doctor off airplane— bogus call—sick man/doctor disappeared
- Found Rasputin house—saw Atcho on same street—old lady morphs into young lady—beats up two guys
- Beat-up man stopped @ Rasputin house to ask about elderly lady—man already known to occupants @ house
- Met people in Rasputin house—grandfather tired of talking— wife friendly and open – husband friendly then tense – said 'elderly lady' was a writer

He sat down, still studying the board. After a while he prepared coffee while his brain cogitated. He had just poured a steaming cup when his eyes went once more to the whiteboard.

Suddenly, coffee forgotten, he ran to the phone and pounded out a number in DC. It was closing time there.

"Tom Jakes here," came the laconic greeting of his editor.

"Don't sign out yet, Tom. It's me, Tony." He instructed Jakes to write down the entries exactly as he had made them on the board.

"Done. So? Where are you going with this?"

He ignored the question. "Study it. Atcho is the only commonality in the first line where Gorbachev and Reagan appear, but Atcho and Rasputin are in the rest of the outline. In other words, Rasputin becomes relevant to Gorbachev and Reagan through Atcho."

"I'm not sure I follow, but go on."

"What's common among those three people: Reagan, Gorbachev, and Atcho? Why would the heads of state of the two superpowers call him in?"

"I don't know."

"I don't either, but the answer must lie in what happened last year. There's a story that got past the news media.

"Think about it. Gorbachev comes to town to sign the arms reduction treaty. He stops to greet people on the street about the same time that a car backfires. Then, a manhunt gins up for Atcho over some real estate transactions. Jakes, since when do the police mount an all-points bulletin for real estate fraud?

"Then, just as suddenly the hunt is called off and the authorities say, 'oh, we made a mistake.' A year later Gorbachev and Reagan obviously bring Atcho to that Long Island estate. Suddenly all this excitement builds around Rasputin, and Atcho is in the middle of it. Doesn't that seem beyond coincidence?"

Jakes had listened with increasing interest. "Are you still thinking that Atcho was involved in an assassination attempt?"

"I don't know. But the guy across the street wound up dead."

"There's something else," Jakes interjected. "Do you remember Sofia Stahl?"

"Sounds familiar. Was she at the State Department?"

"That's her. We did a story about Atcho when he came out of Cuba, and again last January when Reagan honored him at the State of the Union address."

"I remember."

"She was one of the people we interviewed for background on the Atcho stories. She met him when he came through the Swiss Embassy in Havana. That was in 1981 before Castro threw him back into prison."

"Got it. So?"

"She was supposed to marry Atcho next month. She's disappeared."

Startled, Collins sat back in his chair. His cynical mode kicked in. He was not a big believer in coincidence. "Anything else?"

"The investigative and intelligence authorities are keeping very hush-hush about this. No local authorities are looking for her."

"What was her position at the State Department?"

"She was a director in one of the intelligence analysis sections."

Collins leaped to his feet, stunned. "She has high security clearances, and they're not blasting this out complete with a dragnet?"

"That's not all. We've heard from three sources that she's CIA."

Collins looked at the receiver in disbelief. His mind flashed back to the lady he had seen morph from old to young and beat up two guys along the street by the Rasputin house. "What does she look like?"

"We'll get pictures to you."

"Thanks. Anything else?"

"Yes. I told you that local authorities are not looking for Ms. Stahl, but there is a search involving local authorities across Virginia."

"What's that about?"

"Libraries and bookstores are being told to report any lone women that come in asking for a book about Rasputin."

"You're kidding," Collins breathed. "I told you. I told you we were onto something. Here's what I need you to do."

Jakes recited back Collins' instructions. "Anything else?"

"Anything on the CIA guy or the burglary at Atcho's house?"

"We've tracked down where he lives, but he hasn't been home in days. I ran inquiries on him. He was in Cuba with Atcho, but so were several CIA guys. I couldn't find anything current."

"So, another person disappears. Interesting."

After they hung up, Collins made his way back to his hotel. Darkness loitered outside the window, held back by the soft light of two lamps. He pulled Rasputin's biography from his briefcase, and sank into the leather chair by the desk.

"What are you not yet telling me?" he murmured to Rasputin's stern countenance staring at him from its cover. He started to read.

25

Collins glared at the phone on his desk in the hotel room. He was generally a patient man. At least he told himself that—but now he waited for information from members of his own team, specifically Tom Jakes.

He rubbed his eyes. He had slept little, having forced himself to read Rasputin's biography in detail. While much was intriguing, he saw nothing that bore on current events or that might involve Atcho.

He read again the part about the religious sect in Paris, and although interesting, it underwhelmed for current political intrigue. *Why is everyone so interested in Rasputin?*

The phone rang. "Okay, Jakes, what've you got?"

"Geez, guy! Can you say hello! I checked what you asked me to, and came up with good stuff, but it's off the record. The word from the source is that if any of this is published, we get no more."

"Got it. Will it help?"

"You be the judge. All the information came from within the Secret Service. There never was any real estate fraud involving Atcho. That was trumped-up."

Collins' excitement leaped. "Why did they generate the story?"

"Because Atcho punched out one of their guys. There was a body found in a building down the street from where the car backfired during the

Gorbachev visit. The man had a sniper rifle. He was killed by another high-powered rifle from an office across the street. Atcho owns it."

Collins' mind churned. He knew Atcho owned the building, and he knew about the body across the street. He had not known about the rifles or Atcho's interaction with the Secret Service. "How did he end up punching the Secret Service guy?"

Jakes said that when the car backfired, people thought it was a rifle shot. The Secret Service did, too. They fanned out, and several agents went into Atcho's building. They broke the door down to the office directly across from where the dead body was later found. There was nothing in the office, but when they went into the men's restroom down the hall, they found Atcho.

"Atcho? He was there?"

"Yes, and that's where he punched out the Secret Service guy and got away."

"Wait, Jakes. You said the office in Atcho's building was empty, but a minute ago you told me they found a rifle there."

"I'm coming to that. There's more. They found the dead guy across the street because Atcho phoned in a tip about an hour after his escape. He also told them where to find the second rifle. It was hidden in the windowsill in the office in his building. Forensics confirmed it was the weapon that killed the man across the street.

"Right after Atcho's escape, the APB went out for him on real estate fraud charges and was recalled after he called in the information about the body and the rifle. An hour after that, the entire Eastern seaboard went on military alert."

"Why? What happened? How did that get by us?"

"Don't know. The agents we spoke with were on the detail to protect the general secretary. They're not the ones usually close to the president. Those guys won't talk about it, and the military is closemouthed. There's one more thing. Remember the Cuban MiG that flew into Andrews Air Force Base under escort late that night? A helicopter took a lone passenger from the MiG to the White House."

"And that passenger was Atcho," Collins muttered. "I remember that, but how did Atcho go from punching out a Secret Service agent on Pennsylvania Avenue to being on an inbound MiG a few hours later? Where would he have gotten onto it?"

"Well there is one more detail that might fit. It seemed obscure, but might be relevant. That same night, a private jet was stolen from a local DC airport."

Collins considered the coincidence, but dismissed the thought. "That feels like grasping at straws. Do you know if Atcho is a pilot? A jet pilot?"

"No." Both men were momentarily quiet.

"Then what do you make of all that?"

"I'm not sure," Jakes replied. "Instead of trying to kill the Soviet general secretary, it sounds like Atcho might have disrupted an attempt on his life."

"That fits." Collins rested his forehead in his free hand. "That would explain why both Reagan and Gorbachev like him. But what kind of mission would they send him on now?"

"The easy answer is that he'd go after whoever was behind the conspiracy. They're not buying a lone wolf theory."

"Yep. Too much coordination. Had to be an inside Soviet job." An inconsistency tugged at Collins' mind. "If they didn't catch the assassin last year, why haven't they been looking for him all year? Have you heard anything about a widespread manhunt, even on the clandestine side?"

"No," Jakes replied. "Here's something else. I'm not sure how it ties in. Do you remember Lieutenant-General Clary?"

"Paul Clary. I met him a few times. Nice guy. He worked on the arms reduction talks."

"That's him. We tried to call him for an interview. He had met Atcho in Cuba right after Castro took over. Anyway, he's disappeared, too."

"How does a general disappear?"

"Good question. The Pentagon isn't saying a word about it. More pertinent is when he disappeared." He inhaled sharply. "Are you ready for this? On the morning of Gorbachev's visit to DC, Clary went to work and was never seen again."

"What? How could that happen? What about his family?"

"Gone. The house is vacant. It has a 'For Sale' sign, but the listing traces to a nonentity brokerage. Try to find out about buying that place, and you'll get a runaround. We tried."

Collins felt growing frustration. "Let's get back to the present. We think that Atcho disrupted an assassination plot. Because of that, he gained Reagan's and Gorbachev's confidence. Now they have him chasing after the wannabe killer?"

"It seems to fit."

"All right. My head is pounding. Let me wrestle with this stuff a while. Meanwhile, let's stir the pot."

Jakes laughed out loud. "I love when we do that! What do you have in mind?"

"Call the Pentagon. Tell them we want to interview General Clary about his contributions to the arms-reduction process.

"Call the White House with the same message. Tell them that with the first free Soviet elections coming up, we intend to do a series on the history of the Soviet Union, beginning with the fall of the tsars. To develop public interest, we're going to consider the life and times of Rasputin and explore how things might have been different if he had never existed. Let's see what reaction we get."

"Are you expecting a reaction?"

"No, but there has to be a reason why Reagan and Gorbachev met with Atcho, and why he suddenly took an interest in Rasputin."

"What about Clary?"

"A shot in the dark, but he knew Atcho from way back, and his disappearance on that day is too much coincidence. If there's nothing there, it'll all go away and I can come home. By the way, did you find anything new on that retired CIA guy?"

"No. He answers his phone but hangs up when I identify myself. He must have it forwarded, because when we go by his house, he's not there. We'll stay on it. What are you going to do?"

Collins peered at his image in a mirror across the room. The reflection peering back was that of a haggard man, almost a stranger. "I'm going to try to get some sleep. Call me when you have something."

* * *

Several hours later, the ringing phone registered distantly on Collins' sleeping mind. Using most of the vocabulary he repressed back when society had been civil, he picked up the receiver.

"It's me. Jakes. I've been calling for the past twenty minutes."

Collins rubbed his eyes with his free hand, and grumbled something about having been in deep sleep. A sudden thought entered his mind. "Are my travel credentials to Moscow still good?"

"Moscow? We keep them updated for breaking stories. What do you want to do?"

"Maybe I could nose around up there, see what turns up."

"Think again. I did exactly what you told me to do. I called the White House and the Pentagon, and we got a reaction."

Fully awake, Collins felt Jakes' excitement. "What kind of reaction?"

"Wait! Let me fill you in on something else first. Atcho is a licensed pilot and certified for that jet that was stolen. Also, as soon as it cleared US airspace, it turned south."

"You're kidding."

"No." Jakes could barely contain his exuberance. "That airplane had the range to fly all the way to Cuba. No one would say if it was tracked there or not. But I ran a timeline, and Atcho had plenty of opportunity after decking the secret service guy to fly down there, and come back on that MiG by the time it landed at Andrews."

Collins' mind reeled as he juggled the implications. "Your guess was good. Great work! If that was really Atcho on those flights, that would support the notion that he disrupted an assassination attempt. Any idea what he might have done in Cuba?"

"No. Chase the bad guy? That's pure guess. After that, we're at a dead end."

Collins sighed. "All right. Stay on it. What's the reaction to our stirring the pot?"

"You have an invitation to the Oval Office."

"To see Reagan? We're going to interview Ronald Reagan?"

"No. He wants to speak with you."

"About what? We're on a roll. This isn't a good time to pull out. I need to find out what Atcho is doing here now."

"Your Concorde ticket is waiting. You'll meet the president tomorrow morning at ten o'clock. The invitation comes with teeth. If you don't agree, the French will deport you. You're already under surveillance. On arrival, you'll be held in federal protective custody."

Collins fought back a string of expletives. "All right. I'll be on my way."

26

"Why didn't you call me right away?" Atcho barely contained his exasperation. He had called Burly from another room so that Ivan would not overhear the conversation. Rafael would ensure that Ivan did not eavesdrop.

"To tell you what?" Burly retorted. "Keep in mind, buddy, I'm retired. I'm in this because the president thought you'd trust me more than anyone else, particularly on short notice." Irritation tinged his tone. "I called as soon as I had something to tell, which is that we think Sofia is in Paris. She left a message for you." He let that ride. "The truth is the president is wondering how things went to hell so fast. This was supposed to be a quiet project. Now Rafael and KGB-Ivan are there with you, Tony Collins is breathing down your neck, and Sofia's gone rogue."

Atcho fought to control his temper. "You tell Mr. Reagan that if his security had done its job, Collins would never have seen me and we'd have had more time to put nice, neat plans in place. On top of that, if I'd known Sofia's status, we could have told her the truth. Maybe she wouldn't have gone off half-cocked.

"The fact is that Reagan hired an amateur who had to make fast decisions without support. If he wants me off the job, I'm done!"

Burly sighed. "I've already been over that with him. Let's both calm down. I'll tell you what I know."

Despite being on the phone, Atcho nodded. Burly was a rare friend. He had gone to great lengths on Atcho's behalf several times. "What's Sofia's message?"

"When she called last night, she wouldn't say where she was, but she was definitely in France and on a secure line. A good guess is our embassy in Paris. Surveillance cameras there picked up someone that looked like her, and the sign-in log has a scrawl that looks like it could be hers. It looks like it was deliberately obscured. Anyway, she said to tell you that Yermolov is headed to Novosibirsk in Siberia."

"To where? Why? What's there?"

"Novosibirsk. It's in the south of Siberia. A good-sized Russian Orthodox congregation lives there. Some of those people are probably Rasputin followers. Sofia probably doesn't know, but Novosibirsk is a large military center. And, it's the headquarters for the KGB Border Troops."

"Good Lord! Yermolov will walk right into support by elements of the military and the KGB."

"Exactly."

They were both quiet. A question gnawed at Atcho. "How does Sofia know about Rasputin in all of this?"

Burly took in a deep breath. "Her intelligence instincts are well developed. She figured out Yermolov. As for Rasputin," he groaned. "That was my fault, my friend. I pointed her in the direction of the Rasputin biography. I hoped she would go after it in a bookstore or a library around Virginia some place, and we could nab her. Sorry."

Atcho had to grin at the irony. "Sounds like we both have a lot to learn about Sofia."

"I ordered her home. She said she'd come in tonight, but I'm guessing she played me for time. I don't expect her."

"What do we do now?"

"Sofia said you need an ally in the field. I think she means she's going to be out there helping you finish the mission."

"Any idea where she got the information on Novosibirsk?"

"Maybe. We're sending someone from the embassy to the Rasputin house to ask if anyone fitting her description has been there. Next time we speak—"

While Burly talked, Atcho's mind flashed to the scene at the Rasputin house the day before. "Crap!" he exclaimed. "I think I saw her at that house." He described the scene. "She looked right at me."

"It probably was her," Burly grumbled. "When was that?"

"Around mid-afternoon, yesterday."

"Great. Whatever she learned had to come from there. Man, she played me." He chuckled. "You know, bud, if we get through this and you marry her, you'll have one helluva tigress on your hands."

"Let's stick with the present. Where do you think she went?"

"No telling, but stay on mission. Let me worry about finding where Sofia is and what she's up to."

"Good luck with that. I'll get Ivan to plan how we get to Novosibirsk. I need to be ready to move by tomorrow." Another thought struck. "If we're going to have a chance at a raid, it'll have to happen soon. We'll get back out to that hill as soon as we hang up. Anything more on your courier?"

"No."

As he re-entered the room where Ivan and Rafael were, he reflected that Ivan had been remarkably docile after initial anger. Atcho had thought he might try to escape. On second thought, Ivan had no place to go. *He could be biding his time.*

"Have you decided what we're going to do?" Ivan asked. His voice carried an edge.

"Yermolov might be at that place on the hill. We're going to that observation point I found yesterday and try to get positive ID on him. Meanwhile, you need to plan how to get us into Novosibirsk."

Rafael sat up, and Ivan spun around. "Novosibirsk? Why?"

"Can't say right now."

Ivan grimaced. "You want me to get you into Novosibirsk and back out, but you won't tell me why?"

Atcho shrugged.

Ivan's eyes narrowed. "How do you propose I do that? Who will I call? Most people don't take calls from a dead man."

Atcho eyed him. "Assume you're still alive and want to help. How would you do it?"

Ivan drew back. He had expected an angry retort. "Novosibirsk?" He mulled. "Interesting place. A major center of military and KGB activity, but you probably knew that."

Atcho nodded. "You probably have back-channels in place in case you ever had to run."

Ivan smirked. "With as many informants as the KGB has inside the Soviet Union to keep tabs on the rest of us, if I ever had to run, it would be pure improvisation."

"Then pretend you're on the run and believed to be dead. Improvise. You want to stay alive, and you want to get home in one piece. How would you do that?"

Ivan thought over the question. "I'd have to keep a low profile," he said slowly, "and bribe well-entrenched bureaucrats."

"Another question. Would official word have gone to only necessary places about your death by now?" Ivan nodded bleakly. "Or, would every KGB office get the news?"

"I wasn't that important. Most likely, Novosibirsk would not have been informed. So, what?"

"So, you could show up with credentials and throw your KGB weight around."

"That might work, so long as the guy I'm trying to intimidate isn't another KGB officer."

"We'll have to risk it. Think about it while we go out to the hill."

"If I come up with a plan, will you let me make telephone calls?" Sarcasm laced Ivan's tone. "If not, I'm dead weight."

Atcho ignored the pun. "We'll work it out. Let's go."

Ivan got up from the bed. Rafael rose from his seat and crossed to the closet. He reached inside his bag and took out two Glocks. He handed one to Atcho with extra magazines. "We might need these."

Atcho looked at him, surprised. "How did you get those into France?"

Rafael shrugged. "Burly arranged it. One of the president's national security adviser people worked things out through the French Embassy." He handed Atcho a small card. "You'll need this. That's your carry permit."

Ivan was shocked. Since regaining consciousness, he had regarded Atcho as a bumbler and Rafael as his sidekick. *This is the guy who brought Yermolov down in the first place,* he reminded himself. An escape attempt had just become much more dangerous.

The trio drove to the observation point. For an hour, they watched the hill without seeing activity. Then, the shadow of a car appeared at the crest. It cleared the trees and sped down the road through the field. It was the blue sedan. Behind it, another car followed, and then another and another. When they reached the turnoff, instead of turning right, which would have retraced the route of the day before, they turned left and went in the opposite direction.

"They're on their way out!" Atcho roared. He started the car, raced through town at breakneck speed, barreled down the road that led to the turnoff, and then sped in the direction the cars had traveled. When he had gone a few miles without overtaking the other cars and finding no indication of which way they went, he did a quick U-turn, and speeded back to the turnoff. There, he floored the accelerator up the gravel road.

Next to him, Ivan yelled, "What are you doing?"

"Maybe we can catch stragglers," Atcho shouted back.

When they reached the forest, he was forced to slow down by a bumpy road. It curved inside the tree line, and ended in a clearing with a series of cabins. Atcho circled and stopped.

No one appeared. The three of them went from cabin to cabin. They had been recently occupied, evidenced by light trash strewn about, but were locked and empty.

"Missed them," Atcho grumbled.

"What now?" Rafael asked.

"This shoots down the raid idea. We go back to the safe house and let Ivan get on the phone."

They piled back into the car, and Atcho cranked the engine. Just as he set the gear, another car came to an abrupt halt in front of them amidst a swirl of dust. It sprang into rapid retreat.

Atcho floored the accelerator. His car leaped forward. The other car disappeared around the first bend, still in reverse. When Atcho reached the curve, it had almost turned around. Atcho crashed into its bumper, spinning it so that it straddled the road. His car came to a halt.

Suddenly, Ivan punched Atcho hard in the face. Continuing his motion, he grabbed Atcho's pistol and pointed it at Rafael. He moved so fast that neither Atcho nor Rafael had a chance to react.

"Very slowly, toss your gun outside," he told Rafael.

His face a mask, Rafael complied.

"I'm going with him," Ivan said, indicating the other car.

Atcho did not speak. A mark along his cheek began to swell.

Ivan opened the door and stepped out. Keeping the Glock pointed at them, he moved to the second car and spoke to the driver in Russian, instructing him to straighten it out.

Just as the vehicle had completed the maneuver, Atcho floored his accelerator. His car crashed into the rear of the other one, spinning it again and striking Ivan.

Rafael bounded out the back door. The Russian driver gunned his engine, straightened his vehicle, and raced down the road through crunching gravel, and a cloud of dust.

When the air cleared, Atcho saw that Rafael sat on Ivan's chest, his recovered pistol aimed at Ivan's head. He looked back at Atcho and shook his head. "He's not dead," Rafael called. "The car knocked him over. I punched him out. Now what?"

27

Ivan groaned and opened his eyes. He sat with his back against a tree. Rafael stood over him, pistol in hand. A short distance away, Atcho leaned against another tree. Ivan felt the force of his glare.

"What do we do with him?" Rafael asked.

"Drop him at the US Embassy. That's our best bet."

"What about Novosibirsk?"

"I don't know. We'll have to find our own way in." Atcho started toward the car.

Ivan heard them as though through a fog. His head ached and he felt stiffness spreading through his body. "You can't turn me in!" His voice cracked and seemed to come from far away.

"Says who," Atcho snapped. He turned to Rafael. "Any ideas?"

Rafael shrugged his indifference. "Shoot him? Turn him over to the Soviets? Makes no difference to me. We already didn't have a good plan. He made things worse." He jerked Ivan to his feet. "Let's go. The embassy is the best we can do."

Ivan struggled to stand up straight. "Listen to me," he shouted. "I can help."

"Not interested," Rafael growled, jostling him forward.

"They have my family," Ivan bellowed. He pushed against Rafael and planted his feet.

Atcho halted abruptly. "They what?"

"Yermolov has my wife and son. He called a week before Rafael kidnapped me. He threatened them. He has men watching them."

Atcho stared. "Why? What are you supposed to do?"

Ivan heaved a troubled sigh. "Watch you. For Yermolov. He figured I could get close to you." He grimaced. "That was me in your apartment. Your shot grazed my arm."

Atcho's eyes narrowed into slits. "You broke into my home? You planted bugs?"

Ivan said nothing. Rafael moved in, menacing.

"Yermolov thought you could get close to me, and here we are," Atcho muttered. "What do you think you can do now?"

"Execute your plan. I can get to the KGB in Novosibirsk. People there won't know I'm dead. I can strong-arm." He breathed hard.

Rafael squinted at him. "We're supposed to trust you?" He moved in front of Ivan. "What were you intending when you pointed that gun at my head?"

"If I'd wanted to kill you, you'd be dead." Ivan faced Atcho. "I thought that man could take me to Yermolov." His voice took on urgency. "Atcho, if it had been your family, you'd have done the same thing."

Stung, Atcho drew closer, scrutinizing Ivan. "All right. I'll buy that for now. What do we do?"

"I need to call Russia. Take me to the Soviet Embassy."

Startled, Rafael thrust his face close to Ivan's. "Do what?"

Ivan dismissed Rafael with a look. He struggled against the cord binding his wrists behind his back. "Hear me out," he pleaded. "Can I get this rope off?"

Atcho moved in front of him, arms crossed. "I'll listen."

Ivan's shoulders slumped. "We need credentials. To get into Novosibirsk." He looked at Rafael. "You have my papers, right?"

"We left them in your car. Your death had to look genuine."

Ivan rolled his eyes. "That makes things harder. We can get credentials, but it starts at the Soviet Embassy."

Atcho thought that over. "We must have a forger on contract in Paris. Why don't I call DC and ask for him?"

Ivan exploded. "Yermolov is gone! We need credentials now that pass Soviet inspection. You want to leave that to a contractor?"

Atcho shook his head. "How do you expect to pull it off?"

Ivan explained his plan.

When he was finished, Atcho raised his eyebrows. "That's gutsy. Even if I thought you could do it, why would I trust you?"

Without hesitation, Ivan responded, "It's the only chance I've got to save my family. You of all people understand that."

Atcho stared. His own despair when his daughter was kidnapped flashed though his mind. Then, he saw again General Secretary Gorbachev's birthmark against the reticles of his sniper scope, and felt the squeeze against the trigger. How close he had come to completing that heinous act to save his daughter. He turned to Rafael. "Cut him loose."

* * *

Ivan breathed a sigh of relief. He sat alone in the middle of the car's backseat, his hands free. Atcho and Rafael climbed into the front in the mood of futility that follows a strenuous argument. Rafael kept a wary eye on Ivan. "Where to?"

"The Soviet Embassy." Atcho glanced across the left front of the hood. The crash had crumpled it, but the tires were unobstructed. They drove down the hill on the gravel road and wended their way through the city.

Atcho sensed the surreal disconnect known from years ago in Moscow, of seeing ordinary people go about mundane tasks while evil moved in their midst. He had felt it that morning in Washington, DC, when KGB officers drove him to the target site to kill Gorbachev. Today, Parisians could hardly see these three weary men in a beat-up car and imagine that they were at the vortex of a struggle to seize control of the most powerful empire in history.

He stopped by the curb along Lannes Boulevard, two blocks from the Soviet Embassy. "We're almost there. How long will it take?" he asked Ivan. "How do we rendezvous?"

"Three hours. I'll come to the safe house. Wait for me there." He glanced up the street. "I'll walk the rest of the way to the embassy from here. Give me your passports."

"What?" Rafael erupted again.

Ivan ignored him. "I don't have time for this," he told Atcho. "You want to get inside Russia? I need the pictures on your passports for new documents."

Rafael scoffed.

"Give him your passport, Rafi." Atcho handed Ivan his own. Rafael acquiesced.

"We'll wait three hours at the safe house," Atcho said. "Come there. Alone. No calls. Bring our passports. Any deviation, we call curtains on this whole operation and come after you."

Ivan grimaced. "Still no trust." He stepped out onto the sidewalk. "A year ago," he told Atcho in a wistful tone, "I trusted you." He closed the door and walked in the direction of the embassy.

"Do you believe that guy?" Rafael exclaimed.

"I put him here," Atcho replied. He put the car in gear. "I need to call Burly. Fast."

A few minutes later in the safe house, Atcho spoke rapid-fire over the phone. Behind him, Rafael listened while Atcho briefed Burly and told him what he needed. "It's urgent."

"That's a tall order," Burly replied. "I'll do what I can."

"What about Sofia?"

Burly had no new information. "We've widened our search to include embassies and consulates all over NATO."

"Anything new on your courier?"

"No."

Atcho felt no comfort. "If Ivan doesn't come back, what's the backup plan?"

"You're it. You'll have to get to Novosibirsk on your own."

* * *

Portraying a bum, Ivan approached the Soviet Embassy, watchful for anyone taking undue interest in him. He needed no acting. His clothes were disheveled, the side of his face swollen and turning colors. He limped from the stiffness still spreading through his body.

The embassy came into view. Ivan avoided the main entrance, looking instead for private access for embassy staff that must be at the rear. Finding it, he pressed a button on the gate. Moments later, a sentry stepped out. Another stood nearby, his rifle trained on Ivan.

"I am Major Chekov of Section S of the KGB," Ivan announced before the sentry could speak. "Take me to the ambassador."

The sentry looked at him coldly. "Your ID."

Ivan stepped closer. "Do as you're told." He put his mouth close to the sentry's face. "I was captured and beaten, and my credentials were stolen. I am in no mood for shit."

"But Comrade Major, procedure..."

"I understand procedure. The first thing is to get me inside and off this street! Then we can talk."

The sentry nodded. His companion lowered his rifle. Ivan stepped through the gate into a small courtyard with a guard shack to one side. Across the yard, a back door led into the main building. Ivan was certain the executive offices must be close by.

"Take me inside the guardhouse," Ivan commanded. The guards exchanged glances, but did as ordered. The furnishings were sparse. A phone sat on a table. "Call the ambassador's office. Tell him I'm here."

"We can call his secretary."

Ivan glared. The sentry stiffened. "Tell her that Major Chekov escaped and needs to see the ambassador immediately."

The guards glanced nervously at each other. "Shouldn't we take you to the KGB section?"

"No," Ivan snapped. He drew himself to full height. "You are to say nothing of this to anyone, unless you'd like to explain your loose lips to General Secretary Gorbachev himself!" He looked back and forth between them. "Is that understood?"

The two stood at attention, their faces turning red. Moisture formed along their hairlines. "Yes, Comrade," they said in unison. One of the guards jumped to make the call.

A minute passed. Ivan thought he might soon be surrounded and hauled to a holding cell. Then a look of relief showed on the sentry's face. "Yes, he's here." He listened, and hung up. "I am to bring you to the ambassador's office. He was expecting you."

Ivan did his best to mask utter shock. Moments later, the guard led him into a small reception area inside the main building. The door opened, and there stood Vassily Aznabaev, Soviet Ambassador to France.

Ivan had seen him on television many times. The ambassador had been a colleague of Gorbachev's when the two worked together in the Agriculture Secretariat of the Central Committee of the Supreme Soviet. He and the general secretary were known to be fast friends, traveling abroad together on delegations. He had been a strong supporter during the years leading to Gorbachev's accession.

Like his friend, Aznabaev had a charming manner, a new factor in East-West diplomatic relations. He was also known for a hard edge; he knew when to employ the "Nyet" style of Soviet negotiations.

"Major Chekov?" He assumed a professional manner, taking in Ivan's disheveled appearance with a neutral expression. "I was told to expect you." He led Ivan into a large office and pointed to a telephone on his desk with the receiver off the hook. "That's for you."

"Who knows I'm here?" he asked in surprise, but Aznabaev's skeptical glance quieted him. As he crossed to the desk, he saw the requisite portraits of Soviet heroes: Lenin, Stalin, and most of the past chairmen of the Communist Party, including Mikhail Gorbachev. Gone was Nikita Khrushchev, having fallen from grace. *I wonder how many coups we've had since Lenin.* He picked up the phone. "Major Chekov," he announced.

"This is Mikhail Gorbachev. Are you alone?"

Ivan snapped to attention. "Comrade General Secretary. I was coming to call you." He stemmed his shock. Aznabaev tapped his arm and motioned that he was going out the door. "The ambassador is leaving now."

"President Reagan just called. He received a message from Atcho. How can I help?"

Ivan hesitated. When he spoke, he did so with confidence that he did not feel. "Yermolov is going to Novosibirsk. You can guess why."

"Military and KGB assets," Gorbachev replied. "He could gather a lot of capability there."

Ivan explained Atcho's intentions. "We need travel documents to get in and back out. Mine were lost when I was killed." He let the sarcasm linger.

"I heard about that," Gorbachev said without apology. "We must stop Yermolov."

"Do you have a backup plan?"

"Of course." Gorbachev gave no hint about what that might be. Ivan doubted such a plan existed. "Tell the ambassador what you need. He'll see that you get it. Good luck."

"Wait, Comrade! My family—" But the general secretary had already hung up.

Ivan cursed. He sat in a chair facing the desk and closed his eyes. His mind raced. He had only minutes at best. He dialed a number. When it was answered, he spoke quickly.

The call lasted less than a minute. When he was done, he crossed to a small table and poured a shot of vodka. He tossed it, and felt the clear liquid calming his nerves.

The main door opened, and Aznabaev strode in. "Comrade Gorbachev told me as much as he could before you arrived," he said. "Tell me what you need."

Ivan glanced at his watch. He suddenly felt heavy with fatigue, emotionally more than physically. He looked at Aznabaev. "We only have two hours."

* * *

Rafael spotted Ivan first. He and Atcho had left him a note and moved to a café across the street from the safe house after the call to Burly. Nearly four hours had passed since dropping Ivan off. "I hope he follows instructions," Rafael said dryly.

They watched Ivan enter the safe house and shortly re-emerge. He walked to the curb, glanced around, and crossed the street.

"He wasn't looking for anyone," Rafael observed.

"Maybe. He's a pro." As Ivan disappeared into the crowd, they went after him. When satisfied that no one followed, they confronted him in the café specified in their note.

"You're late," Atcho said.

"Getting three sets of documents to travel inside the Soviet Union isn't easy," Ivan snapped. "Glad to see the trust factor went up."

"Get on with it."

"Fine. The general secretary sends greetings." He read their skepticism. "He said you sent Reagan a message. Thanks for the help."

Atcho remained stone-faced. *Burly got through.*

From inside his jacket, Ivan produced two sets of papers, including their passports. "Welcome back to the KGB, Atcho." His tone bordered on sarcasm. "You are now Colonel Nikolina. Rafael is Colonel Ovinko. With these, we can travel anywhere in the Soviet Union. I'll do the talking. All you have to do is look stern. Can you handle that?"

Rafael glared at him.

Ivan ignored Rafael. "We have a direct flight to Moscow tonight. We connect to Novosibirsk three hours after landing. We'll be there tomorrow night."

28

Yermolov strode into a staff conference on the airbase in Romania. Transport from Paris had gone off without a hitch. A Soviet cargo plane with French markings had flown them from a private airstrip. It demonstrated strong support within the Soviet Union.

Safely in a Soviet satellite state now, half the forces that sought Yermolov were neutralized. The US did not know his whereabouts. He could scarcely believe the distance he had come since lying near death in Havana. He regretted telling Chekov, "I will have my day." He had expected to die. Now the statement seemed foolish.

The first time the Soviet Ambassador to Cuba had visited him at the clinic, the bustling outside Yermolov's door ceased. The ambassador had come alone. Yermolov sensed someone by his side. The ambassador sat in the same chair that Ivan had used a few days earlier. He leaned in. "How are you feeling, General?"

Surprised at the expression of respect, Yermolov opened his eyes to see a man he did not recognize.

"I am Ambassador Jeloudov. Don't speak. I came to say that you are among friends. Many of us object to Gorbachev's policies."

As soon as Yermolov was out of danger, the ambassador moved him to Soviet VIP quarters in a secluded part of the embassy. The few conversations between them were short, but productive. The ambassador's behind-the-scenes maneuvering became evident. He had reported Yermolov dead, and certified documents to that effect.

"Castro is no friend to Gorbachev," Jeloudov said. "If the Soviet Union crumbles, so do subsidies to Cuba. He ran interference in case Soviet authorities demand your body."

During another conversation, Yermolov asked, "Do others support my return home?"

Jeloudov did not hesitate. "Why else would I take the risk?"

Yermolov studied him. "How do we bring this off?" he asked slowly.

"We're both exposed here. We need to get you out of Cuba." He planned to fly Yermolov to Nicaragua, and then to Europe. "You'll be able to hide in plain sight while you make contact in Russia, assemble a staff, and get ready to transfer home."

Yermolov studied the ambassador. He was a small man who could pass for Latin nationality, which might be why he was effective with Cubans. "Why would you help me get back to Russia?"

Jeloudov chose his words carefully. "I'm a diplomat, not a warrior. You're experienced in the Cold War." He raised his eyebrows. "From inside both superpowers."

Yermolov acknowledged the comment, and Jeloudov continued. "Gorbachev's policies will destroy the Soviet Union. Russia will lose its dominance over Eastern Europe and will be vulnerable to Western ambitions. Napoleon and Hitler both demonstrated how ruinous that could be for Moscow. I don't want to see the chaos that is certain with the Soviet Union gone."

Yermolov sat quietly, formulating his next question. "What do you expect to see if I return to Russia?"

Jeloudov responded without hesitation. "The restoration of our country's greatness and stability."

Yermolov nodded slowly. *This man is skilled. Better watch him.* "You could not have kept me alive, certified my death, and hoped to move me to Europe without help from KGB and Party officers here in Havana." His comment was more a question than a statement.

Jeloudov displayed an amorphous smile. "As I said, you are among friends. We believe you can make a change."

Yermolov tapped his fingers as he contemplated what Jeloudov had said and the implied possibilities. "How do I hide in plain sight?"

Once again, Jeloudov exhibited an enigmatic smile. "How well do you know the story of Rasputin?"

* * *

Yermolov pulled himself from his reflections back to the present at the airbase in Romania. His staff was prepared to brief. Only Colonel Drygin was missing. "Does anyone know where the executive officer is?"

"Yes, sir," the adjutant spoke up. "He was on the phone just before we came in. The call seemed serious."

"All right." In the practiced manner of Paul Clary, Yermolov set aside his annoyance. "What is the plan for getting to Novosibirsk?"

The operations officer stood. "We can go as early as tomorrow." He briefed that on arrival, a bus would take them to a local village. Only KGB and army personnel who were vetted supporters would move them. The village was populated with Russian Orthodox Christians, many of whom still hoped for the return of the Romanovs and believed in the legend of Rasputin. "Leaders are ready to spread support to other communities."

"Excellent!"

Drygin entered and took his seat. He looked tense. "If that's all," Yermolov told the staff, "execute the plan. We move tomorrow."

As the staff officers filed out of the room, Yermolov kept his seat and turned to Drygin. "Did you have something for me?"

"Yes," Drygin replied. "You'll recall that we left my driver, Yegor, behind outside of Paris to handle loose ends." Yermolov nodded. Drygin continued. "He was in the village to get supplies for a few days. When he went back, another car was already there. Yegor says it looked like the one we thought was following me yesterday. It rammed him."

Yermolov's brows arched. "What happened?"

"I'll fill you in on the details. You should hear this first." He set a recording device on the table. "We had a phone in the operations cabin with a number to give outsiders."

Yermolov nodded, recalling that he had given the number to Major Ivan Chekov. Drygin pushed the play button.

"General Yermolov," a disembodied voice said. "This is Major Chekov." Stunned, Yermolov looked at Drygin. Ivan's voice continued. "I am alive. I was kidnapped. I am coming to you."

"He's alive!" Yermolov drew back. "We suspected that."

Drygin played the tape several times. "Sounds like he tried to escape," Drygin observed. "Obviously, he was stopped."

"That's the way I see it. When did the call come in?"

"Sometime between our departure and two hours later."

"Maybe he escaped again," Yermolov reflected. "He must be concerned about his family. I doubt he just became an ardent supporter. Bring his wife and son to Novosibirsk. High priority."

"Yes, General."

Yermolov reflected a few more minutes. "Major Chekov said, 'I am alive.' Why would he think we know about his fatal accident?"

"Maybe he's assuming."

Yermolov remained in thought. "Maybe. He was at our cabins in Paris. He thinks we know about his death. And he said he's coming to me, so he thinks he knows where we are going. That's three data points. How did he get them?" He sat quietly with his thoughts for a few moments. Then he faced Drygin directly. "Do you think we have an informant?"

Drygin responded calmly, but with a slight edge in his voice. "I hand-picked these men. They detest Gorbachev's policies and worry about the future of our country."

"I appreciate that." Yermolov breathed a sigh. "It was a thought. Issue an alert to be on the lookout for Chekov. When do we depart?"

"Tomorrow morning. We will be in Novosibirsk by nightfall."

29

The commanding general of Western Siberia Military District, Colonel General Kutuzov, met Yermolov at the aircraft when they landed in Novosibirsk. "Welcome, General," Kutuzov greeted. "We flew you to a different airfield than the one planned. Ride with me. Your staff will meet you in the village. We can talk."

Yermolov did not like operational surprises. Without his own security, he felt vulnerable. He returned Kutuzov's greeting in equal measure, but as he did, he saw in Kutuzov's light-green eyes a man practiced at providing requisite expressions for any occasion.

Yermolov carried with him the briefcase delivered in the tavern two nights earlier. Kutuzov reached for it. "My men can handle that."

"No, no," Yermolov responded in his most amiable tone. "I prefer to carry this one. It has personal effects." Colonel Drygin took note.

Kutuzov showed him to a waiting limousine. "This runway belongs to an aircraft manufacturing plant," Kutuzov explained as they rode away. "Fewer eyes are watching it. Fewer questions."

Yermolov remembered Kutuzov from years ago. His rise in the Soviet Army to command this vast region in Siberia affirmed his brilliance. Still, this was the Soviet Union where everyone was watched, where watchers watched watchers, and where a shift of political wind could find people at any level banished, imprisoned, or dead.

As the limousine left the airfield, Yermolov noticed a massive airplane gleaming in the sun across the field. Its nose and cockpit were rotated over its roof, revealing a cavernous cargo hold.

"What is that?" Yermolov asked in amazement.

"Beautiful, isn't it?" Kutuzov responded. "That is the Antonov 225 Mriya. It's built to carry the Soviet space orbiter, our version of the Boeing 747 that ferries the American space shuttle around."

"What's it doing here?"

"It's been here a few weeks to be checked out at the aircraft plant. It's brand new. In a few days, it'll go on a check ride for its full range, and then fly to Moscow for commissioning." He nudged Yermolov conspiratorially and lowered his voice. "Excitement about this aircraft will provide cover for our movements."

Yermolov drew back, but said nothing. Kutuzov turned to him as if to change subjects. "Before I came to pick you up I had this car swept for listening devices. My driver can't hear us." His face grew serious. "Tell me. Why should I support you?"

Yermolov stymied a rise in irritation at the abruptness of the question. "You have me at a disadvantage."

"You must have thought about it," Kutuzov rejoined. "I've gone this distance because I have faith in our mutual friend in Cuba, Ambassador Jeloudov, and because I'm familiar with what you did in the United States." He reached over and grasped Yermolov's forearm. When he spoke again his low, slow speech added gravity to his voice. "I know the whole story." He withdrew his hand and looked out at the passing fields of snow and ice. "I wish you had succeeded with the assassination. I don't see how the Soviet Union can survive Gorbachev's policies. I'm not alone."

Yermolov relaxed. Instead of putting him on the spot, Kutuzov opened to him. "I agree," he replied. "The plan was developed over months at senior levels in the government and the Party. To have gunmen in place at the precise moment that the general secretary's motorcade stopped in that exact spot took unbelievable coordination. Monumental, really, that we kept it a secret. That's the depth of feeling against the general secretary and his policies."

Kutuzov nodded. "Do you know about the unrest in Moscow?"

"The protests in the streets? They should be put down."

"Agreed. The more freedom Gorbachev allows, the more people demand. The buffer states are starting to push for greater autonomy. If this continues, the Soviet Union will dissolve. Russia's underbelly will be laid bare." He shook his head. "Already the Baltic states demand independence, like Poland."

Yermolov chuckled. "Soviets seek freedom, and Americans seek more free stuff." He became serious. "We're all anxious. I had time to think in Cuba. I'm happy to lay out my ideas, but between here and the village I can give only an outline."

"Please." Kutuzov appeared eager to listen.

Yermolov took a moment to formulate his thoughts. "My plan revolves around three tenets: restoring military strength, clamping down on political dissent, and loosening economic freedoms."

Surprised, Kutuzov turned on Yermolov. "I like the first two," he remarked, "but loosening economic freedom? Have you forgotten that you intend to lead a communist country?"

Yermolov laughed out loud. "I assure you I haven't. I'm a pragmatist, not an ideologue. Ronald Reagan started this arms race to bankrupt us. But the US is creating its own financial crisis, and with patience, we can exploit it."

"Explain."

"The US keeps putting expensive social programs in place that never go away. Add that to their defense spending, and at some point, the US economy will crash under them. We'll be there to pick up the pieces."

For the duration of their ride to the village, Kutuzov listened, captivated by Yermolov's strength of knowledge. "The American Constitution is a big problem for them, because it stands in the way of the government doing what it wants."

"I've never understood that document," Kutuzov replied.

Yermolov laughed out loud. "Not many Americans do either," he chortled. "Fewer every year. Someday, it will die a quiet death. We Russians have a different problem. We need to ditch ideology. It's nothing more than acting with confidence on what we think we know. But what if we're wrong? It's costly and gives little benefit."

Kutuzov was disconcerted. "We stop being communists?"

"Call it whatever we want," Yermolov replied, "but look for what works. We can't have factories that manufacture only left shoes and expect to progress. That's a waste of resources." He returned to discussion of the military buildup. "For a while, we keep first-strike nuclear capabilities, but we don't expand or improve them."

Kutuzov recoiled. "You're getting close to heresy."

Yermolov saw that he was not smiling. "I know the Americans," he said in his most reassuring voice. "They won't strike first. They're deathly afraid we will. We already have a nuclear arsenal larger than theirs. If we keep them spending their money and stop depleting ours, we gain ground. Meanwhile, we beef up conventional forces to keep control over the satellite states. Then by applying the results of my third tenet, we'll have resources to overtake gaps, if they still exist. Some fools in the US want to disarm unilaterally."

They both laughed, and Kutuzov regarded Yermolov with a new light in his eyes. "I'm starting to see. But I don't understand the part about loosening up on economic freedoms. Won't that cause more trouble? We were just talking about the problems with people demanding more freedom in Moscow."

"Think China," Yermolov said flatly.

Kutuzov looked doubtful. "That's a communist country."

"They call themselves that, but China implemented capitalist methods on a large scale over a decade ago. With over a billion people to feed, they had no choice. If a fraction of their population starves, their whole power structure crumbles." Yermolov paused a moment. "They already had a taste of that during the Boxer Rebellion when there were so many dead bodies floating on the Yangtze River that they choked it." He lowered his voice above a whisper. "Chinese citizens are allowed no political freedom at all. They can make as much money as they want, engage in whatever stupidity they desire, buy toys, go to the hairdressers, but if they criticize the government or dissent in any way, they pay holy hell."

Kutuzov sat in quiet contemplation. "And you think that could work here?" He looked dubious.

Yermolov nodded. "The Soviet Union has more oil reserves than Saudi Arabia. If we present a less hostile face to the US and become friendly to investors, we can rebuild defenses and develop our oil industry with their money."

Kutuzov rubbed his chin and turned to glance at the passing countryside. They were approaching the village. "What about our social spending? Won't we face the same challenges as the US?"

Yermolov's eyes burned with malicious delight. "My friend," he laughed, "we can stop spending on any program, at any time. No one in the Soviet Union has rights to life, liberty, or the pursuit of happiness. We'll take spending down to levels they need to be, and if the people cry too loudly," he looked intently into Kutuzov's eyes, "they can protest with sticks and stones, and we can shoot them, drive tanks over them, even bomb them to hell, and we won't worry about choking a river."

Kutuzov listened intently. He studied Yermolov with a poker face, as though trying to see into his mind.

They arrived at the compound. "After I drop you off I must report on our conversation," Kutuzov said. "Others are keen to know about your ideas. I'm meeting with the commander of KGB Border Troops tonight. If you're not too tired, you should come along."

"Of course." Yermolov tried to discern Kutuzov's enthusiasm for their discussion, but saw only a neutral face.

"You can settle in," Kutuzov said. "I'll pick you up in two hours."

After Kutuzov left, Yermolov surveyed the compound. At one time, it might have housed a crude restaurant with adjoining rooms for travelers. The structure was nondescript: concrete walls set up in functional form around a courtyard.

Drygin came to meet him. "Everyone arrived," he said. He again noted Yermolov's briefcase. "The rest of your things are in your room." He reported that he had integrated the staff with the local KGB unit, and had assumed responsibility for perimeter security. "Did you want a staff meeting?"

"Is there anything new to discuss?"

"No. The local leader of the Rasputin group wants to meet with you here tomorrow morning. We'll arrange that and let you know the time."

"That's fine. Any word on the whereabouts of Chekov, Atcho, or Ms. Stahl?" His feeling of unease settled in again as Drygin shook his head at the mention of each name.

"The KGB unit has pictures of all three. They know to be on the look-out, and they've spread the word."

"Let me know when anything turns up. General Kutuzov will pick me up later for a meeting with the KGB Border Troops commander. I'm sure that's the next step in a vetting process."

Drygin nodded. "I think you're right."

* * *

Two hours later, Drygin watched as the limousine carrying Kutuzov and Yermolov drove away. He was angered by Yermolov's suspicions after the staff meeting last night in Romania. He was further troubled by the general's anxious insistence on receiving constant updates regarding Atcho et al.

A measure of distrust had been expected as a Soviet staple. Drygin recalled a photograph of Joseph Stalin taken during the early days of that dictator's reign of terror. In the photo were three other men who had been early supporters, and had followed Stalin into power.

The photo was widely circulated. Over the years, each of the other three men disappeared from the photo in sequence as they fell out of favor with Stalin, and their lives were forfeited. In the most recent version of the photo, Stalin stood alone.

Stalin was not unique in history. Drygin's study of world upheavals often revealed the premature demise of early followers of dictators. History contained myriad examples, but one fresh in Drygin's mind was Saddam Hussein, the reigning tyrant of Iraq. When Hussein seized power, he had his best friend summarily shot along with others considered to be either less than reliable or potential rivals. *And then there was Castro and Che.*

Drygin had been a primary contact for Yermolov within Soviet intelligence for several years while the Soviet general doubled as General Clary. He was thus taken aback when Yermolov questioned the possibility of an informant among his group. The general's suspicions were aimed at men who had taken great risks to forward his ambitions, and Drygin was currently closest to him. From his perspective, Yermolov already showed indications of suspecting him of subversive acts.

The irony was that not only had Drygin set up the arrangements with the Rasputin sect in Paris, but he had also initiated and managed the contact with the commander of KGB Border Troops, Lieutenant General Fierko. Fierko had arranged for Yermolov's smooth re-entry into the Soviet Union. More importantly, he had a direct link with the chairman of the KGB, Nestor Murin, without whose support no coup was possible.

None of the men Drygin had brought to form Yermolov's initial staff were hard-core ideologues. Each had been in the group that provided intelligence, security, and logistical support to Yermolov during the assassination attempt. Most ironic was that Yermolov's plan for seizing power was Drygin's plan. The colonel and his staff had developed it.

Drygin went to Yermolov's room. The door was locked, but Drygin had a master key. Seconds later, he stood in front of a padlocked wall locker. When he could not open it, he took care to relock the room, and went to place a call.

* * *

Yermolov observed the passing countryside. Dusk approached, and shadows already cut visibility. "Is this meeting part of vetting that began with you this afternoon?" he asked.

Kutuzov eyed Yermolov. "You didn't expect us to hand over the keys to Moscow easily?"

Yermolov shook his head. "Knowing the process would be helpful."

Kutuzov studied his face. "Your loyalty and dedication are not in question. We are considering capability. The question is, can you deliver a new direction? I'll leave it to the KGB to explain how vetting works for our purposes. Do you mind a piece of plain advice?"

"Go on." He masked his irritation.

"I am a soldier, first, last, and always," Kutuzov began. He searched for words. "Communist Party officers have interfered with my operations over my entire career, but if I had ever said so, I would have been in a *gulag* long ago." He looked intently at Yermolov. "Part of the mission of the KGB is to protect Party ideology. Without them we have no chance of success. You have to sell your plan to General Fierko, and he is KGB."

"Understood," Yermolov said as amiably as he could over his annoyance. "Thank you. And so, the politics begin."

30

Yermolov extended his hand to Lieutenant General Fierko, Commander of the KGB Border Troops in the Novosibirsk Oblast. "I'm pleased to meet you, Comrade."

"You are welcome here, General." Fierko spoke in a perfunctory manner, with a thin voice.

Yermolov could not read Fierko, and that puzzled him. Fierko was a small man, but anyone judging him on that basis would err. His reputation was that he had risen on intelligence and political savvy, not lack of them. Ambassador Jeloudov had worked through Fierko to make Yermolov's transit preparations from Cuba.

Fierko circled to the opposite side of his desk. "Please sit down." Even though both generals held one rank higher than his own, he obviously felt secure. Yermolov's formal rank in the KGB had disappeared with his flight from capture following the failed assassination. Referring to him as "General" was a courtesy until he was formally reinstated.

Fierko directed a penetrating gaze at Yermolov. "My job tonight is to explain the process of assessing you and your plans." He chose his words carefully and nodded in Kutuzov's direction. "If we had received a less-than-favorable report from General Kutuzov, we would be pursuing a different course of action."

"I understand. Who is we?"

"As you know, I report directly to Chairman Murin. For any plan to succeed, he must be at the center of it. He will be here tomorrow."

Yermolov's face registered surprise, bordering on shock. He had not anticipated Murin's involvement at this stage. "He will be here?"

"Yes. Officially he's coming to review new border security procedures and address a conference of senior commanders."

Yermolov watched Fierko closely. He lacked passion and humor, and seemed incapable of pretense. *A bureaucrat's bureaucrat showing no indication of who is pulling the strings.*

"Chairman Murin's actual purpose is to meet with you," Fierko went on. "I operated under his general guidance to bring you back in country. Any further actions will rely on his specific order. I hear that you and he are old friends."

Suddenly, Yermolov understood Fierko's dilemma. All KGB involvement in bringing Yermolov home had emanated through Fierko so that Yermolov would believe him to be the originator of support. Murin already supported the coup conspiracy, but was keeping himself hidden. If this went south, Fierko would be the fall guy.

Yermolov pictured Murin. From rare photographs in newspapers, Yermolov had seen that he had become a man of rotund proportions. That had not been the case when the two of them had been early in their careers. Murin had been Yermolov's handler in Cuba back in the days when Yermolov doubled as young Lieutenant Paul Clary of the United States Air Force.

Discussion between the two resulted in inquiry to learn if the anti-Castro resistance leader, Atcho, could be the same man who had graduated from West Point. When investigation confirmed the fact, they speculated over the value of Atcho, if he could be turned.

Murin had developed the idea of kidnapping Atcho's daughter, but the task fell to Yermolov to implement. Last year, Murin had devised the plan to assassinate Gorbachev, and had survived above suspicion after it failed.

Yermolov saw clearly that he had been set up from the beginning. The plan had gone smoothly right up to the moment of execution. When it failed, Yermolov took the blame.

No one had foreseen that Atcho, the intended assassin, would turn the tables and lay bare Yermolov's role. Thus, as a "rogue general," he had shielded Murin's involvement. Now the task fell to Fierko to be Murin's shield. Clearly, Murin expected to be the power behind the throne when the plot succeeded.

Fierko studied him. "Did you have a question?"

"No. I'm flattered that he would come this distance to see me."

"Instructions are tight. Actions must be completed long before the elections. Otherwise, establishing legitimacy will be far more difficult.

"You must gather support of at least two-thirds of the military commands including army, navy, air force, et cetera. What's left won't be difficult to pull into line. We'll release commanders who went to prison last year…" He paused, picking his words carefully, "…in the last attempt to correct our current destructive path."

Yermolov thought a moment. "How do we get that support?"

"Murin expects it won't be difficult. Assuming we go forward, he'll personally vouch for you. Your education, training, and experience are well suited to the job, and your background is known. That leaves managing the economy and governing. You'll have to address those issues convincingly."

He nodded toward Kutuzov. "General Kutuzov indicated that your ideas have merit. That message was forwarded to Murin. The conference tomorrow afternoon will be for senior leaders known to oppose current policies. Your job will be to convince them that you have a better way."

* * *

Fierko stood at his window and watched Kutuzov and Yermolov enter the limousine and drive away. Directly across the plaza stood the indomitable statue of Vladimir Lenin, his bronzed cape furling in a permanent wind, his eyes gazing into his utopian vision.

Fierko had been a good student of communism at the University of Moscow. He was part of the vanguard that Lenin introduced into doctrine to propel communism across the globe. No one rose to Fierko's level without being embroiled in it. "It has its rewards," he muttered. "But hell, it sure carries its risks."

He crossed to the door and closed it. Then he sat behind his desk and placed a call over his secure line. He recognized Murin's voice as soon as he heard it.

"They just left," he said without bothering with niceties.

"What is your impression?"

"General Yermolov looks in good health. He is a commanding figure. His mind is fully alert and capable. He contains himself well, and showed no concern over the short time to prepare for the conference. General Kutuzov respects him. That is huge for bringing the other commanders on board. We're ready for your visit."

"Do you recommend going forward with the next step?"

Fierko saw that Murin was establishing deniability, but also knew that he could not hesitate, and that his voice must convey confidence despite the way his stomach churned. "Yes. The risk can be contained. The plan starts to correct the direction of the Soviet Union. Before we make a final determination, you should know about a call I received from Drygin."

"What did he want?" Murin sounded more curious than annoyed, but Fierko knew that he was probably both.

"He was concerned that the information leaked out that Yermolov is alive. The Americans know Yermolov plans to re-enter Russia with help from the Rasputin group, so Secretary General Gorbachev probably does too. They must have pieced it together."

Fierko heard the chairman chuckle low in his chest. "Don't worry," Murin rumbled in a voice that cracked from years of heavy smoking. "I personally informed Gorbachev about Yermolov's 'sighting' in Paris. I couldn't let him think our intelligence services were asleep on the job.

"If the plan fails, our ambassador in Cuba will do the honor of accepting responsibility." He chuckled again. "You see, I take care of my protégés. Besides," he added with a draconian shift in tone, "the man who saw Yermolov in Paris will tell no one else."

Fierko was stunned by Murin's revelation of how Gorbachev became aware of Yermolov's continued existence and the intent to let Jeloudov take a fall. Fierko and the ambassador had been classmates in Moscow and had followed parallel careers until Jeloudov transferred to a diplomatic path. Murin had to know that.

"What was Gorbachev's reaction?" Fierko could think of nothing else to say.

"He was angry, but not surprised," Murin replied. "I committed to a low-key investigation into Yermolov's escape. I assured him we would find him and bring him in."

"What about the Rasputin group?"

"That was a ruse." Murin chuckled again. "I set that up with Yermolov years ago, complete with documents to show him as heir of both Rasputin and Tsar Nicholas. We spun a story that Rasputin had a secret marriage to the tsar's daughter, Anastasia, and that she had his child. That would be Yermolov's father.

"We did that to give Yermolov a place to disappear, if he needed it. We kept the rumors of the existence of such a man alive all these years without revealing his identity so that group members would be happy to receive him if the time came."

He was quiet, and Fierko waited. "You know," Murin mused, "we came up with this ploy to get Yermolov away from authorities if he needed to escape. We never dreamed that we might use both the Rasputin and Romanov names to..." He coughed. "...correct the direction of the Soviet Union."

Fierko contained his further astonishment. "I thought Ambassador Jeloudov came up with the idea of having Yermolov pose as Rasputin's heir."

Murin laughed out loud. "We must allow Jeloudov to continue thinking that. The suggestion was easy to plant in his creative mind. We found a biography written by an author in California that was supposedly coauthored by Rasputin's daughter. It made its way to the embassy in Havana, and in conversation with Yermolov, the plan was born—that's what Jeloudov thinks." The tone of Murin's voice suddenly changed. "Did Drygin have any other concerns?"

"Yes. Yermolov somehow acquired another briefcase. He didn't have it when he arrived in France, nor when they moved into the cabins outside of Paris. He won't let anyone carry it, and keeps it locked up in his room."

"Hmm, that is concerning," Murin replied. "Does Drygin have any idea what it could be?"

Fierko hesitated. "He's an intel guy, and he said to remember that. He's trained to consider all aspects. He's not saying the briefcase is a bomb, but thinks that's a possibility."

Murin scoffed. "What would he be doing with a bomb, and how would he get one?" He was quiet a moment. "My guess is he has those documents in there that show his ancestry. I'd be protective of those too. Anything else?"

"Just one. Drygin thinks that Yermolov perceives leaks coming from his own men; that Yermolov might even suspect Drygin."

Murin scoffed again. "Tell Drygin his services are appreciated. Yermolov was an intelligence officer in deep cover for his entire career. His job was to be suspicious, and he was under constant stress. Anyway, it's good that Yermolov feels a little off balance."

Once again, Fierko felt startled. He said nothing.

"Drygin has nothing to fear. I'll vouch for him," Murin went on. "Tell him that the Soviet military and intelligence services will soon experience what Americans call 'upward mobility.' His contributions will make him a rising star."

"So, is the plan going forward? Will Yermolov—"

"Of course." Murin's gravelly voice was ebullient. "He has as much or more qualification than anyone in the country. We can use the Rasputin followers and the Romanov name to great advantage. That will help establish legitimacy quickly." He suddenly switched subjects. "I'll need a new deputy. Are you up to the job?"

31

Dawn broke. Yermolov carried his coffee onto the porch in front of his temporary headquarters. He kept his expression impassive, but his impatience grew as he watched a group of Russian Orthodox Church members plod toward him through the snow. To him, meeting with these Rasputin followers was a waste of time.

He wore the uniform of a Soviet Colonel General, and his bearing expressed full appreciation for all that meant. He noticed, as though observing himself, that he felt a sense of satisfaction in the uniform. It fit in a way that the Unites States Air Force uniform he had worn for nearly thirty years never could. He felt genuine, and he reveled in the sensation.

Feeling at all was unusual for him. He knew what he was: a sociopath motivated by the love of power. Over decades he had tasted growing authority as he rose simultaneously through the ranks of the KGB and the US Air Force. His power had been exercised primarily through influence as a leading expert in nuclear weaponry.

He cared little for creature comforts or the family he had lost. They had been nothing more than props lending credibility to his role as a respected member of Western society. Where he slept or what he ate had no relevance as long as he progressed in his quest for power. *Except for that damn fish soup!* He growled at the thought.

The exercise of power was the single source of joy that drove him, and he saw the pinnacle of national power to be the only achievement that might satiate his hunger for it. To get there required patience, and in the guise of Paul Clary he had learned that the exercise of patience was one of the most necessary and effective survival skills.

Nevertheless, he felt impatient. When he and Murin developed his escape plan through the Rasputin group years ago, they had joked about it. The need to implement it had seemed farfetched.

While convalescing in Cuba, Yermolov endured Jeloudov's self-congratulating overtures while leading the ambassador to the notion of arranging Yermolov's escape to the Rasputin sect. In Paris, he had even had to eat some of that vile fish soup at the house of a group member while the staff organized and prepared the cabins.

While still at that house, Yermolov received the documents establishing his connections to Tsar Nicholas and Rasputin. He saw the look of awe and fear in the eyes of his hosts when they viewed them. He understood then that they would assume any risk to move this perceived demigod back into Mother Russia. Now, as the Rasputin group reached the stairs leading to the porch, he recognized the worshipful expression on their faces: hope, awe, and fear.

For the space of seconds, Yermolov knew the feeling of possessing charisma. He felt a tingling of rare enjoyment, and for a fleeting moment he saw a vision of himself in the Kremlin.

He shook himself back to the present and fought down rising impatience stemming from the charade imposed by the necessity to engage with the Rasputin followers. *Fools! How can they carry that garbage about Rasputin through generations?*

He fought off the sense of what he knew must be hubris, a danger to survival. Then he adopted the countenance of a senior general of the Soviet Army mixed with the professional amiability he had affected as General Clary. He walked down the stairs to meet his guests and extended his hand. "Welcome," he said warmly. "I am so pleased to meet you."

The leader of the group, in priestly robes with well-groomed graying hair that extended to a full beard, stopped almost in shock. Russians were not accustomed to being treated with courtesy by government officials, much less a senior officer of the Soviet KGB. He maintained reserve more than the others in his group, and observed Yermolov with an attempt to hide skepticism. He reached up to grasp Yermolov's hand, hesitance registering in the anxious look in his eyes.

As Yermolov had done in such practiced manner in the halls of the Pentagon as General Clary, he drew the priest's hand in and took his elbow. "You are kind to meet with me." He saw the change in the man's expression that told him he had won him over.

Yermolov led the small group into a dining hall that served as a conference room. There, already laid out, were four documents. The priest drew close and studied them. His eyes grew wide, his expression one of wonder. He gazed at Yermolov and then moved aside for the others to see.

All four documents looked old. Two of them looked ancient and contained ornate print. One of the two more recent documents was a birth certificate, that of a male child born in Akron, Ohio. The child's name was Paul Clary, born to Peter and Maria Clary.

The second was an immigration form from Ellis Island in 1925. It recorded "Peter Clary" as the name of a boy entering the US. The certificate further showed that the child's name had previously been Pyotr Rasputin. The collective expression of the group when they saw it was one of amused skepticism.

The third and fourth documents arrested their attention. The visitors looked back and forth between the papers and Yermolov, their disbelief turning to wonder. Both documents were deeply yellowed by age, almost orange. The smaller of the two was another birth certificate. It recorded the birth of Pyotr Rasputin and showed the names of his parents, Grigori Rasputin and his wife, Anastasia Romanov. The men gasped when they read the names.

The fourth document was grand with flourished writing, and scrollwork adorning the margins. On seeing it, the visitors gaped. It recorded the marriage of Grigori Yefimovich Rasputin to Grand Duchess Anastasia Nikolaevna of Russia, daughter of Nikolay Alexandrovich Romanov, Emperor of Russia. Both documents bore a waxed double-headed eagle, the seal of Imperial Russia.

* * *

"How did things go with the Rasputin group?" Kutuzov asked when he stopped to pick up Yermolov that afternoon.

"Who knows? They seemed suitably impressed. That was an unnecessary annoyance."

"I've watched Gorbachev's rise," Kutuzov replied. He explained that Russian Orthodox activism brought about the move to return property to Church control. "That shows effectiveness. The Rasputin bunch is a tiny splinter, but they're not outcasts. If they promoted support among other congregations across the Soviet republics, the Church could be valuable in establishing legitimacy."

"I see." *Drygin thinks the same thing.* "What should I expect at this afternoon's conference? I didn't have much time to prepare."

"Don't worry. You're a legend among senior commanders." He grasped Yermolov's shoulder. "Unbelievable! To be on the US side of the table at nuclear negotiations, while looking out for the interests of the Soviet Union. No one can duplicate that. You're not a rogue general. You followed orders." He watched the passing landscape. "I vouched for you already. Murin supports you. Repeat those things you told me, and the group will be prepared to act."

Yermolov looked out the window. Bleak stretches of snow met his gaze. "We've gone a good distance down a risky road. To use an American colloquialism, why are you sticking your neck out?"

Kutuzov rested his elbows on his knees. "For my entire career, I've defended my country." He spoke with unguarded passion. "Russia is my country, not the Soviet Union. Invaders lay waste. Right now, America threatens nuclear devastation, and they are well aware of our petroleum and mineral deposits.

"Those other countries that make up the Soviet Union—Latvia, Czechoslovakia, Kazakhstan, the others—they're defense mechanisms. If we lose control of them, doing damage to Russia becomes much easier." He paused to gather his thoughts. "When Gorbachev's policies destroy the Soviet Union, rich countries will look at Mother Russia with lust for rape. That can't happen."

A Russian patriot? Yermolov thought. *Who knew any still existed?*

Kutuzov spoke again. "I reached a position far beyond my expectations. I'm content to remain where I am, retire, or serve in another capacity. I live to serve Russia." His intense green eyes bored into Yermolov. "Putting me somewhere that doesn't keep me in command of soldiers serves no one. You're welcome to my service, and if that doesn't please you, you're welcome to my head."

Yermolov drew back. *He just told me that he's not afraid of me! I'll deal with that later.* "I appreciate your dedication." He feigned the warmth of General Clary and nudged Kutuzov's arm. "We'll have to put thought into where you can best serve. For the immediate future, keeping you where you are makes sense."

They reached the security gate at the army base. A sentry saluted and waved them through. "We're just in time," Kutuzov exclaimed, glancing at his watch. "Chairman Murin and the generals are assembled."

32

When he entered a small theater-like room, Yermolov recognized his old comrade, KGB Chairman Nestor Murin, on a raised stage, obviously engaged in informal discussion. Thirty of some of the top Soviet generals were already seated in the first three rows.

Hearing the door open and close, Murin looked over and saw Yermolov, and his face lit up. He stood and approached, arms extended. "Comrade, it's good to see you safe inside Russia. Among friends." He grabbed Yermolov in a bear hug.

They both faced the audience. "I give you a man who needs no introduction," Murin announced, "Borya Yermolov."

The generals stood and applauded, but their expressions revealed reserve. When they had quieted down and were seated, Murin took Yermolov's arm and guided him around a table on the stage. He offered Yermolov the center seat. Then he took the chair to Yermolov's left. Kutuzov took the one on the right.

The symbolism was not lost on Yermolov, nor was the nature of the welcome he had received. To the assembled senior military leadership, the message was clear: This is our guy. Ask what you will, but be prepared to support.

Yermolov gazed across the assembly. Looking back were faces that bore gradations of hope, tenacity, and skepticism. *This is my coup to lose.* Lieutenant General Fierko stood there in full uniform with KGB insignia. Two KGB colonels flanked him. *Murin stacked the odds in my favor.*

Nearby, but slightly apart, a civilian stood alone. With lights shining in Yermolov's eyes, he could not make out the man's features. However, he bore the unmistakable presence of high-level seniority, the Politburo.

Yermolov felt satisfaction, but almost instantly sensed that gnawing unease that seemed a constant companion. He shook it off.

Murin stood, but remained behind the table. "Every man in this room is at risk," he said. "If we're discovered, we will be considered co-conspirators, and," he smacked his hands together, "we'll be executed." His face grim, he continued. "We came voluntarily, but as of now we're all in. No one can pull out." His words hung in the air and he attempted to look each man in the eye. "You came to hear General Yermolov, not me." He turned to Yermolov. "General, tell us why we should support you." He sat down.

No one stirred. Yermolov remained silent, observing each man in the room. He rose to his feet and strode to the front of the platform. "Thank you to all of you for your dedication to the Soviet Union." He paused and gestured toward Kutuzov.

"I'm in the presence of greatness. I'm among men who put country and service ahead of personal ambition. Colonel General Kutuzov is a comrade who has no ambition beyond being a great soldier. He has already accomplished that."

His arm swept toward Murin. "I've had the privilege of working for the chairman, who always provided the support I needed while in foreign lands on national business." He let the veiled reference to his espionage in the US sink in. "He asked me to tell you why you should support me." Yermolov dropped his hands to his sides in a posture of utter defenselessness. "My answer is simple. You should not."

He watched the looks of confusion. No one spoke. In the second and third rows, some looked at each other in consternation. They leaned forward, eager to hear what he would say next. *I guess Paul Clary learned a few things in those dreary US Air Force classes.*

"Your allegiance belongs to the country, and we should never follow a man who seeks self-aggrandizement. Your questions need to be: Is this General Yermolov—who has been absent from our country for so long—capable of leading our nation? Does he have the right ideas to restore our defenses, our economy, our greatness?"

He spoke with increasing intensity, looking from man to man as he inflected his voice for greatest impact. "You should ask if he is the most qualified potential leader. Does he understand the profound questions that plague us; does he have the knowledge of nuclear defenses and conventional forces? Can he beat the United States in this game called the arms race?" Yermolov's voice reached full volume. "Can he lead?"

He let the thought linger. "If you think this Borya Yermolov is competent in every one of those areas, then considering him would be an intelligent move." He dropped his voice to almost a whisper. "If you have doubts in even one of those areas, then you should seek someone else. The stakes are too high."

The room was silent; no one even coughed. "Yesterday, General Kutuzov asked me the same question: Why should he support me? He asked for specifics. I gave him three." He paced. "Hear me out on each point. The third one will cause raised eyebrows. Is that right, General?" Kutuzov confirmed with a solemn nod.

Over the next hour, Yermolov explained his tenets. He watched the faces of the generals, but knew that any outward expressions were masks of their true thoughts. Their careers had been forged in a brutal system that rewarded bureaucratic manipulation, political skill, and blatant corruption.

As much as any of them might consider country, the truth was that they saw a plebiscite looming that they felt to their marrows would seal the fate of the Soviet Union. Chaos lay on the other side.

Coupled with that pragmatism was the perception that Murin had skillfully cast the die. In a culture where personal loyalty was in short supply and always unreliable, Murin had used the power of his office to coerce, intimidate, or otherwise coopted these senior leaders to hatch a coup. Regardless of patriotic fervor, they were bound together. They dared not resist.

Yermolov glanced at Kutuzov. He might be an exception.

The concept of loosening economic freedom seemed to be understood, even welcomed. "Does that mean that my wife can sell the produce from her garden, and I can keep the profit?" one old general quipped. "I'll put her to work tomorrow. If I can make her shut up, so much the better." Laughter spread through the room.

The humorous remark broke the tone of gravity and brought more jesting comments. Yermolov took questions until they seemed to have been exhausted. Then he turned to Murin, who rose from his seat, rounded the table, and gripped Yermolov's hand.

"Thank you, General," Murin said. "General Kutuzov, Comrades, please help me welcome General Yermolov home." The audience rose as a body, applauded, and formed a line to shake Yermolov's hand. Within minutes, only a few generals still waited to formally greet Yermolov. Those who had already paid homage grouped around him.

Soviet democracy in action. Yermolov felt hubris again, more intensely. This time he relished it.

When the last of the generals had gripped Yermolov's hand, he called across the room. "Comrades, please take your seats."

When they were ready, he addressed them again. "Our plans are impossible to hide indefinitely." He turned to Murin. "We need to act sooner rather than later?"

"Gorbachev knows resistance is growing," Murin agreed. "If the elections take place, he'll think he's succeeded. Establishing legitimacy for a democratically elected government toppled by a coup is tough in the international community."

"The international community." Yermolov almost sneered, but stopped just short. "How soon can we execute?"

"On command," Murin replied. "We have everything in place."

"Good. Then we'll execute within two weeks. In particular, the nuclear response capability cannot have a lapse."

Murin nodded agreement.

"The general secretary will be given two alternatives. Either he can retire to his dacha to recover from illness, or he will disappear."

The room was deathly quiet. Yermolov went on to say that simultaneously with removing Gorbachev, unreliable military commanders would be replaced. "Furthermore," he continued, "by mid-afternoon on the day we execute, ambassadors will seek formal recognition from respective countries. Any ambassador who resists will be replaced. At that point, the future of the Soviet Union will be secure."

When the meeting adjourned, Colonel General Borya Yermolov appeared firmly in charge. Murin took note.

33

Collins wiped his palm across the top of his head to ensure that his few straggling hairs were in place. Upon receiving his boarding pass for his flight to rendezvous with President Reagan, he meandered toward the gate. He was tired, and boarding the Concorde was always easy.

He chose not to think much about his impending visit to the Oval Office. In his profession, access was everything, and a meeting with the President of the United States was the holy grail of journalism.

The president knew him by name, as they had met on more than one occasion. He had also interviewed another president several years ago in the Oval Office, so the trappings of neither the office nor the man awed him. From Collins' perspective, they each performed their respective jobs as best they could. Still, the honor was great, even under these circumstances.

He stopped in a store and browsed the books; he might need a novel to help him sleep on the flight. Finding a suitable one, he moved to the checkout counter. Other customers were ahead of him, so he let his mind wander while he glanced about at passengers hurrying past the store.

Perhaps because of the intensity of three men moving toward the Aeroflot gates, or maybe because his subconscious mind recognized something familiar about them, they captured his attention. He almost gasped.

One of them was Atcho. The other two were the men he had helped from the plane two days earlier. They looked tired. The one who had been sick on the flight from Washington looked like he had been beaten, and he walked stiffly. *So, that* was *Atcho at the airport, and he's with those guys.*

With a line of customers still in front of him, Collins knew he would lose them if he did not move; but, recalling that Jakes had said he was under French surveillance, he was careful to appear unhurried. He left the queue, returned the book to its shelf, and meandered back out into the terminal.

He hung back and stopped occasionally to observe a piece of airport art or sculpture as he followed them. Soon they arrived at a seating area at one of the passenger waiting areas and settled in. He noted the gate number and went to one of the arrival/departure displays out of their sight. Their plane left in two hours, bound for Moscow.

He briefly considered confronting Atcho in the gate area, but dismissed the thought as unworkable. Atcho would stonewall, an unpleasant scene could ensue, and Collins would walk away knowing no more about what the men were up to than he currently did. He glanced at his watch. His own flight was scheduled to close its doors in another twenty minutes.

For the benefit of whoever tailed him, he exaggerated his gestures of concern and stepped up his pace. He arrived at his gate within five minutes, sweating and puffing, and was immediately shown aboard. There, he waited another ten minutes, rose from his seat, and made his way back to the front.

"Ma'am," he said to the attendant, "I am so sorry, but I'm feeling sick." Sweat still trickled from his forehead. He pulled a handkerchief from his pocket, wiped his brow, and blew his nose. Then he pretended an imminent nausea attack.

The young woman was aghast. "You can't fly that way, sir. The other passen—"

"I know," he interrupted. "I'll forfeit the ticket."

Without waiting for a response, he left the plane. He ducked into a narrow space behind the ticket desk and sat on the floor with his back to the wall. He waited there until he heard the jet engines revving, and then ambled into the waiting area. It was empty. He took the nearest seat, stayed long enough to see that no one paid attention to him, and walked into the main terminal.

Ten minutes later, he purchased an Aeroflot ticket to Moscow on the same flight as Atcho and his companions. As Jakes had said, his credentials were up-to-date.

When he arrived back at their gate, Atcho and the two men still sat where he had left them. He moved to the opposite end of the waiting area, and sat where he could watch them without being obvious.

His stomach churned. *You just stood up the president of the United States! You threw away access that people give their right arms for. On top of that, you're flying into Moscow, and no one knows where you are. Count on consequences.*

He tried to dismiss his concern. He had acted on instinct in pursuit of a story; in his mind, the right call. Still, his nerves felt raw when he contemplated his current position. To professional peers, his action would seem bizarre. If no concrete story surfaced, he might have just seen the apex of his career pass in front of his eyes.

He managed to board ahead of Atcho and sit ten rows behind him and his companions. As the plane took off, he knew he would not sleep, and regretted not purchasing the novel.

* * *

Dawn broke rending scattered flame-colored clouds against a blue, early morning sky. The Aeroflot jet descended into Moscow.

Inside the terminal, Collins located Atcho and his companions, and followed among the passengers trailing behind them through the vast hall. They stopped and inspected a departure bulletin board. Collins realized with dismay that he would lose them; he was not credentialed to fly anywhere else in the Soviet Union. He followed them anyway, until they disappeared into another departure gate. Glumly, he looked at the sign announcing the destination of their flight. It would leave in three hours, bound for Novosibirsk.

Then, he felt a surge of excitement. After going through customs, he looked for the first place he could find where he could sit and drink a cup of coffee. There, he pulled the Rasputin biography out, and flipped through the pages.

He glanced up at one point and saw two men watching him. *My "minders" have arrived.* They were Soviet officials detailed to watch him, as was customary in communist countries. They caused him no concern. He had been to Moscow before, and was accustomed to their shadowing behind. He could not imagine a more boring job.

He flipped pages until he found what he was looking for. The connection was beyond coincidence: Novosibirsk, Rasputin's birthplace.

He headed for the exit, hailed a taxi, and gave the driver the address to the *Washington Herald's* local office. As he rode through Moscow's streets, he was too engrossed in thought to notice his surroundings. *Why would Atcho and those two men have such interest in Rasputin's birthplace?* A link had to be there somewhere, connecting Atcho's role in stopping Gorbachev's assassination to Rasputin and Novosibirsk. *I'm missing something.*

He pulled out the biography and re-read the part relating to the mystic's relations with the royal family. That ran into a section regarding Rasputin's contempt for aristocrats and how he humiliated them by flaunting his sexual proclivities. Collins wondered idly whether Rasputin had ever fathered a child by a member of the royal family. Suddenly, he sat bolt upright.

What if he did? What if Rasputin fathered a child with one of the tsarinas? What if such a child survived the royal family's massacre?

The taxi rolled to a stop. Collins looked up expecting to see the plain façade of the *Washington Herald's* Moscow office. Instead, parked in front of the taxi was a police car with its lights blinking. His two minders from the airport approached the taxi.

Collins jammed the book into his briefcase. One of the minders opened the door and motioned for him to exit. Bewildered, he complied. One of the minders took his arm and led to a black official-looking sedan behind the taxi. A man stood next to an open rear door. He pushed Collins into the middle seat and entered behind him.

Another grim-faced man sat on the other side. "Don't talk," he said in heavily accented English. Collins sat in silence, more curious than concerned at that point. Even Soviets were cautious when handling the international press, particularly with the advent of *glasnost*.

The car sped off. Collins tried to take note of his surroundings. Despite that the side windows were heavily tinted, he saw when familiar dark red walls appeared. He had never fathomed the acts of cruelty directed from this repository of classical Russian art that those bulwarks protected—the Kremlin.

Then to his astonishment, the driver pulled up to a side gate, and they entered. Consternation overtook curiosity. Collins had no idea where he was being taken.

The sedan steered into a short tunnel to an underground parking area. Collins' captors ordered him out of the car. They set a brisk pace as they entered a massive building through a back door and climbed many stairs. For a fleeting moment, Collins thought he might be going to see General Secretary Gorbachev. Just as quickly, he dismissed the thought. *I'm not a big enough fish, even if I did ditch the president.*

They reached a landing with a single door where the lead escort motioned for Collins to enter. When he did, his jaw dropped. The office in which he found himself was huge. Emblazoned on the opposite wall was a carved symbol of the Soviet Union. Behind a desk was the red national flag, with the hammer and sickle. Collins' attention focused on the man advancing toward him, Mikhail Gorbachev.

"Sit down, Mr. Collins." He indicated a seating area around a small table with a pitcher of water and some glasses. His manner was courteous but stern, and he did not offer to shake hands. Collins took the seat. Gorbachev sat opposite him.

"We don't have much time," Gorbachev said. "Mr. Reagan passes along his regrets that you did not accept his invitation." He spoke in English, which surprised Collins at first, but then he remembered that the general secretary had spoken English with Margaret Thatcher prior to taking office, and had only confined himself to Russian since then.

Still in mild shock, Collins could only manage, "I understand."

"I hope you do. This is not the United States. There is no record of the ticket you purchased in Paris last night, or of your having boarded the flight

to Moscow. You were last seen getting on the Concorde, and then you disappeared. No one knows you're here. This is the Soviet Union."

"Is your intent to intimidate me?"

"Am I succeeding?"

Collins bestowed a wan smile on him. "Yes, you are."

"Good, then let's get to business. Why did you divert to Moscow?"

Collins was at a loss for a response. He breathed deeply and finally
asked, "Do you know who Atcho is?" Gorbachev nodded. Collins went on,
"I saw him and his group in Paris, waiting on a flight to Moscow."

"You followed them. I see. I know where they are. Mr. Reagan said you
intended to inquire into related matters, things he wanted to discuss with
you. Tell me what you think you know. Be thorough."

Collins looked around. He had been a reporter too long for his
emotions to run rampant, but he could not recall a more pressured situation. He indicated the pitcher of water on the table. "May I have a drink?"

"Of course. Allow me."

That General Secretary Gorbachev of the Soviet Communist Party
poured his glass of water was not lost on the reporter. He took a sip. "Where
should I start?"

"At the beginning. Tell me what you think you know."

Collins nodded and took another sip. "I saw Atcho in New York at a
meeting with you and President Reagan. No conjecture." Gorbachev did
not react. On impulse, Collins said, "I can either take you step by step
through each detail, or I can tell you my conclusions. I think I have a good
understanding of what is going on."

"By all means, tell me your understanding." Gorbachev's tone bordered
on condescension.

"There was an assassination attempt on your life last year in the United
States. Atcho stopped it. For that reason, he gained yours and Mr. Reagan's
confidence." Collins searched the general secretary's face for a reaction, but
was met only by a steady gaze. Collins took a mental leap. "Someone inside
your country is pushing a credible claim to being a descendant of both Tsar
Nicholas and Rasputin." He looked for an expression of ridicule on
Gorbachev's face, but again saw only impassivity. *I'm in the ballpark!*

He took another mental leap. "That person is tied in with the assassination attempt last year. You can't turn to the KGB because some elements support him. The CIA can't help because it's an internal matter here in your country." No reaction. "You turned to Atcho because he knows who the assassin is, and both you and Reagan trust him."

Gorbachev scoffed. "Those are interesting conclusions, but not plausible. Is that all?"

"No. Atcho is headed to Novosibirsk, Rasputin's birthplace."

"What do you think this supposed assassin might do, or who he might be?"

Collins sat deep in thought. "I don't know." He suddenly thought of the conversation with Jakes about Paul Clary's disappearance, and his pulse surged. He spoke slowly and deliberately now, and watched the general secretary closely. "You probably know that a US Air Force general disappeared last year. Completely vanished, and his family, too." He thought he saw Gorbachev's eyes narrow. "He was last seen on the same day as the assassination attempt. I'm betting that the missing general is tied in with all of this."

Now Collins' mind raced, his speech speeded up, and he leaned forward in his seat. "That's it, isn't it. General Clary was a nuclear arms expert. Was he KGB? Then he must have worked—" His voice rose in excitement. He stopped and stared at Gorbachev. "Was he the assassin? Is he planning a coup?"

"Mr. Collins!" The general secretary spoke sharply. He returned the reporter's startled gaze without speaking. Then he leaned forward. "Your conclusions are preposterous, but let me ask you this: if you print articles along the lines of what Mr. Jakes indicated to the White House, and if any part of what you say is true, what do you think might be the ramifications?"

Collins settled back in his seat. He was embarrassed. Getting carried away was unusual for him. *But I have the story. I'm certain of it.* "Impossible to say for sure. This individual could be alerted to efforts to stop him. He might move up his timetable."

"Then you see that turning the story loose could be damaging?"

Stunned, Collins took another moment to think. *Did he just tacitly confirm my theory?* "If you ask Mr. Reagan, he will tell you that I've held back stories that could cause public harm."

Gorbachev studied him a moment. "I know," he said in a low voice, "which is why we are talking. Otherwise, I would have taken different measures."

Collins felt a sudden pricking across his forehead, an involuntary reaction to what the chairman had just said. He started to speak. Gorbachev cut him off. "Listen carefully. I will tell you what is about to happen."

Collins felt the bristles rise on his neck.

"You will be escorted from here to the airport where you will be kept under armed guard, until you board the most direct flight to Washington. Members of both my personal security detail and US State Department security will be on the airplane. When you arrive, you will be taken to meet with President Reagan. Is that understood?"

Collins nodded.

"Mr. Reagan assured me that he will convince you to use good sense and keep your suppositions to yourself. And you and I never had this meeting. Is that clear?"

Collins met his steady gaze. "We are a long way from printing a story. Fact-checking will be extensive."

"Good. If a time ever comes to break a story, we might invite you for interviews. But, we will see your articles before publication. If you had stood me up, your treatment would have been quite different." He glowered. "I'm certain that your actions will cost you, even with Mr. Reagan."

Despite the ominous comment, Collins felt a spark of excitement. *I'm going to get the story.* "I understand."

For the first time, Gorbachev allowed a faint smile, and started to rise as if to terminate the meeting. Lost in thought, Collins kept his seat.

"Is there something else?"

Collins snapped back to the present. "Sorry. I had a thought. Maybe I could help?" The general secretary settled back into his chair.

* * *

When he landed around noon at Washington Dulles International Airport, two Secret Service agents met Collins at the gate. They escorted him in a dark sedan to Dogwood Cabin at Camp David, the retreat of US presidents in the Catoctin Mountain Park, Maryland. The situation chafed the charm. His escorts silently indicated that he should vacate the car and enter the cabin.

A grizzled, Irish-looking man waited for him at the door as he tramped through the snow up the walkway. Collins scrutinized his face.

"I've seen you before," Collins said. "You were with Atcho in New York at that Long Island estate." On instinct, he asked, "Are you his CIA buddy?"

Burly said nothing, but gestured for Collins to enter. Then he led into the living room and indicated a chair.

"Where's the president?" Collins asked. "I'm here to see him."

Burly grunted. "You're here to do exactly as you're told," he said, and there was nothing friendly in his manner.

Collins stared, and then stood. "I'll be going now. Tell the president I'm sorry we missed each other."

"Suit yourself," Burly said. "Those guys will be very happy to lock you in a cell."

Collins glanced out the window. The Secret Service sedan was still there. *Where did you think you were going anyway?* He sat back down. "Are you going to tell me what's going on?" He felt like a misbehaved schoolboy about to be scolded.

"Yeah," Burly replied. "I'll tell you what's going on. You're going to stay put right here at Camp David until this whole mess blows over. You can stay here in this warm, comfy cabin, or you can stay in a cold room with bars. Your choice."

Burly seemed to be warming to an argument. He pulled himself forward so that his eyes were level with Collins'. "Where do you get off blowing off the US president? You've been tromping all over the world disrupting sensitive operations and putting friends of mine in harm's way."

Collins felt a flash of ire. "I'm a reporter. I go after the story. That's what I do." He lowered his voice. "I did not intentionally disrespect the president. The story ran in a direction that did not go through the Oval Office."

Just then a young Secret Service agent, identified by his dark suit and curly wire behind his ear, burst through the door. His face serious, and without saying a word, he moved from room to room in the cabin, and then called, "Clear!"

A moment later, Ronald Reagan strode in. Collins sprang to his feet. "Mr. President!"

"Tony," the president responded coolly, ignoring Collins' outstretched hand. "How was Moscow?" His irritation was palpable. He settled onto a couch. "Mr. Gorbachev briefed me on your conclusions. He also filled me in on your idea. We need to talk about that."

"Yes, sir."

Collins sat in an overstuffed chair across from him, and watched for signs of Reagan's waning lucidity as reported in the news.

The president seemed sharp enough today. He sat eyeing Collins, clearly irritated. "Mr. Gorbachev told me you want to write a story," he said. "If that's all we needed, what makes you think we couldn't pull in a reporter? On either side of the Atlantic?"

Collins sat back. He had not seen that question coming. "You could do that," he replied slowly as he gathered his thoughts. "I'm guessing that the wayward general who wants to spring a coup is already in Novosibirsk, and that Atcho is there to disrupt him."

That statement was pure speculation. At the time, Collins knew only of the existence of Paul Clary, not Yermolov. He surmised that someone led the conspiracy, and that Paul Clary was implicated with members of the KGB and the legend of Rasputin. *Atcho must have* some *reason for flying to Novosibirsk.*

Reagan held his steady gaze. "So? Why do we need you?"

Collins flared. "Because I'm the reporter who knows the story. I know what to do. Now."

Reagan looked doubtful.

"I'm known," Collins persisted. "I have an international following." Reagan did not appear impressed. "Look," Collins said, approaching exasperation. Before he could continue, Burly stirred in his chair and shot him a menacing glance. Reagan waved Burly back with his hand.

"This is a shot in the dark," Collins went on. "I might provide a disruption, or at least a distraction, or I might have no effect at all." He explained the idea he had outlined to Mikhail Gorbachev.

Twenty minutes later, Reagan leaned back in concentrated thought. "All right," he said at last. "It's worth a try, but here are the conditions: you'll stay here at Camp David and use my staff for whatever research you need. We'll provide a direct, secure line to your editor so that you have unimpeded communication—"

"Why stay here?" Collins interrupted. "I can get—"

Reagan stopped him with a raised hand. "That's not negotiable." He turned to Burly. "Tell him the repercussions if he declines."

What Burly said was terrifying to a reporter. He told Collins that if he refused the conditions, that his passport and press credentials would be suspended until the entire matter was settled. The president would issue an order prohibiting federal employees from granting an interview with him or providing information on any story, on or off the record. Indefinitely.

As he spoke, Collins felt redness creeping up the back of his neck and into his cheeks. His eyes narrowed. He stared at the president.

"If that's not enough to hold you," Burly concluded, "we can look at other measures." While Burly spoke, Reagan's expression changed to one indicating that he was done with discussion.

Collins was not done. He gestured toward Burly in disgust. "You make me a prisoner, and let this man threaten my livelihood?" Burly glowered at him.

Reagan drew back. His eyebrows tightened. "You compromised a sensitive operation." His tone was terse. "We can implement your idea with or without you. You choose."

Collins grimaced. "What if I give you my word to stay in my office?"

Reagan dropped his head. When he looked up, his eyes had regained their famous twinkle. The edges of his mouth held the hint of a smile. "How about if you accept my invitation to stay here for a few days?" His smile broadened. "As my guest."

Despite his frustration, Collins could not help but return the smile. *I'm outgunned.* "Am I free to leave whenever I choose?"

Reagan threw his head back and laughed. "Of course. This is a free country." Without losing his jaunty smile, he continued, "If you leave, you just won't be able to work on this or any other story involving the federal government, until it's all over."

Collins gave him a sidelong glance. "Can I use my own research staff?

I've got to get the articles to them for publication anyway. Your guys can monitor our calls. I'll keep my nose clean."

Reagan considered that for a moment. "All right, we can do that."

Collins shifted his glance to the snow beyond the window. He let it rest there and then looked around the room. "How's room service? Can I get beer and chocolate doughnuts?"

"I think we can handle that?" Reagan replied congenially.

Across the room, Burly shook his head, obviously not impressed.

* * *

Late the following afternoon, Collins called Jakes. He had worked all night and through the day. "Did you get everything?"

"We did," the editor replied. "We included the final edits and two side stories just before press time. They're out to all the news wires. Moscow will wake up to them on the first page of *Izvestia* and *Pravda*. The main story will show above the fold as a side column. It should get a lot of attention."

"Great! I'll kick back, watch TV, and wait for sparks to fly."

34

As her plane circled above Moscow on its flight from Bern, Sofia looked across the frozen city. She had no way of knowing that Atcho and his companions—and Collins—were also landing on a flight from Paris.

Minders would follow her; that was certain. She traveled under her own identity using her diplomatic passport, so her priority was to visit the US Embassy. Government personnel of her stature and level of security clearance were required to register on arrival in the country. Her minders would expect her to go there. To do otherwise would invite unwelcome Soviet security attention.

As soon as she processed through customs she spotted her two minders. Later, when she emerged from the embassy without incident, she spotted them again. She made her way to the Metropol Hotel, the architectural treasure built before the Russian Revolution. Inside, she sensed the gloomy supremacy of a tyrannical bureaucracy over creative craftsmanship; the once majestic building still adorned with fading classical artwork was in a deplorable state of maintenance.

The next morning, she came awake with a start after a restless night, and sat up with the sheets draped over her legs while she contemplated her next move. The implication of Burly's statement that Atcho would need a

NukeX bore down on her, but for the moment, that was beyond her ability to affect.

She was certain that Yermolov believed himself to be descended from a Romanov and Rasputin; that he intended a coup in the Soviet Union; and that Mikhail Gorbachev and Ronald Reagan found the threat credible enough that they cooperated to stop him.

She found outlandish the idea that the erstwhile General Clary, aka Yermolov, might attempt a coup—and might be carrying a nuclear device. She remembered meeting him at a barbecue at his home on a beautiful spring afternoon in Washington, with laughter, and the aroma of sizzling beef floating on the breeze. She had met his wife, Peggy, and their daughter Chrissy. They had been so wholesome. He had seemed so normal, so pleasant. *How could General Clary and General Yermolov be the same person?* She had been dumbfounded to learn of the dual life.

She shook off the thought. "You're in the intelligence business, lady," she told herself. "You see a lot of strange things."

The thought that had developed as she made her way from Bern to Moscow was that Yermolov seemed intent on using members of the Church to advance his agenda. *Maybe I can make contact within the Church to give warning in Novosibirsk.* The most famous Russian Orthodox cathedral in the world was barely a half a mile from the hotel. Although it was now a museum, she might pick up a piece of information there that could help.

She left the hotel and walked in that direction. Behind her, the two minders struggled to keep up. Soon, she came into view of the Kremlin. A little farther on she entered Red Square, site of massive military parades, complete with rockets, intended to project Soviet strength. At the far end was the splendid St. Basil's Cathedral, Sofia's destination.

Her minders hurried to keep up as she crossed the huge square, entered the cathedral, purchased a ticket and joined a tour. Then, they stayed nearby, maintaining bored attitudes.

Sofia went to ask the tour guide a private question. It was innocuous, but she wanted to see the minders' reactions. They moved in closely, and when she had finished her conversation and rejoined the group, one of them stayed nearby while the other spoke quietly with the tour guide. *They're monitoring closely.*

She approached them. "Would you help me?" she asked in English. "I'm studying the history of the Orthodox Church in Russia and the Soviet Union. Where can I get information?"

The minders looked at each other with some confusion. "Do you understand?" Sofia asked. They nodded, but she saw reluctance in their eyes, and thought she understood the reasons.

A year ago, she might have been arrested for asking the same questions. The minders could have found themselves in trouble for giving assistance. With Gorbachev's *glasnost* policies, magnificent cathedrals were to be returned to their parishes across Russia. New rules for what interactions were allowed had not been promulgated. The minders seemed unsure of what to do. They conferred privately, and one pointed at the tour guide.

"I should speak with him?" Sofia asked. "It's okay?"

The man nodded. "Anyway, I'll ask him what you talked about," he replied in heavily Russian-accented English. They exchanged wry grins, and Sofia went to speak with the guide.

"That man said I could ask you a question about Church history," she said. She pointed at the minder. The guide looked cautiously at the man, who nodded and shrugged as if to say, "Why not?"

"What do you want to ask me?" the guide spoke in lightly accented English.

"I won't get you in trouble," she assured him. "Is there a Russian Orthodox cathedral close by that was already returned to its parish? I'd like to speak with anyone who lived through the history of state control."

The guide was young, maybe a graduate student. He wrapped his hand around his narrow chin and rubbed the stubble while he thought. "There are several Church sites close by, but they've been destroyed or fallen into ruin. Mr. Gorbachev has not yet returned them to Church ownership. What would you like to know?"

"I'm researching the interrelated histories of the Russian Orthodox and the Catholic Churches," Sofia said. "I'm interested in the time span when the Church couldn't operate."

"Are you looking for specific information?" He studied her.

"I'd like to speak with old members of the Church. People who remember as close to the beginning of the revolution as possible." She hesi-tated, and then plunged. "I need to find Rasputin followers."

The guide glared at her. "Ah!" he exclaimed. "You make fun."

"No. This is serious." She struggled to maintain a pleasant demeanor for the sake of appearances, and saw that he did the same. "Does the name Aleksey in Paris mean anything to you?"

Startled, he drew back. "Should it?"

"He made the fish soup for the mystic." Sofia saw that the point regis-tered. "I visited him two days ago."

"How long will you be staying in Moscow?"

"As long as I need to. I'm at the Metropol."

"I'll have someone contact you. Be at dinner in the restaurant this evening." The guide shot a furtive glance at the minders. "We need to end this. Point at something and ask me about it."

Sofia did, and the guide engaged others in the discussion. Soon she was in the middle of the group, just another tourist.

* * *

Burly could not believe his ears. "You're calling from Moscow?" He spoke on a secure line from his office in the basement of the White House.

The voice on the other end of the line sounded irritated. "Yes. My name is Zane McFadden. I'm the CIA Station Chief. I'm calling because of your high-priority message to embassies."

"You saw Sofia Stahl?" Burly massaged the back of his neck.

"As I said, she's on our surveillance tapes. She came in yesterday morning."

"You're sure it's her?"

"I'm sure," McFadden replied. "We double-checked."

"Do you know where she is? I'd like to speak with her."

"No. She came and left without signing in. We checked with all our offices. She's not here."

"All right. We've got to find her. Let me fill you in."

"You just landed a whopper in my lap," McFadden said when Burly had finished. His tension was unmistakable. "I'll get my guys out searching immediately. Do you know what she intended to do?"

"No."

McFadden sensed the distress in Burly's voice. "All right. I'll keep you posted. Out."

* * *

At seven o'clock that evening, Sofia ordered dinner in the restaurant at the Metropol. Two new minders sat across the lobby. The minor chords of Russian classical music floated through the air, played by a group of string musicians. The mix of sweet and mournful melody that played in counter-point to Russian harmony evoked a visceral sense of the ageless Russian struggle, and reflected her mood: melancholy.

Thoughts of Atcho lingered. She remembered the first time she had seen him: gaunt, undernourished, and unkempt. But, even as a just-released political prisoner in Havana, he had carried himself with grace and dignity. His eyes had shown an indomitable spirit, yet unspeakable sorrow.

Sofia felt her throat constrict and her eyes moisten. She straightened in her seat to regain poise. The waiter brought her meal and set it in front of her, carefully moving the bowl to reveal writing beneath it on a napkin. Sofia read it: "Go to the restroom." Her heart raced.

Keeping her composure, she finished her dinner and left for the ladies' room. As she crossed the restaurant, she noticed a man observing her with the detached alertness that she had come to recognize among operators in the intelligence community. He reminded her of a scaled-down version of Burly, and he looked directly at her. "Sofia?"

She smiled down at him. "Yes." She replied in her most friendly manner. "Do I know you?"

The man smiled, and stood. "My name is McFadden. I work at the emba—"

"I was just going to the restroom," Sofia interrupted with a despairing expression, "and I really don't want to embarrass either of us. I'll be right back, and if you'd like, you can join me at that table right over there." She pointed with a cutesy flick of her wrist.

35

Sofia's heart pounded as she hurried out of the restaurant. She feared McFadden might stop her or follow her. Out of the corner of her eye she saw him sit down, and she breathed a sigh of relief.

She found the women's room down a poorly lighted corridor. As she entered, she heard a hiss behind her. The face of the guide from St. Basil's appeared in a doorway across the hall.

"This way," he whispered. He led through deserted passages past loading bays at the back of the hotel. A car and driver waited there.

"Get in," the guide said, opening the rear door.

Startled, Sofia pulled back. "No way. Who are you?"

The guide looked disconcerted. "You asked for help," he hissed. "This is dangerous for us too." He scanned the darkness. "We can't stay here. Your minders will be looking for you."

"I don't know anything about you."

"You knew that when you approached me at St. Basil's." He looked disgusted. "And when you read my note and followed me out here." He looked around again. "I am Marat. I made a call to Paris today and spoke with Aleksey. He confirmed that a lady came to his house two days ago asking about Rasputin." He peered at her through ambient light. "I want to know why you're here. I don't believe you're researching Rasputin or the Church. The risks you take are too high for that."

Sofia started to respond.

"We can't talk here," Marat interrupted. "It's too dangerous. Either come with me or go back inside, but do it now."

Sofia took a deep breath. "Let's go." She climbed into the backseat. *Every security procedure I know just went out the window.*

Marat got in, his driver gunned the engine and the car moved off. As it joined general traffic, Marat turned in his seat. "Tell me what's going on."

Sofia summarized what she knew of Yermolov; what she had learned about Rasputin; her journey to Paris and what occurred there; and her conclusions. She deliberately omitted any mention of the nuclear device. *That might be a bit more than they can handle right now.*

Marat listened intently. When Sofia finished, he asked, "Do you think Yermolov's ancestry claims are genuine?"

"I don't know," she replied, "what matters is if Rasputin's followers believe him, and help him."

"What do you think Yermolov will do?"

She told him, again not revealing the bomb concern. When she had finished, Marat scoffed. "You think he can stage a coup?"

"He spied in the US for nearly thirty years," Sofia retorted. "He reached the most senior levels of US nuclear defenses. He almost succeeded in assassinating your general secretary in the US. And, he escaped from Cuba. What do you think he's capable of?"

Marat raised his eyebrows, and then was quiet while the driver maneuvered through nighttime winter traffic. "So," he said finally. "What do you want us to do?"

The driver spoke. "Never mind, Marat." He startled Sofia. He was white haired, and Sofia realized quickly that Marat deferred to him. "My name doesn't matter," he said quietly. "You are very brave."

In the dim light, Sofia could make out only the outline of his profile. His voice was kind. He seemed to try several times to turn to see her, but was constrained by a peculiar bend of his neck.

"Do you know that many Russians would welcome the Romanovs back to the throne?" It was a rhetorical question. The old man did not wait for a response "We've seen nothing but more dictatorship and bigger bombs for the past seven decades. Our people might look to Yermolov for deliverance."

He tried again to turn to see Sofia, but gave up the effort. "You are right that Novosibirsk is Rasputin's birthplace, and the group that believes in his legend is quite large there." He paused in thought. "It's also the birthplace of Saint Alexander Nevsky. He is the antithesis of Rasputin and a much-loved figure among Orthodox believers, including those that revere Rasputin."

He sat in quiet reflection, and tried one more time to see Sofia. "We know what we have to do." His voice was resolute. "You can't go back to the Metropol. You've been out of sight too long. The KGB would take you into custody immediately."

Sofia stared into the dark. "Tell me how I can help. Then take me to the US Embassy."

"That's easier said than done," Marat interjected. "The KGB will be looking for you there."

* * *

McFadden glanced across the lobby at Sofia's minders. They fidgeted. Ten minutes had passed since she had gone to the restroom. He went to find her. Thirty minutes later, he called Burly from the embassy. "She gave me the slip," he grumbled. He related what had happened at the Metropol.

"She's done it to the best of us," Burly groused.

"I went all the way to the loading docks at the back of the hotel," McFadden told him. "She had to have gone out that way. Which tells me, she had help."

* * *

The next morning, Sofia melded into the crush of Moscow's rush-hour pedestrians heading to their destinations. Her heart beat faster as the consular entrance of the US Embassy came into view. Already, a line of people seeking entry had grown.

Last night, Marat and the kindly old man provided shelter. This morning they dropped her off near the embassy to immerse herself among people doing routine business with the embassy's consular services. Dressed in a heavy coat, fur hat, and knee-high boots that Marat provided, she looked like any woman bracing Moscow's icy cold.

Chiefly on her mind was how to get by the Soviet guards. She looked ahead and saw that two of them stood on either side of the line about fifty feet in front of the embassy entrance. She sucked in her breath. They were checking identification documents.

To one side about one hundred feet away was a dark sedan with two civilian men. They watched the crowd. She glanced along the line of people behind her. None were leaving. She moved to the inside of the queue and stood at an angle to appear as though she were with a group of people.

The plainclothesmen by the car scrutinized the crowd, but had not taken note of her. The line proceeded. The guards studied the faces and papers of each person.

Sooner than she could have imagined, Sofia was one person behind the head of the line. She reached along the front of her coat and unbuttoned it, and stole another furtive glance at the plainclothesmen. One seemed to concentrate on her. She turned slightly as if looking inside her coat and slipped one arm out of its sleeve, but kept the coat over her shoulders.

She glanced again at the two plainclothesmen by the car. One of them pointed at her.

Now! Sofia shoved the person in front of her against the nearest soldier. Both staggered, and became entangled as they tried to regain balance. Yanking the coat from her other arm, Sofia threw it over the second guard and jammed a knee into his stomach. He clutched the air and crumpled to the ground.

To her left Sofia heard a startled cry. From the corner of her eye she saw the two plainclothesmen running toward her.

The first guard recovered his footing. He lunged at Sofia. She spun out of reach and swung around, kicked a foot high in the air, and brought it down on the back of his neck. He fell to the ground.

Hurried footsteps drew close. Without looking back, Sofia took off in a dead run toward the entrance to the embassy. Ahead of her, American Marines, alerted to the commotion, drew their weapons.

"I'm an American," Sofia yelled. "I'm an American." She threw her hands high in the air and continued her headlong sprint.

A strong hand grabbed her shoulder from behind. She dodged, and stooped as she slowed her forward momentum. When her pursuer lunged past, she shoved her right foot down on the backside of his left knee and drove it into the ground. The man cried out in pain, rolled over, and grabbed his injured leg.

The second man was older, heavier, and slower than the first. He slowed to a trot when he saw his companion go down, and closed the distance cautiously.

Sofia spun on her heels, and sprinted the few remaining yards into the entrance. As soon as she cleared the threshold, she threw herself on the ground, spread-eagled. "I'm an American!" she shouted. "My passport is in my back pocket!"

While one Marine stood over her with his Beretta pointed at her head, another extracted her passport and examined it briefly.

"It's her." He helped Sofia to her feet. As she stood, she saw a third Marine pick up the receiver on a wall phone. He spoke in muffled tones. Moments later, McFadden tramped in front of her, hands on hips, his face angry.

"We met last night," he said unceremoniously. "Follow me." He led through a maze of halls, past a reinforced security door, and into his office. He pointed to a phone on a massive desk with the receiver off the hook.

"That's for you." He sat down and directed a steady gaze at her. "My orders are not to let you out of my sight, and to hold you by force if necessary."

"You and whose army?" She picked up the phone. "Sofia Stahl."

For a few seconds, she heard only breathing on the other end of the line, and then Burly's voice. "I'm glad you're safe." He spoke slowly and steadily, but his anger came through. "You're under arrest. Do you understand?"

"I knew what to expect when I came here. Are you ready to listen?"

Burly was quiet a moment. "Go ahead."

"Was that tip about Novosibirsk good?"

"I don't know. You missed Atcho in Paris. He saw you in front of that Rasputin house, but didn't know it was you. He flew out of Moscow to Novosibirsk yesterday."

For a second, Sofia felt a hollow sense of lost opportunity. Atcho had been so close, twice. "Is he alone?"

"Rafael and Ivan are with him. Rafael is the guy—"

"I know who they both are," Sofia interrupted. "Listen carefully. Last night I met the head of the Russian Orthodox Church in Moscow. He's a honcho."

"So?"

"He can contact the head of the church in Novosibirsk." She filled Burly in. "The congregation there is active and effective. The patriarch will use his influence to stop any help that Yermolov could get from the Rasputin sect."

"Okay, got all that. You stay put in Moscow until this is over. You've done enough. McFadden has strict instructions in your regard."

Sofia scoffed and eyed McFadden. "Like that'll have any effect." She sighed. "OK. I'll be good. I don't want to put Atcho in greater danger." Her voice broke as pent-up emotion and the strain of days suddenly released. "Can you tell me more about the situation with the NukeX?"

"No. We're still working it." He heard Sofia sniff. "We'll get Atcho back," he said gruffly. "Hang tough."

When they hung up, Burly whirled on his staff. "What's the latest on that briefcase nuke?" he demanded.

"It's been delivered. That's all we have."

"And the NukeX?"

"They've been working through a technical glitch, but expect to have it fixed within hours. It should be ready to ship to Moscow by tomorrow."

"OK. Make sure McFadden knows all that stuff."

36

A day earlier, as Atcho's trio flew from Paris to Moscow, Atcho felt plagued by several issues. Flying into Cold War enemy territory was no small matter. This war was fought in shadows on clandestine battlefields, but the casualties were just as dead.

He reflected on his comrades next to him, and on Burly and Sofia. He had been terse with Burly, doubted Sofia, dragged Rafael into enemy heartland, and manipulated Ivan. Self-doubt gripped him. With nightmares of the past replaying on his mind in concert with those thoughts, he fell into restless sleep, and stayed that way for most of the trip to Moscow. He did not see Collins, seated ten rows behind, nor as the reporter exited the airplane for his unexpected rendezvous with Mr. Gorbachev.

After they had landed, they made their way to the gate for Novosibirsk. Fortunately, their KGB credentials had allowed them to travel with their weapons.

Ivan commandeered a vacant VIP room with a phone and placed a call. He spoke for fifteen minutes in Russian. Almost as soon as he finished his call, Ivan paced near another door situated on the opposite wall. He looked at his watch and then the door, and repeated those actions for the next hour, stopping occasionally to stare out a glass wall overlooking the airport.

"Did you see when our flight leaves?" he asked Atcho.

"We have two hours. Why don't you sit down?"

Ivan ignored him and resumed pacing. Atcho glanced at Rafael, who watched Ivan through half-closed eyes.

The door near Ivan opened. A Soviet Army colonel walked in, accompanied by a US Army colonel. Startled, Atcho started to rise.

Ivan's eyes opened wide. He motioned for Atcho and Rafael to stay seated.

"Are you Major Chekov?" the Soviet colonel inquired.

"I am."

"Are we ready?" the US colonel queried. "I have my orders."

Ivan glanced nervously at Atcho. "The others haven't arrived yet."

Just then, the door opened. A Soviet captain entered, escorting a pretty woman in her mid-thirties and a young boy in his early teens. Seeing them, Ivan's face lit up.

"Lara, Kirill!" He ran to them and engulfed them in his arms.

Lara threw her arms around Ivan's neck and sobbed. "Ivan, what's happening? They told us you were dead!" She pulled back to look into his face through tear-filled eyes. With rushed and staggered phrases, she told him that Gorbachev's personal security had taken them from their home at night and brought them here. "We had no time. We left everything." She broke into sobs once more.

Ivan caressed her face. "I know, darling. I'm so sorry." He held her gently. "I can't explain now. Please go with this American and do as he says. He'll take care of you. I'll join you in a few days." Then he turned to embrace Kirill, pulling his son's face into his chest. "I love you," he said softly, and his face showed his pain. "Take care of your mother."

"When will we see you, Papa?"

"Soon," Ivan promised. He stood back, nodded to the colonel, and held his wife and son one more time. "Go. I love you."

Lara pulled away, wiping tears from her eyes. After gazing at his father, Kirill followed. The colonel pointed the way, and the door closed behind them. Ivan remained in place, staring at the door.

Atcho stood and walked across to Ivan. "What was that about? Was that your wife and son?"

Ivan nodded. His face contorted with struggling emotions. "That," he rasped out, "was the price of my willing cooperation." He walked over to stare at the airport scene beyond the glass wall. Atcho crossed the room to stand near him. Rafael studied him.

After a time, Ivan half-faced Atcho. "I hate the way our people have to live." His voice shook. "I dreamed that Lara and Kirill could live in the US. Now they will, courtesy of Mr. Gorbachev and Mr. Reagan." He closed his eyes momentarily. "I hope they'll be safe."

"How did you do it?" Atcho asked in disbelief.

"I made the agreement at the Soviet Embassy in Paris. That was my condition for coming back to help you." His voice took on a note of disdain. "I spoke on the phone. In Russian."

Atcho started to place a supporting hand on his shoulder, but Ivan glared, and shoved Atcho's arm away. "Don't!" he hissed. "Do you see what your foolish haste did?" He was silent a moment. "My family is terrified. This was not the way I hoped to bring them to America." His anger was palpable. "I might never see them again. They know that." He turned to stare through the glass.

Stung, Atcho backed away and went to sit near Rafael. An hour passed. Ivan took a seat. Atcho waited for a few minutes, and went to sit next to him. Ivan did not immediately look up, but his fury seemed to have receded. "What now?" Atcho asked.

Ivan glanced at him, his face neutral. "My family is safe," he said, "so you have my willing cooperation. That was the deal. But," his voice took on a tone of ferocity, matched by his change of expression, "the mistrust must stop. I had no choice in coming here. You did."

Atcho started to apologize. Ivan cut him off with an upheld hand. "Don't. If I meet hostility or disrespect again, you'll find your own way out of Siberia." He gestured at Rafael. "That goes double for him."

Atcho stared. "Got it. Now, how do we do this?"

Ivan gathered his thoughts. "Yermolov couldn't hope to bring off a return through Novosibirsk without high-level military support in place, so he must have gotten some already.

"He must have similar support from senior levels in the KGB. Moving that entire staff secretly across the border wouldn't be easy, so KGB Border Troops had to have arranged entry.

"He'll need popular support to gain legitimacy, particularly with the coming elections. The Rasputin sect could help with that. His advantage is that anyone who might oppose him probably doesn't know he exists.

"Incidentally, I don't think he'll try a tactical nuke to blackmail Moscow. He might like to try to steal one, but he's pragmatic. He wouldn't be the first guy to think of that. Soviet safeguards are in place. If he tried, he'd alienate support.

"Whoever masterminded his escape thought long and hard about how to do it. Matching Yermolov with Rasputin followers was ingenious. So was planning his campaign to start in Novosibirsk."

"Do you believe he's a descendant of the tsar and Rasputin?"

Ivan shrugged. "The sect believes him. That's all that matters."

"How do we proceed?"

"He'll need a meeting of top commanders. He'll have to control elements where commanders oppose him soon, or he could find units shooting bullets at each other. That's civil war. He'll avoid that. So will Gorbachev, which is why there's no force going to Novosibirsk to arrest the bastard." He yawned. "Let me think. By the time we land in Novosibirsk, I should have something."

Atcho stood to stretch and glanced at his watch. Another thirty minutes remained before boarding. "Can I call the US from here?"

"Would you want to? I can route it to appear to originate somewhere else, but it'll be monitored by unfriendly people."

"I know. I'd still like to try."

Ivan placed the call and handed the phone to Atcho. When it was answered, Atcho blurted out, "This line is not secure. No names."

"Got it." Recognizing Burly's voice, Atcho breathed relief. "Glad you called," Burly said. They spoke in cryptic terms, and when they hung up less than a minute later, steel talons seemed to have gripped Atcho's stomach. Burly had just told him that Sofia was in Moscow, and still operating on her own.

At that moment, an attendant appeared in the doorway. "It's time to board," she said. "Follow me."

* * *

What is Sofia doing in Moscow? The thought plagued Atcho on the flight to Novosibirsk. He pushed his worries from his mind.

Tensions had dissipated between members of his team, but Atcho still had only a vague notion of how to proceed. "Tell me about the Russian Orthodox Christians in Novosibirsk," he told Ivan.

Ivan searched his memory. "There are a lot of them. Saint Alexander Nevsky was born there."

"I read that Rasputin was from there too," Atcho interjected.

Ivan nodded. "The cathedral was named for Nevsky. The Soviet government closed it years ago, along with all the cathedrals in the Soviet Union. Gorbachev recently encouraged parishes to apply to return them to local ownership. I'm sure the parishioners in Novosibirsk did that."

He recounted Nevsky's story, a military hero so revered by the populace that he was canonized two hundred years before Rasputin was born. "Nevsky cared about people," Ivan said. "Christians who know both stories will not revere Rasputin."

"That's interesting Russian history," Atcho said after a while, "but what are we going to do when we get to Novosibirsk?"

"You're missing a point," Ivan said. "We have a strong argument for turning members of the Rasputin sect at the Nevsky Cathedral. They could help us get close to Yermolov. Isn't that what you want?"

"That could take a while. Yermolov is in country. He won't wait for the elections, or for us to change minds about Rasputin. There must be a faster alternative."

Ivan gave him a sidelong glance. "There is."

* * *

Evening settled shortly after landing in Novosibirsk. News of Ivan's demise had not yet made it to the local station. He secured a KGB vehicle without difficulty.

"Tell me again what we're going to do," Atcho said.

"We're looking for the highest commanding general in the area," Ivan replied. "I'll show him a letter from Gorbachev requiring full cooperation, and say we need assistance to monitor Russian Orthodox Church members who might be overly aggressive in pressing for more religious freedoms ahead of returning the Nevsky Cathedral to Church control."

"And you have such a letter?"

Ivan produced it from a pocket inside his overcoat. "I requested it at the embassy in Paris. We don't know what we might need or when, so it was written broadly to require cooperation of anyone we present it to."

Rafael whistled from the backseat. "Whew! That is some pull."

"Right," Ivan replied. "It'll get us help, or get us killed."

"Won't the commanding general wonder why the local KGB isn't handling it?"

"He might, but he probably won't ask. It's Gorbachev's initiative, and for him to take personal interest wouldn't be unusual."

Atcho considered that. "What do we hope to accomplish?"

"You said we want to get ahead of Yermolov. He must be working through the KGB Border Troops. He might not have direct contact with the military yet. We need surveillance on the Rasputin group and military units related to last year's conspiracy, as quickly as possible."

"But you're a major. Won't the highest military commander—?"

Ivan produced a new ID card. "They made me a colonel too."

They headed southeast toward Novosibirsk. Atcho watched absently as snow-blown fields and forested hills slipped by, creating a sense of desolation in a hostile land. The heater barely worked, and cold crept into his skin.

Ivan noticed his discomfort. "Welcome to the achievements of a great socialist power. We make substandard cars, and you only have to wait three years to get one." He laughed. "People think that Soviets don't have money. We have plenty of rubles. There's just nothing to buy. And it's all poor quality." He was on a sarcastic roll. "What economic power can match that?"

Atcho held himself against the cold. "You're an unusual KGB officer. You admire our Western decadence."

"You lived in Cuba," Ivan rejoined. "You know what it's like. Americans forget what they have." His jaw tightened. "You built a society where anyone can prosper. That's why I sent Lara and Kirill there. I want a good life for them."

Atcho regarded Ivan soundlessly. *What have I done?*

Streetlights blinked on as the little car puttered into the city. Ivan turned into a checkpoint at the entry of an army base. When he pulled up to the guard shack, a sentry spoke with him and checked their IDs. Moments later the sentry returned their credentials, and waved them through.

"Gentlemen," Ivan announced. "Welcome to the belly of the bear. This is the headquarters of the Soviet Army Regional Commander, Colonel General Kutuzov."

37

Yermolov felt a strange sensation as Kutuzov guided him through the halls back to his office—hubris eroded by anxiety. "We're on our way," Kutuzov exclaimed. They had just left Murin and the conference of generals.

"I don't want to celebrate yet, but thank you for your enthusiasm."

"Securing our country's rightful place is worthy of sacrifice."

"I agree." He looked at Kutuzov. *Does an honest patriot still reside in this country? Poor fool—but a useful one.*

Five loose ends bore on Yermolov's mind: Atcho, Chekov, his family, Collins, and Sofia Stahl. He had heard no news about them in two days. He hated loose ends.

They entered Kutuzov's office from the rear. It was large but spartan. A double door encased in the far wall was the main entrance. Yermolov assumed that it led into a reception area.

"I'll pour some vodka," Kutuzov said. They had just clinked glasses, when they heard a rapid knock. The door from the reception area burst open. An orderly appeared, looking flustered.

"I'm sorry, General," he blurted. "Three KGB colonels are in the foyer. They've been here for an hour and insist on seeing you."

Before he could say more, the door swung wider, and three tough-looking men entered, wearing civilian clothes. The first walked over to

Kutuzov and was about to speak, when Yermolov rose from his seat. Hearing the chair scrape, the man looked past Kutuzov and made eye contact with Yermolov. With no change of expression, he diverted around Kutuzov, strode over to Yermolov, and presented himself at attention.

"Major Ivan Chekov reports," he announced in Russian.

At the door, Atcho and Rafael froze, staring at him with questioning eyes. Ivan gestured toward them. "I said I would come to you, General Yermolov. These are my prisoners. Both are posing as KGB colonels, and they are armed. Please take them into custody."

Without hesitation, Kutuzov pulled his Makarov and pointed it at Atcho and Rafael. Then he barked an order to the orderly, who hurried into the foyer.

Within seconds, two armed guards took up positions inside the door. Kutuzov turned to Yermolov, his face a mask of fury. "Someone tell me what's going on in my headquarters. Who are these men?"

Yermolov's face hardened as he recognized Atcho. "This is the man who stabbed me." He crossed the room to within inches of Atcho. "I see there is still fire in those eyes."

Atcho stared back into eyes devoid of emotion. Then he struck, hard and without warning, landing his right fist on the left side of Yermolov's jaw. He followed with a matching left blow to the right. Then he stepped in, grabbed Yermolov by the collar and delivered multiple punches to the stomach. The general doubled over, and Atcho brought a knee to his chin that sent him careening backward, landing in a heap.

Yermolov's back had been toward Kutuzov and Ivan. Atcho attacked so fast that neither saw what took place, until Yermolov fell.

Atcho stepped forward, intending to continue the beating, but Ivan tackled him and pinned him to the floor. Rafael jumped to Atcho's aid, but the guards grabbed his shoulders and pointed pistols in his face. Kutuzov pulled the charger on his pistol and aimed at Atcho's head. The sharp metallic click resounded through the room.

"Don't shoot him!" Yermolov gasped. He raised himself to one knee while regaining his breath. Ivan clambered up. Atcho got to his feet. He glanced at Rafael, who stared at the floor.

Yermolov regained composure. Then he stood in front of Atcho, glaring wordlessly. Suddenly, he delivered a powerful punch to Atcho's face, his knuckles striking between the eyes. Atcho reeled against the wall, blood trickling from his nose. His vision blurred.

Yermolov panted heavily. "Major Chekov, you redeemed yourself. General Kutuzov, confine these two. I'll clean up. Then we can discuss." He turned to Ivan. "Major, you'll join us."

* * *

"I understand," Kutuzov told Yermolov in his office an hour later, "Major Chekov and Atcho came after you in Havana last year."

Ivan sat next to Yermolov across the desk. "I did my duty."

Kutuzov waved a hand. "Of course, and Atcho was the intended assassin." Yermolov walked him through the details, then Kutuzov asked, "How did you, Comrade Chekov, come to be working with them this time?"

"I did not work with them." Ivan replied. "I was kidnapped, my death faked. I was coerced. Atcho's idea was to get as close as possible to General Yermolov in Novosibirsk. We didn't know the two of you had already linked up."

Yermolov's impatience showed. "I want to know three things: How did Atcho track me to the hill in Paris? How did he know we were coming to Novosibirsk? And how did he know to check out the Rasputin group in Novosibirsk?"

Ivan recounted what he knew. "I'm not clear on how he traced you to the hill in Paris. It had something to do with fish soup?" He intoned the statement as a question, and shrugged.

Yermolov growled, "I knew that soup was going to be trouble."

Kutuzov reacted with curiosity.

"I'll fill you in later," Yermolov said, and turned back to Ivan. "Go on."

As Ivan explained, Yermolov listened for indications of a leak within his own organization, particularly any that pointed at Drygin. They talked for hours, at the end of which Kutuzov exclaimed, "That is one hell of a story. Wish we had Atcho on our side. Rafael, too."

"Atcho's a bumbling fool," Yermolov snapped. "I'll interrogate him personally, then make sure he never interferes again."

Kutuzov looked up sharply. "Do we need to be that extreme? We could trade him for one of our own held by the US."

"Sometimes we must take hard actions," Yermolov said slowly. "Atcho sees our situation as personal. He won't rest until I'm dead. We need to remove the blight now."

"May I offer an observation?" Ivan asked. When Yermolov nodded, he went on. "I've watched Atcho closely for the past several days, under pressure. He is both instinctual and logical. He weighs what he knows and then acts." He addressed Yermolov. "You might have trained him to do that."

When Yermolov looked surprised, Ivan went on. "For all those years, he had no one to counsel with. He learned to go on his own judgment, and act without hesitation. He's dangerous to our cause."

"I'm pleased to hear you refer to 'our cause,'" Yermolov interjected. He turned to Kutuzov. "You're reluctant to end this problem." His voice took on stern overtones. "I intend to interrogate him tomorrow morning, and then I'll make a final determination. If you have a good reason to object, let's hear it. Otherwise, he will cease being a threat by tomorrow afternoon."

Kutuzov took a hard look at Yermolov. He chose his words carefully. "I don't take life wantonly," he said. "Today, many major military commanders joined with the KGB and the Politburo and selected you to lead us. We expect you to apply sound judgment."

His green eyes bored into Yermolov as he continued. "You know far more than I do about the facts concerning this Atcho. I would be imprudent to substitute my judgment over yours. National security must be our top priority."

Yermolov listened to each word. He flashed an ingratiating smile. *I'll be damned! The guy is a politician after all—and I've lured him into my corner.*

"I'm curious." Kutuzov returned his attention to Ivan. "How were you chosen to capture General Yermolov last year?"

Ivan took a deep breath. *I knew this was coming.* He shook his head. "Luck of the draw. It was my turn for duty, and that's when the shit hit the fan—excuse the American expression. It fits."

He turned to Yermolov. "When I came after you, sir, I had no idea who you were. I only knew that I had orders to capture or kill a rogue general. I oppose Gorbachev's policies, and apologize for what took place. If you're going to put me away, do it now."

"That would be a mistake," Kutuzov interrupted. "We have few men with character in our country who'll do what's right. Leave him in my command. I'll make sure he behaves."

Yermolov studied them both. "No need to make decisions now." He let a measure of Paul Clary's good nature show through. "We can find a role for our young major that makes best use of his talents." He spoke to Ivan again. His tone was borderline friendly, but his eyes pierced. "I promised to keep an eye on your family," he said. "Your wife and son are well and safe."

Ivan resisted a ferocious impulse. "Thank you, sir."

Yermolov studied him.

* * *

Drygin waited outside Fierko's office. Events raced to a climax, and he was out of the loop. After this afternoon's conference, Yermolov's stature would take a quantum leap, *but he's suspicious of me.*

He proceeded into cold calculation. *Yermolov will try to take me down. I won't let that happen.*

Fierko opened his door and gestured for Drygin to enter. "You sounded concerned."

"I won't mince words," Drygin replied. "I'm in trouble."

"You said so on the phone. I passed your concern to Comrade Murin. He said to reassure you that you would be a rising star."

Drygin sat deathly calm, understanding the weight of what he was about to say. "Our enemy is no longer only the US. It's also the Soviet regime. Now is not the time to threaten Stalin-like purges."

He looked around as if searching for words. "I've been in close quarters with Yermolov a long time. He only cares for power. He projects a reasonable image, but goes into rages. Just as quickly he reverts to courtesy. I think he's insane."

Fierko listened intently. When Drygin had finished, he stared without expression. At last he spoke. "The die is cast. We've crossed the Rubicon. Pick your metaphor. We can't reverse."

Drygin returned his stare. "We're between the potential extinction of the Soviet Union, or a return to a Stalinist era like never before. Comrade Murin must be informed."

"I can tell you only that elements are in place to contain Yermolov," Fierko said. "Meanwhile, you'll have to rely on Comrade Murin's statement that you'll be a rising star." There was no more insight he could offer. They both knew it.

Fierko escorted Drygin out. "Anything more on that briefcase?" Fierko asked as they reached the door.

"No. He locked it away on arrival, and I haven't seen it since."

"Well, maybe it was just as Chairman Murin guessed—he's being protective of his documents."

* * *

Yermolov's eyes blinked open. He sat up in bed. *Major Chekov couldn't get travel documents so rapidly in Paris without high-echelon help—ambassador-level help. Why would the ambassador help him?*

As soon as he formulated the question, the answer flashed in his mind. *Aznabaev is one of Gorbachev's best friends.*

He dressed quickly and went to Drygin's room. "Call a staff meeting. Do it now."

Thirty minutes later, Yermolov watched as Drygin and the primary staff officers filed half-asleep into the conference room. He felt in better control among his own staff, despite that he had selected none of them.

When they were seated, he addressed them. "We need to review our situation." He steeled himself to remain calm, knowing that if his staff sensed his anxiety, word would spread.

He smiled easily in his best Paul Clary guise, and looked at each of them. "I'm sorry I didn't brief you immediately on my return from the generals' conference. The meeting went well. We received the support of each of the major commanders present, as well as the KGB, and the Party member representing the Politburo. We are moving forward."

Several staff officers thumped the table and nudged each other in approval. The mood in the room brightened a bit.

"We can't celebrate yet," Yermolov went on, "but there was a development you'll want to know about. Earlier tonight, Major Chekov delivered Atcho and his partner to us, in Kutuzov's office. Chekov wasn't dead after all, and he performed a tremendous service."

Amid exclamations, Yermolov briefed the events of the evening. "We have loose ends," he said, after he had concluded. He turned to Drygin. "Is there any news on Ms. Stahl or Collins?"

Drygin shook his head. "Negative. The last time we saw either of them was four days ago, in Paris."

Yermolov's eyes almost closed as he dropped his head in thought. "I don't like it. They're not going to stop whatever they're doing. We need to know where they are, and why. What about Chekov's family? I ordered them brought here."

"We went through Fierko's office to accomplish that," Drygin responded. "They've disappeared."

"What do you mean?" Yermolov snapped.

Drygin kept his expression dry. "They are not in their house. They disappeared the same night you issued the order. The officers spoke with neighbors. No one knows where they went. A woman said she saw them taken away in dark cars. That's all the we have."

The muscles in Yermolov's face rippled into controlled anger. *Does Chekov know?* "When did you intend to tell me?"

Drygin leaned forward. "I'm telling you now." The staff members froze. Deathly quiet permeated the room. "The order went out as soon as you issued it. Yesterday we moved from Romania to here, and today you were in meetings." He pressed forward, and his posture expressed that he was coming to the end of patience. "We've followed up diligently, and tonight received the word I just gave you. I had intended to inform you at our first meeting in the morning, and that's what I'm doing now."

Yermolov studied him. *This man openly defies me. I'll make an example of him after the coup.* "All right. Keep me informed." He looked around the room. "We've made progress, but we're not home yet. If anything, our security must increase." His eyes bored into Drygin, who returned his gaze, unblinking. "Find them!"

Drygin nodded.

"I'm going to interrogate Atcho later. Colonel Drygin, you'll come with me. I want you to keep an eye on Major Chekov. I don't trust him.

"Also, we need to reach out to Rasputin's followers, to generate good-will." He instructed the adjutant to put together a reception for the sect leaders. "It should be low-key, but provide our guests an opportunity to feel important. You're all expected to be there." He smiled in his best Paul Clary style. "Be friendly. That'll be a new skill for many of you, a valuable one." His expression returned to stone. "Colonel Drygin, we'll leave right after the regular staff meeting."

38

Atcho sat in the corner of a dark cell in the basement, two floors below Kutuzov's office. Rafael sat across from him. They had watched in alarm when, on entering Kutuzov's office behind Ivan, Yermolov rose from his chair. Their apprehension grew to dismay when Ivan reported to Yermolov at attention. Neither needed to understand Russian to realize what was taking place.

When Yermolov had stood with his face so close that Atcho could feel and smell his rank breath, fury rose to explosive levels. It was Yermolov who had controlled Atcho from shadows for so many years. It was he who had kidnapped Atcho's little girl; imprisoned Atcho; laughed at the death of Atcho's best friend, Juan; and coerced Atcho into the assassination conspiracy.

Rage unleashed, Atcho had struck on instinct, inviting a bullet with each blow. Now, Atcho tried to see Rafael through the darkness. "Rafi, what are you thinking?"

"That our gooses are cooked," Rafael called back. "Or is it that our geese are cooked?"

Atcho chuckled. "That's what you're thinking right now?"

A guard rattled the door. Rafael paid no heed. "What does he think he's going to do, send us to Siberia?" He laughed. "Yeah, I'm thinking about those geese right now. That and what I'll do to Ivan when we get loose." He smacked a fist into his other hand, and then grinned in the dark. "I knew you were trouble when you showed up at the Bay of Pigs with that tank!"

"I'm sorry—"

"Don't go there. You tried to send me home when we were back in Paris." He chuckled. "But did you have to antagonize our host?"

The guard rattled the door again, and opened the hatch. Rafael clambered to his feet, strolled to the door, and raked the dark space beyond. "You aren't going to shoot me."

The guard flipped a switch that illuminated his face. He raised a pistol, aimed it directly at Rafael, and pulled the slider. In perfect English, he said, "My orders are to use any force required to keep you from talking."

"Oh," Rafael said. "Time for a snooze." He ambled back to his corner, lay down, and closed his eyes. The guard flipped the switch, immersing the cell in darkness once more.

For a while, Rafael thought of his long friendship with Atcho. He had been amazed when Atcho had blazed through massive fire in the jungle near the Bay of Pigs in Cuba, in a recaptured American tank, delivered it to Rafael's unit in Brigade 2506, and then almost as rapidly, had disappeared. Atcho's legend had grown such that he was a hero among the counter-Castro fighting forces, and he was feared among Castro's own soldiers. He had been a ghost, and even after capture, he had spent nineteen years in the dungeons without Castro ever learning that Atcho was his prisoner. Only on his arrival in Miami did he become known for who he was, and received a hero's welcome.

In the intervening time since their jungle encounter, Rafael had languished a year in the same prison where Atcho had spent most of his time, though they never saw each other there. When Rafael was released with the rest of Brigade 2506 under terms of agreement with Cuba negotiated by President Kennedy, he settled in Miami, where he had built a successful real estate brokerage.

Rafael had always felt that he owed Atcho. Unfortunately, the Kennedy agreement did not cover political prisoners, like Atcho, who had still lived in Cuba prior to the invasion, and so he continued to suffer in Castro's dungeons. Rafael had thought about Atcho often during the intervening years, and had been thrilled to see that he finally gained freedom.

When Atcho had been honored by President Reagan years later, Rafael had been thrilled to fly to Washington to be present at the reception where they renewed their acquaintance. Later that year, when Atcho called upon Rafael to protect his family while he broke Yermolov's assassination conspiracy, Rafael had been happy to help, and found volunteers from veterans of Brigade 2506 eager to keep Atcho's family safe. They had provided effective security under the noses of Yermolov's men and the Secret Service, without detection.

Now, despite his affection for Atcho and his own outward show of bravado, he was worried. He too had a wife he loved, and sons and daughters and now grandchildren, whose lives would be upended if he should not return from Siberia. *Atcho, I hope you get us out of this. But I'll never let you down.*

* * *

Atcho was sleepless. An indeterminate amount of time had passed. He peered in Rafael's direction. More time passed. He stood, and running his hand along the wall as a guide, he walked to the front of the cell.

There, he felt along the hatch in the door, estimating its dimensions. Then, he jerked it. Clanking steel resounded through the cell. He heard the guard outside stir in response. He jerked the door again, and kept shaking it. The clanking reverberated.

The hatch in the door slid open. The guard's silhouette appeared against a dimly lit background. "Quiet!" he ordered. "Do that again, and ..." He left the threat unspoken.

"We need blankets."

"No blankets." The guard reached up to close the hatch.

"You're *Spetsnaz*, aren't you?" Atcho called out to him.

"What?"

"You're *Spetsnaz*. Elite troops, like the US Special Forces."

The guard grunted derisively. "They wish!"

"I was trained by the *Spetsnaz*," Atcho went on. "Years ago. The KGB brought me to one of those camps outside of Moscow that don't exist. They trained me to spy in the US."

The guard peered at him. "So what?" He reached up to close the hatch. Atcho grabbed the sides of the door and shook it again so that it clanged loudly. "Now look," the guard bellowed, and he brought his face close to the opening.

In a flash, Atcho threw his arm around the guard's neck, and pulled it to the narrow opening. "Listen carefully," he hissed, his mouth only inches from the guard's ear. "You can die right now, or you can save yourself. I don't care either way. All I have to do is jerk down. You'll suffocate; your neck will break; or both. Your choice."

The guard gurgled a response.

"Give me your pistol. Right here in my hand. You can shoot me, if you want my dead weight on your neck. But you'd better not miss." He felt the guard move. Seconds later he felt the cold steel against his hand.

Atcho took it with his free hand. "Rafael," he called above a whisper. "Wake up. Come over here."

"I'm right behind you. Who can sleep with all that clanging?"

"Unlock the door," Atcho told the guard.

The hapless man attempted to shake his head despite the pressure on his throat. Atcho pressed the pistol against his head. "Open this door, now!"

"No key," the guard gurgled.

"Rafi, shoot the hasp. Don't worry about noise. If we don't get out of here now, we're dead."

Seconds later, the sound of a shot exploded through the cell and echoed down the corridor. The guard struggled, but Atcho held his throat pinned to the edge of the opening.

Rafael tried the door. It held firm.

From down the hall, they heard shouts and running footsteps. Rafael put the pistol to the hasp and fired again.

Atcho's ears rang, but when he pulled the door, it gave way. As it swung, he dragged the guard with it and applied greater pressure to the man's throat, blocking his airway. Within seconds, the guard blacked out. Atcho released him, and he slumped to the floor.

The running footsteps drew closer. They slowed to a walk as they approached the cell door. Atcho peered around the corner.

"Come out," a voice commanded. It was Ivan's. Rafael swore. Someone flipped the switch, throwing dim light along the corridor.

Moments passed. "You can't escape," Ivan called. "I have three guards with me. They will shoot to kill."

"We don't have a choice," Rafael whispered to Atcho.

"I know. Let's go."

Rafael threw the pistol into the corridor. Ivan picked it up and slid it into his belt. Then Atcho and Rafael came out. Two guards moved behind them.

Ivan waited while the guards handcuffed them and handed him the key. "We'll take them to a more secure place," he said. He peered inside the cell at the unconscious soldier, and waved one of the guards to attend to him. "You. Stay here until he wakes up."

He picked out the biggest of the three guards. "You come with me to escort the prisoners. Bring your weapon."

He turned to the third one. "Bring the staff car around front. Then report to the sergeant-of-the-guard that Colonel Chekov took the prisoners into custody for transfer to KGB headquarters." He looked between the guards. "Do you understand your instructions?" When they nodded, he gestured to Atcho and Rafael. "Let's go." Rafael shot him a deadly glance.

* * *

While Ivan covered his prisoners with his pistol, the big guard drove through empty streets toward the main thoroughfare that would take them to the regional KGB headquarters at Lenin Square. Atcho and Rafael sat in the tiny backseat, their arms handcuffed behind them.

"When I get free, I'm going to break your neck," Rafael growled.

"You'll try." Ivan kept his pistol pointed at them. He said something to the guard, who steered the vehicle through a left turn onto a secondary road. Soon the city fell away, and snowy fields on either side of the car reflected the light of the full moon.

Ivan seemed to be looking for something. He spotted a road and told the driver to take the turn. The gravel lane was narrow and led into low, forested hills.

Atcho and Rafael glanced at each other. The driver squinted at Ivan as if to confirm instructions. Shortly after entering the forest, Ivan told the driver to turn the car around and pull over.

When the car stopped, all were silent a few moments. "Sit still," Ivan commanded his prisoners. Then, he turned and shoved the muzzle of his pistol against the guard's neck, and spoke to him harshly in Russian. The soldier looked terrified. He handed his Makarov to Ivan.

In the backseat, Atcho and Rafael exchanged stares. "Is he doing what I think he's doing?" Rafael muttered.

"Shut up," Ivan called back. "Don't screw this up."

The guard clambered out of the car and trudged up the road, continuing in the same direction they had come. Ivan got out and watched him until he disappeared over a moonlit, snow-covered ridge a quarter mile away. The cold moon observed, uncaring.

Rafael called to him. "Are you going to take these handcuffs off?"

"Be quiet. I'm thinking."

"I sure thought you had sold us out."

"What did you want me to do?" Ivan's voice was thick with irritation. "Yermolov was right there."

Ten minutes later, Ivan drove the car onto the main highway going away from Novosibirsk. Atcho sat in the passenger seat, and Rafael stretched as best he could in the rear. Both were free of handcuffs, and Ivan had returned their Glocks and spare magazines. He kept the two Makarovs he had taken from the guards.

"Yermolov ordered your execution," he told Atcho. "He wants to be rid of a threat that won't go away."

"Does that let me off the hook?" Rafael bantered. He rubbed his wrists to restore circulation.

"No. You'd have been condemned by association."

"They'll be after you too, Ivan," Atcho remarked.

Ivan shrugged. "They haven't picked a date to put their plan into motion, but it's predictable. I learned a lot last night."

Kutuzov had revealed that in five days, Gorbachev would go on vacation to his dacha by the Black Sea at Foros in the Crimea. While there, the general secretary would be reported sick and under a doctor's care.

The KGB would cut his communications and isolate him from the news. Meanwhile, the rest of the military would be co-opted. "When he returns to Moscow, he'll be forced to resign in favor of Yermolov. The public will be told that he's too sick to continue in office."

"What if he refuses?" Atcho asked.

"He'll need medical treatment for real—or an undertaker."

Atcho absorbed that. The cold crept in deeper, and he folded his arms for warmth. "What do we do now?"

"I got you close to Yermolov," Ivan replied. "It's your call."

Atcho nodded. The impossibility of what he was to accomplish bore down. Sofia tugged at his mind, and he briefly thought about Collins. *He's probably long gone.* "Yermolov doesn't know that we're just three guys in a tiny car in the snows of Siberia, with no plan or support," he said.

"True," Ivan agreed, "but now they have confirmation that Gorbachev knows Yermolov is alive, in country, and intends a coup. Before, they had only an unconfirmed report that Yermolov was seen in Paris."

Atcho thought out loud. "How could we get word out about their plan?"

"I can command a telephone at any police station."

"You're a KGB major on the run."

"My ID says I'm a colonel. It'll be hours before that soldier gets back to his unit and sounds the alarm. We've got time. I can throw some weight around."

"Who would you call?"

"Gorbachev."

Startled, Atcho asked, "You can call him directly?"

Ivan shrugged. "He sent down a personal number while I was at the embassy in Paris."

Rafael stared at him. "And you didn't tell us?"

"A matter of trust," Ivan retorted.

Rafael scoffed. "Murin will love bugging that conversation."

"Murin won't expose himself," Ivan replied. "The generals won't cross him. They know he could deliver a deathblow to any of them. He has deniability through a Politburo member that attended the conference, and he commands the largest single military-type unit in the Soviet Union, the KGB. He's covered his tracks."

"Can you get us to Moscow," Atcho asked, "or Crimea?"

"They're nearly nine hundred miles apart. What happens if they switch the plan to Moscow, and we're in Crimea?"

Atcho sat deep in thought. The little car puttered through the half-light of a full moon over a desolate road traversing fields of snow. "We definitely need to inform Gorbachev," he said after a time. "But he still doesn't know who might betray him. Yermolov thinks he's won. We might have forced him to change his plan, but he'll keep on." He faced Ivan and Rafael in the moonlight. "Here's what we're going to do. Turn around."

Ivan shot Atcho a wondering glance, but maneuvered the car on the narrow road to head in the opposite direction. In the backseat, Rafael half-grinned. "Here we go again."

As they drove back toward Novosibirsk, Atcho explained. When he had finished, Ivan said, "That's risky."

"Compared to what?" Rafael muttered.

"The fast alternative nearly got us killed," Atcho said. "We'll have to get to Yermolov the slow way, and we don't have much time."

A few miles further on, they stopped at a nondescript town whose primary feature was a police station. There, Ivan used the full force of a KGB colonel to demand a private office with a telephone. After impressing on the senior officer the consequences of eavesdropping, he placed a call to Gorbachev.

The general secretary answered on the third ring. Ivan explained Yermolov's plan and identified as many participants in the conspiracy as he knew of. Gorbachev listened intently. When Ivan mentioned Kutuzov and Fierko, he expected a reaction, but Gorbachev remained ominously silent.

"They'll move against you either in Moscow before you leave, or while you're on vacation at your dacha."

"Move against me," Gorbachev repeated brusquely. "We'll see. I can take action to shake that up." He did not explain.

They went over Atcho's plans for Novosibirsk. Gorbachev grunted. "I don't underestimate Atcho."

* * *

Collins felt restless as he waited for news. The phone rang. "It's me. Jakes." The editor sounded tired.

"What's up?"

"The articles are published. In a few hours, they'll appear under your byline in *Pravda* and *Izvestia* in Moscow."

"Thanks. I'd like to know that they're effective."

"We'll know soon. Bye."

* * *

Sofia stepped into the CIA station chief's office. She had received a message that he wanted to see her.

"I thought you'd want to know about this," McFadden told her. He held out a newspaper. It was in Russian. In the far-right column was a pencil-sketched visage of Rasputin. "This is today's *Pravda*," he said. "The article is about fake Rasputin descendants. It was written by a *Washington Herald* reporter, Tony Collins." He held out a photograph. "Is this the old man you met the other night?"

Sofia peered at the sketch. The man was grayed and bent, but he portrayed dignity, undiminished by the penciled rendering, or his simple clothing. "It could be. Do you have a photo from the side? I met him in the dark."

McFadden produced another likeness, this one in profile. The two images were unmistakably of the same man, but in the photo his head was canted at a peculiar angle, perhaps because of age, or from injury. "Yes! I'm sure that's the man I met. His neck had that angle. It was like he couldn't move it out of that position."

"Lady, you sure get around. That's the top guy of the Orthodox Church in Moscow."

"I told Burly that. You heard me."

"That I did. We need to make sure he sees this article. Quickly."

"Okay, I can do that. Tell me—"

"We'll handle it," McFadden said firmly. "There's another issue." He looked grim. "Burly told me that you know something about the NukeX."

Sofia nodded. McFadden produced a box from his drawer. "This is the NukeX. It arrived by diplomatic pouch last night. Burly didn't want to mention it or the nuke to Atcho until he could either send it, or find out that it wouldn't be available. Then Atcho left Paris before expected.

"We need to get the device into Atcho's hands and warn him about the nuke. I need to know everything you know about where he might be and what he looks like, and the same stuff for the two guys that are with him. Gorbachev will provide transportation out there."

Sofia stared at him. "You're kidding."

McFadden gave her a grim look. "I wish I were. The threat's been confirmed. Atcho will have to locate Yermolov, and disarm the bomb with the NukeX. If he doesn't..." McFadden puffed out his cheeks and let the air escape through pursed lips.

"Send me," Sofia exclaimed.

Startled, McFadden stared at her. "No way. You're too personally involved. You've done your part. Time for someone else to step in."

"Send me," Sofia insisted. She gripped the desk, and leaned over it with a fierce expression. "Look, we still have to find Atcho, and when we do, he has to trust whoever we send. We might only have seconds. He knows me. He doesn't know anyone else here, and right now we don't have direct commo."

McFadden regarded her stubbornly. "No. You're an analyst."

"Listen to me." Sofia circled the desk and stuck her face up near McFadden's. "I'm a trained officer with over ten years of field experience, and I'm fluent in Russian." She saw him still hesitate. "I stayed ahead of the whole CIA all the way here, and shook you off. Do I need to remind you how I got into this embassy?"

If her comment irritated McFadden, he did not show it. He continued to study her.

"Send me," Sofia repeated impatiently. "We don't have time for debate. There's no one here more ready than me to do this mission." She reached up and shoved McFadden's shoulders with the open palms of her hands. "Brief me. Let's go."

39

Yermolov's eyes blinked open again. He sat up. Feelings of overwhelm approached. Loose ends were beyond his control. Having Atcho and his sidekick in a cell was good. *But where are Tony Collins and Sofia Stahl?* He lay back in his bed and tried to sleep, but then sat up again sharply. *Where is Ivan Chekov's family?*

Just as troubling, Drygin barely disguised his hostility. For the moment, Yermolov was powerless to act. But in a few days... He exulted momentarily over a mental image of subjecting Drygin to his will from the Kremlin.

He looked at his watch. It showed seven o'clock, an hour before the staff meeting. From there, he and Drygin would go to interrogate Atcho. *I want to see Atcho die, to be sure it happens.*

An hour later he entered the conference room where Drygin and the staff were already assembled. "What's the progress on Collins, Sofia Stahl, and Chekov's family?" He asked the question abruptly, and without regard for normal staff-meeting protocol.

"No change." Drygin regarded him with his steady, unwavering gaze. "But, we received an article on the front page of *Pravda*. The story came from one of the newswires, so it's out internationally. I think you'll want to see it." He held up a typed set of pages.

Yermolov gave Drygin a caustic glance and turned to his adjutant. "Get me some coffee." He read the paper's first line, and blanched.

"Fake Rasputin Descendants Proliferate," the headline proclaimed. The name of the author arrested his attention: Tony Collins.

The adjutant arrived at Yermolov's elbow with a mug of steaming coffee, and reached around to hand it to him. In a surge of anger, Yermolov knocked the coffee away. It spilled across the adjutant's arm onto the table, with some of it splashing into Yermolov's lap. He leaped to his feet, his eyes bulging in rage.

The adjutant was a decorated major. He held his arm, and although he did not cry out, his face showed excruciating pain.

Yermolov tried a Paul Clary compassionate response, but his voice sounded terse. "My fault. Get that arm seen to right away." He turned to Drygin. "Get a car. We're going to see Kutuzov. Now."

* * *

Colonel General Kutuzov watched through his second-story window as Yermolov arrived. Today's *Pravda* rested on his desk. In the far-right column above the fold was the sketch of Rasputin. Kutuzov had scanned the article. It was innocuous, telling only of the mystic's life and influence on Tsar Nicholas. The main thrust, however, was that over the years, people had claimed direct ancestry from Rasputin, just as they had from the Romanovs. Those claims had been debunked.

Side articles added depth. One went into detail about methods of aging paper and ink. Another discussed techniques used to dispel doubt about the age of almost any object, including documents.

The combined thrust of the articles seemed to have purposes beyond informing the public. No such pieces could have appeared on the front page of official Soviet newspapers without Kremlin sanction—or more specifically, without Gorbachev's consent. They constituted a warning: the general secretary's suspicions were high and pointed in a specific direction; and they derided anyone making or believing such ancestral claims. They threatened to isolate Yermolov from the Rasputin group and the Russian Orthodox Church. That an American received credit for the main article published in Soviet flagship newspapers implied close cooperation between the United States and the Soviet Union.

Yermolov entered with Drygin. "Sorry to barge in," he said with forced affability. He glanced at the desk, and his attention landed on the issue of *Pravda*. "You read the news. What's your take?"

"It's a setback," Kutuzov replied. As Yermolov and Drygin took their seats, he sat down behind his desk. "I don't see it as a major blow. The Rasputin group's part is done. They gave you a haven and finance during planning, and helped stage your move back here. Any more support from them was peripheral, and no longer needed. We didn't mention them to the generals at the conference."

Yermolov listened without immediate response. Then he exhaled, genuinely relieved. "I'm glad we agree." He turned to Drygin. "Call Fierko. See what he thinks."

Drygin started to rise, but before he was fully standing, Kutuzov cut in. "There's something else you need to know. Atcho and his companion tried to escape last night."

When Kutuzov saw Yermolov's eyes widen, he raised his hands in a placating gesture. "Major Chekov caught them right after they overpowered the guard. He transferred them to KGB headquarters. That facility is much more secure."

"Chekov?" Yermolov growled. "Let's get that interrogation done." He turned to Drygin. "Find out about Atcho's status."

Drygin moved rapidly. He told the soldier at the front desk, "I need a room with a secure line." Moments later, two junior officers in the intelligence section vacated their office, leaving Drygin alone.

"I'm at General Kutuzov's office with General Yermolov," he said when Fierko came on the line. "They want your views of this morning's article in *Pravda*."

"I just read it, but haven't analyzed it. Tell them we should talk in person this afternoon."

"I'll pass that on." Drygin's adherence to decorum declined. "They want to know the status on Atcho."

Fierko was not amused. "What's an Atcho?"

"The man who caught Yermolov in Havana last year." Drygin gave a quick rundown. "Yermolov wants to interrogate him."

"Give me a minute." When Fierko came back on the line he sounded agitated. "No one came to our facility last night; no KGB major, no Atcho, no anybody."

Drygin sat forward in his chair. "Are you sure?"

"I'd know if someone were to be interrogated in my facility, particularly when it's this sensitive."

"My mistake." Drygin felt low-key elation. The *Pravda* article and Atcho's disappearance were two chinks in Yermolov's armor.

When he relayed the message, Kutuzov placed an immediate conference call to Fierko. "Where are the prisoners that were taken there last night?"

"I'd like to know," Fierko replied, his voice icy. "No prisoners arrived here, and no major. They must have left your location eight hours ago. I assume they escaped. Your major could be dead."

Yermolov felt pincers tighten in his stomach. "I'm coming to your headquarters," he announced. He modulated his voice to sound authoritative without being tyrannical. "We need to discuss the *Pravda* articles and have a phone call with Chairman Murin."

Fierko was quiet. "Be here in an hour," he said at last. "I'll inform Comrade Murin that you, General Yermolov, requested a conference. I'll let him know of Atcho and his disappearance. Meanwhile, I'll send out investigators to find out what happened with the prisoners and the major. Anything else?"

With each point, Yermolov felt anxiety rise. "You stated the issues. Do you have any questions?"

"No, but for your information, Gorbachev cancelled his vacation in the Crimea. Think about it. He allowed those articles onto the front pages of the newspapers, and then he changed plans with no explanation. His radar is up."

And the two men who caught me last year are loose. Together.

40

An hour later in Fierko's office, the three generals viewed each other guardedly. "Do we know anything about the whereabouts of Atcho and Chekov?" Yermolov asked.

Fierko turned to Kutuzov. "He was your prisoner. A single guard accompanied the transfer. Chekov had an ID showing he is a colonel. Have you heard anything about the soldier?"

Kutuzov took his time to reply. "My staff is working on it," he said coldly. "I came to discuss the *Pravda* article. If that's not why we're here, I'll go back to my command." He directed his eyes to Yermolov. "I assume that Chekov, whatever his rank, was helping Atcho."

Yermolov returned Kutuzov's steady gaze. "I requested a conference call to Chairman Murin." He turned to Fierko. "Place the call." His command brooked no challenge.

Fierko stared back, and then dialed the number. Murin's smoke-worn voice sounded over the voice box. "General Fierko, do we all know the same things?" There was no sound of warmth.

"Yes, Comrade. Unless you have new information."

"None. General Yermolov, what's on your mind?"

Yermolov straightened his shoulders and moved close to the speaker. "Comrade Murin, it's time to accelerate. Nothing on Gorbachev's itinerary should cause delay. He seems aware that something is taking place, but doesn't know what, when, or where. By waiting, we give him time to mount counteractions.

"Even if we assume that Chekov betrayed us, anything he thinks he knows is conjecture, and if we move up our timetable, his knowledge will be outdated."

He paused to gather his thoughts. Murin's silence felt ominous. Yermolov's voice took on a firm note. "The Rasputin group was ancillary. Soviet power never relied on the Orthodox Church. We have the critical pieces in place. It's time to move. The future of the Soviet Union rests on what we do now."

When Murin responded, his voice was low and cautious, almost challenging. "Are you ready?"

Yermolov drew to full height. His eyes exuded fire. "I'm ready." His fate rested with Murin.

"General Kutuzov, what is your assessment?"

"No change. As General Yermolov stated, no strategy was grounded on Church support. It was nice to have. That's all."

"What about your escaped prisoners?"

"At best, Chekov was overpowered. At worst, he helped. We'll intensify our search. That should not affect our plans."

"General Fierko, what do you think?"

Fierko exhaled. "If we stand down, we'll face massive retribution. Our best defense is to stay on offense. We have no time to waste. We should press on. Now."

Yermolov regarded Fierko with surprise. *The guy has guts.*

Murin spoke again. This time, his voice carried gravity, even deference. "General Yermolov, let me be the first to welcome you to Moscow. I'll meet you in my office at noon the day after tomorrow." He hung up.

The office was deathly quiet. Yermolov stood still, a solitary figure. Then he started a slow turn, taking in every detail in the room. As his eyes bore on General Fierko, the KGB general came to attention.

Yermolov acknowledged him. He continued his turn until his eyes rested on Kutuzov.

"General Yermolov," Kutuzov said, standing at attention, "My command is at your service."

* * *

Drygin noticed the change in deference when the two generals returned to Kutuzov's headquarters. Yermolov was clearly in charge.

"We're moving up the schedule," Yermolov told him. "I leave for Moscow tomorrow. As of this moment, you're released to General Fierko. Thank you for a job well done." *I'll deal with you in a few days.* He entered Kutuzov's office without further comment.

Watching him, Drygin smiled, his eyes narrowing to slits. He glanced up and saw Kutuzov studying him.

An hour later, he sat in Fierko's office. "Colonel Drygin, welcome to my command. We're accelerating the plan. I leave for Moscow tomorrow. Chairman Murin wants you there tonight."

Drygin maintained his calm. "Is there something for me to do?"

"You'll monitor security arrangements. I'll do the same from this end until my departure. We can't afford mistakes."

Barely twenty-four hours had passed since Drygin had voiced his concerns to Fierko. In this cold emotionless way, steps seemed to have been taken to insulate and even advance him, though he wondered about the concept of keeping enemies closer.

He had weathered many KGB political storms. He foresaw the one roiling on the horizon to eclipse all others, and made his own assessment about where personal loyalties should lie.

* * *

Late that night, Yermolov's eyes blinked open yet again. This time, a sense of exultation worked his mind, and he basked in it. He had learned before going to bed that the triumphal chariot carrying him to Moscow would be the magnificent Antonov 225 Mriya, the new aircraft he had seen on the runway when he and his entourage arrived in Novosibirsk.

"Gorbachev must know where I am by now," he had told Fierko. "Won't he suspect if the Mriya flies to Moscow a day early?"

"At this point, he'll suspect anything that moves," Fierko said. He related that Murin felt the flight was easy to justify. The aircraft was a terrorist target, and would be best protected in Moscow.

Fierko had briefed Yermolov on the movement plan. On arrival in Moscow, security teams would board to clear the aircraft. "One of them will escort you to your car. You'll be taken straight to the Lubyanka." The next day, Murin would accompany him to a meeting in Gorbachev's office at the Kremlin.

"The general secretary will suffer a heart attack, and will be unable to carry out his duties," Fierko said. "Murin's handpicked security detail will take action to safeguard the life of the general secretary to ensure the continued functioning of the Soviet Union."

Yermolov enjoyed the music of what he had just heard, essentially the Soviet version of, "The king is dead. Long live the king!" Despite the pleasant scenario, he alternated between exuberance and unease. "Do we have any news of Chekov or Atcho?"

Fierko shook his head. "Speed and surprise are our greatest weapons now. In two days, you'll have the full might of Soviet forces to unleash on the fugitives."

You don't know Atcho. Yermolov had dismissed the thought. Now, in the still of the night, it returned full force, displacing hubris.

To Yermolov, Atcho was an enigma. He never quit. Through twenty-seven years of manipulation and imprisonment, his spirit had never broken. His tenacity bordered on lunacy. More problematic, his motivation stemmed from principles, and most high among them were protecting family and country.

Yermolov contrasted himself against Atcho. Only the drive for power had guided the general's career. He had affected humility, compassion, understanding, and other virtues as needed. He had even convinced a wife, a daughter, and a community that he was a loving husband and father. His family had been a prop to maintain his cover, nothing more. He had left his house early on the morning of the assassination attempt, and never looked back.

Now, when he was so close to reaching absolute power on a world stage, he felt the overwhelming emotion he most scorned. Fear. "Damn you, Atcho."

41

When Colonel General Borya Yermolov strode into Kutuzov's office the next morning, he had shaken off the terrors of the night, and wore the full-dress uniform of the Soviet KGB. He arrived at the army post without bothering to obscure his presence, and when he entered Kutuzov's office, he did so with only a perfunctory knock. He carried his briefcase with him.

Kutuzov rose to greet him. "At last this day is here." He shook Yermolov's hand firmly. "Maybe we can right this ship-of-state."

Recalling how easily Kutuzov agreed to Atcho's execution, Yermolov regarded him with hidden contempt, while feigning warmth. *You're as dirty as the rest of us.* "Where is General Fierko?"

"At the airstrip. We've tightened security, so we'll be traveling in a motorcade."

When they arrived at the airfield, both generals could only stare in wonder at the elegance of the Antonov 225 Mriya. Yermolov exited the limousine, carrying his briefcase with him. Kutuzov followed.

As they approached the aircraft, a crew van drove up on the opposite side. Three members of the ground crew hopped out and inspected the landing gear.

Yermolov paid them no mind. He was too taken with the Mriya. As a former US Air Force officer, he appreciated the fine lines and aerodynamic detail. It was designed for heavy lift, dwarfing the Boeing 747, yet its steep tail allowed for shorter takeoffs and landings than would be expected of such an enormous airplane. Nevertheless, with a full load it needed a two-mile runway.

"This is a work of art," Kutuzov breathed, "in classical Russian tradition."

"Agreed," Yermolov said. *But the Ukrainians built it.*

The crew van drove between them and the aircraft, and the driver rolled down the window. "Lieutenant-Colonel Zhukov will be here in a few minutes. We have ground crew doing final inspections." He drove on.

Yermolov noticed that two members of the ground inspection team on the other side of the aircraft were near the crew door, and appeared to be opening it. He could see only their legs. The third had gone to the front landing gear, and was inspecting the tires.

Just then, an air force officer approached from the operations building. He stood at attention and introduced himself. "I am Lieutenant-Colonel Stephan Zhukov, the pilot. Would you like to board now? We're waiting for General Fierko and then we'll be ready to start the flight." He seemed unsettled.

"Are you nervous?" Yermolov asked.

"A bit," Zhukov replied. "This is an important flight. I'm watching the ground crew to make sure they're doing things right."

"They seem thorough." Yermolov glanced at the man inspecting the front tires, and then at Kutuzov. "Let's board."

As they started toward the front of the aircraft, Fierko hurried from the operations building. "I've been on the phone with Murin." He turned to Kutuzov. "He insists that you fly in a separate aircraft."

Yermolov and Kutuzov were both puzzled. "Why?"

"He's concerned about security. He thinks that with this plane being such a high-priority target, having three senior-level officials aboard is inviting fate. He wants me to handle security for General Yermolov when we land. Also, if things go badly on arrival, he doesn't want the army implicated by having another general on board."

Kutuzov looked at Yermolov. "That makes sense," he said, reluctantly. "What do you think?"

Yermolov's survival warnings blared in his head, but he saw no alternative. "I'll see you in Moscow."

"There's another plane inbound to pick you up," Fierko told Kutuzov. "You'll land within minutes of us."

Yermolov boarded the Mriya with Fierko and Zhukov. A crewmember met them at the top of the stairs on a crosswalk in front of the flight cabin and cockpit.

"This is my senior engineer," Zhukov told them. "He'll show you to your compartment. I'll leave you now." He disappeared through a door into the flight cabin at the center of the crosswalk.

The generals settled into their cabin. They sat on two couches facing each other, with a table between them. Soon, the plane hummed with the high-pitched whine of generators followed by a deep throaty roar as one after another, six engines thundered to life.

"Do you recall the estimated flight time?" Yermolov asked.

"About three hours." He was not conversational. Although Yermolov did not object, he made a mental contrast between Fierko and Kutuzov. He had found his discussions with Kutuzov valuable. They gave him a sense that he knew the man. He had no such insights into Fierko.

"Do you have any reservations about what we're doing?"

"No, sir," Fierko said after an extended silence. Yermolov took note of the deference. It was qualitatively different from Kutuzov's. "I've long admired you," Fierko continued. "As I told Chairman Murin, you have the skills and experience for the job, and you bring insights no one else does."

Yermolov acknowledged the comment. *Is that sincerity or lip service?* "What security concerns are you expecting on arrival?"

"None in particular. I sent Colonel Drygin ahead to be sure. He was closest to your operation in the US, and knows the security requirements. Murin wanted him there."

"Drygin." Yermolov's sense of alarm ignited. *Why did I turn him loose so soon?* "Good man."

The Mriya's engines roared, and the big plane crept from its parking place on the tarmac to a position at the end of the runway. In the cockpit, Zhukov heard a transmission from ground control, "Antonov 225 Mriya, please hold your position. We have an inbound Sukhoi making an emergency landing. Wait until cleared."

Moments later, a small fighter streaked low over the Mriya. It settled to the ground, decelerated rapidly, and came to a halt a few hundred yards down the runway. As it did, several trucks and an ambulance rushed toward the aircraft. Zhukov saw the canopy on the fighter pop open, and two figures jumped out while emergency personnel started their procedures.

General Yermolov appeared in the flight cabin. "Trouble?" he asked, scanning through the windshield.

"An emergency landing," Zhukov replied. "Probably a hot-shot pilot overstraining his engine. We'll be set to go shortly."

Twenty minutes passed. A tow truck pulled the fighter off the runway, and ground control cleared Zhukov for takeoff. The Mriya rumbled down the runway, lifted its nose skyward, and pulled its massive bulk into the morning air. Watching from the operations building, Kutuzov thought the plane seemed like a magnificent white eagle soaring into the clouds. "So, it begins."

42

On the morning that Yermolov, Kutuzov, and Fierko conferred with Murin over the likely impact of the *Pravda* articles, Atcho and his companions witnessed an unexpected event. From the little car, they watched as a man used wire cutters to snip the rusted, aging strands of barbed wire strewn on the fence and the gate of the Nevsky Cathedral in Novosibirsk. He pulled the wires apart, leaving them in two piles on either side of the entrance. Then he pried the gate open with a crowbar, and walked into the courtyard.

While they watched, the church's dark red bricks came to light, illuminated by advancing rays of dawn. Despite being muted by decades of neglect, the golden main dome glinted in the morning sun, decked with yet more twisted barbed wire.

Minutes passed. Another man walked past the piles of cut wire. Shortly, an elderly couple followed. Soon a stream of people filed through the stately redbrick gate.

Atcho and his companions stepped out of the car, shivering against the cold. "What do you think?" Atcho asked. "I was hoping to find a caretaker. I hadn't expected to see people going to mass."

"I didn't know Gorbachev's policies had gone this far," Ivan exclaimed. They approached cautiously, adopting the demeanor of those ahead of them. Inside, Atcho led them into an empty row of pews near the back.

Around them, congregants either stood with bowed heads, or looked about as though observing changes in an old friend. Time and neglect had taken their toll but had not destroyed the magnificence of the building, from the carvings that adorned the columns to the sculptures that overlooked the altar.

They heard rustling behind them. A priest in flowing red robes walked down the center aisle, flanked by two acolytes. He made his way to the altar and faced his parishioners.

"Welcome," he said with a solemn smile. "We received the news last night that General Secretary Gorbachev let us into our church a few months early. Our people are once again welcome in the Cathedral of Saint Alexander Nevsky." He prayed. Men and women let tears run down their faces, celebrating a day they'd thought would never come.

When the sermon was finished and the people had left, Ivan spoke with the priest. Abruptly, the cleric motioned for Atcho and Rafael to join them, and led them into a darkened corner. "I am Father Matfey," he said in heavily accented English. "The patriarch in Moscow called last night. He passed the word from Gorbachev to open the church. He said to expect three men. One is called Atcho."

"That's me."

Matfey studied him. "He told us about a few articles in *Pravda*. They make anyone look silly who believes claims of descending from Rasputin. Some members had parents who revered the mystic. They were poor and accepted hope where they could find it."

"What about someone claiming to be descended from both the tsar and Rasputin?" Atcho asked. He recalled his own incredulity when Burly had explained Yermolov's alleged background.

"There was a Soviet general in Novosibirsk yesterday who made that very claim. He had strong documents, but last night, the patriarch in Moscow called to warn us about him specifically. The general's name is Borya Yermolov."

Atcho's pulse raced. "What did you think about the newspaper articles?"

"If we hadn't heard about them directly from the patriarch, we would have viewed them as propaganda. Our people would have helped Yermolov."

"Did you know that Yermolov intended to use Rasputin's followers to spread his support to other parishes?"

"Yes. That plan was cynical, and now it will fail." The priest looked around his church disconsolately. "I hope we're not outlawed again." He sighed. "By the way, his staff called this morning to invite us to a social event with him. We don't know when it will be. It's still in planning."

"As soon as you know the details, please let us know."

* * *

Hours later, Atcho awoke from sound sleep. He stared up into darkness. He felt someone shaking him, and then heard Matfey's voice. "Sorry to bother you." They were in a room on the cathedral grounds. The priest spoke urgently. "Yermolov cancelled the social event. His staff is packing up."

Atcho's eyes adjusted to faint light filtering through the open door as his mind grappled with what he had just heard. Across the room, Rafael sat up and stretched. Ivan yawned.

The priest tugged at his shoulder. "Yermolov is leaving. They cancelled the event."

Suddenly, Atcho's mind grasped what the priest had said. "He's moving," he thundered. "Yermolov is moving. Father, get the news to your patriarch. Ivan, wake up! You've got to get us to Moscow."

"I have to do what?" Ivan came fully awake with a start.

"That article spooked Yermolov," Atcho declared. "He's moving."

"That's a leap," Ivan replied. His voice carried his skepticism. "Maybe he's relocating to the army post. He had his big conference. He might feel more secure."

"No, he's moving on Moscow," Atcho insisted. "Yermolov didn't just postpone the social event. He cancelled it. He knows Gorbachev is taking active steps. The *Pravda* articles told him that. He wants to preempt Gorbachev."

Ivan still looked dubious. "Even if you're right, what do we do?"

"We'll take it step by step," Atcho growled. "We have to get ahead of Yermolov. Reagan wants him brought to the US alive."

Ivan whirled on him. "I'm still a loyal Russian. If we capture him, he should be turned over to Gorbachev."

"I work for Reagan," Atcho reminded him sharply. "Yermolov has our military secrets."

Ivan started to protest, but Atcho silenced him with an upraised hand. "We don't have time to discuss it. Either way, we have to get in front of him. If we can't return him to the US, I'll kill him."

Ivan stared at Atcho, and nodded. "Fair enough." He pondered the difficulty of getting to Moscow. "We can't drive there fast enough, especially in a stolen army car. If we go commercial, we're likely to get caught. Atcho, you flew that private jet down to Havana last year to capture Yermolov. If I get you into a Soviet plane, can you fly it?"

"Maybe, if you translate the switches and buttons. That's not a safe alternative. Frankly, I'm seeing only one option with a chance of capturing Yermolov. We have to be on the same flight."

Rafael, Ivan, and Matfey stared at him. Ivan scoffed. "Since this just turned into a suicide mission, why don't we shoot him on sight?"

Atcho ignored the dark humor. "He has to be going on a military flight, and not a regularly scheduled one. The crew won't know they're carrying the next wannabe general secretary. We should be able to spot an unscheduled plane at the airfield prepping to fly to Moscow."

"I can do that," Ivan said. "Our KGB credentials will get us on the airfield. I can handle it from there."

Matfey interrupted meekly. "May I offer a suggestion?" Startled, the others regarded him with courteous skepticism. "There's a cargo plane parked on the runway at the aircraft plant. They say it was built to fly the Soviet space orbiter around. I've never seen one so big. It was supposed to fly out for a check-ride tomorrow, but the schedule was changed. Instead it will go straight to Moscow."

Atcho stared at him. "Are you sure? How do you know that?"

"Some of our church members work at the plant. The schedule change was ordered a few hours ago. The ground crew will prep it tonight."

"And it's supposed to fly to Moscow tomorrow?"

Matfey nodded.

Ivan suddenly looked excited. "Is that the Mriya?"

Matfey shrugged. "I suppose so. The plant workers were talking about it for weeks. They were so excited to see it."

"Do you know why the schedule changed?" Rafael asked. The priest shook his head.

"That's got to be Yermolov's ride," Atcho exclaimed. "The *Pravda* articles came out yesterday, and then the schedule changed."

"That's a fantastic aircraft," Ivan broke in. "It's the biggest plane in the world. It can fly a third of the way around the earth at the equator without refueling." He turned on the priest. "And it's here?" His eyes gleamed. "I never expected to actually see it!"

"We'll do more than see it," Atcho said. "That's how they're going to Moscow, and so are we. Let's get moving."

While they gathered their things, Matfey left. He returned minutes later, his face ashen, his eyes wide in terror. "Please, Atcho, I need to speak with you." He tugged at Atcho's shoulder. Seeing the priest's distraught state, foreboding gripped him. He followed the priest into a corner away from the others. They conferred in hushed tones, and Atcho's head jerked up sharply. When he returned to his companions, he looked grim. Meanwhile, Matfey left the room.

Atcho set his jaw. "Ivan, if you can get me on the plane, I can finish things. You'll have to get the two of you out of the country." He smiled. "Lara and Kirill will be happy to see you."

Rafael and Ivan stared at him, eyes wide. "What the hell?" Rafael asked.

"Father Matfey received a phone call from Moscow," Atcho said. He related the conversation he had just had with the priest. "Yermolov has a briefcase nuke. I'm supposed to disarm it."

Rafael reacted first. "You mean a bomb? Yermolov has a bomb?"

Atcho nodded.

"How big is it?"

"Big enough to take out the Kremlin and everything around it for a mile. Then there's the fallout. The US Embassy is in the area."

"You were right that he intended to blackmail with a nuke," Ivan said, alarmed. "And he bypassed Soviet protocol. Brilliant. How are you supposed to neutralize it?"

"Overpower him, I guess." He thought of the NukeX, wishing he had one now. "Someone is supposedly on the way with a device to do the job, but we don't have time to wait. Yermolov is moving."

"Whew!" Rafael exclaimed. "That's a lot to take in." He faced Atcho while shaking his head. "Look, I'm afraid of heights, small spaces, and things that go bump in the night," he said, "but nothing scares me as much as facing Sofia if I show up back home without you. I'm going with you."

Atcho started to protest. Rafael stopped him with an upraised hand. "Don't. We've known each other too long. Save your breath."

"I can get you on the plane," Ivan cut in. He looked grim. "What happens then? I didn't volunteer for this." He looked back and forth between Atcho and Rafael. "What happens if you fail and Yermolov succeeds? You'll be dead, and every KGB officer in the Soviet Union will be after me. A madman in the Kremlin will threaten my family along with the rest of the world. I already saved your skins once. I'll stick around to make sure you don't screw up again. Besides, I won't let this maniac blow up Mother Russia. Now let's get on with it."

Atcho stared at them. "All right then." They started picking up their things. Father Matfey knocked on the door.

"Come in, Father," Atcho called, "and thanks for your help."

"I am so sorry," Matfey said anxiously. "I forgot to tell you this morning when you first came in. There's a lady waiting for you at the US Embassy in Moscow. Her name is Sofia Stahl."

Atcho felt the blood drain from his face. He turned to his companions with a grim look. "Let's go."

* * *

Two thousand miles away, McFadden faced Sofia on a windy runway at an airbase east of Moscow. Next to them stood a Soviet Air Force general, a member of Gorbachev's inner circle.

"You understand that this is going to be a very uncomfortable ride," McFadden yelled against the wind and the roar of jet engines. Out on the runway, a Sukhoi 35 jet fighter was surrounded by technicians and crewmen working busily around it. "Novosibirsk is at the edge of this aircraft's range, but it was the only one immediately available that could fly that far without refueling. The crew is removing every piece of equipment possible to extend its distance, and it's not carrying ordinance. But there is still very little room for error. Also, it's a one-seater, so they're taking out everything they can from behind the pilot's seat. You'll have to scrunch in, but it flies at Mach 2, so the flight will only take a little over an hour. They've jerry-rigged a second oxygen supply." He scrutinized her face, and saw subdued fright overridden with resolve. "Are you sure you can handle this?"

Sofia nodded vigorously, even as her gut took a turn. She glanced at the aircraft, heard its roar, smelled the exhaust, and saw the heat waves distorting the view behind its engine. The crew was clearing away the last pieces of equipment. "Looks like they're ready for us. Let's go."

"Wait!" McFadden called out. "Are you sure you know how to use that NukeX?"

Sofia nodded again. "Hold device down firmly against trigger area. Red button powers. Yellow button tests. Black button executes. Keep downward pressure until..."

McFadden grinned roguishly. "You got it. If we don't see a red glow in the east, we'll know you succeeded."

"Thanks." She turned and strode across the tarmac dressed in a Soviet colonel's uniform. McFadden walked next to her. "I'll be in radio contact with you on a dedicated encrypted frequency that the pilot can't access. Right now, his flight plan calls for him to land at the Novosibirsk aircraft manufacturing plant. You might have to commandeer a vehicle. Are you sure you can do that?"

Sofia's gut took another turn, but she nodded.

"From there, head straight to the Nevsky Cathedral in Novosibirsk. As far as we know, that's where Atcho is now. We'll try to get a better fix on his location, and get word to you, and if that changes, we'll let you know."

They arrived by the aircraft. The thunderous engine made further conversation impossible. McFadden clapped her shoulder, and she climbed the short ladder. The pilot stood in the cockpit and pointed to the incredibly small area into which she would squeeze herself.

McFadden watched as Sofia placed one leg into the cockpit behind the pilot's seat, and then the other. Then she put on a helmet, attached a hose and communications wire to the aircraft where the pilot indicated, stooped, and disappeared backwards into the cramped space. Moments later, the SU-35 roared down the runway, and then hurtled almost vertically into the night sky.

43

Atcho sat in the passenger seat of the little car. Rafael scrunched across the rear seat. They had a clear view of the airfield at the manufacturing plant as Ivan trudged through snow to the operations office.

On the runway stood the Antonov 225 Mriya, the most magnificent aircraft any of them had ever seen. It looked longer than a football field. Six jet engines hung from its wings. Its nose cone was rotated above its fuselage, revealing the gaping cargo hold.

"We can get lost in that thing," Rafael remarked.

Atcho caught movement in his right peripheral vision. When he focused his attention that way, his blood froze. Approaching the gate a mile off was a convoy of military vehicles illuminated by floodlights along the access road. Near the front of the column was a limousine. That could mean only one thing: Yermolov's arrival.

Atcho jumped from the car and shouted to Ivan, who continued trudging to the operations building. Atcho took off in a dead run, shouting until Ivan heard him and turned to look his way.

Atcho waved both arms and pointed at the convoy. Ivan turned and stared. The lead vehicle approached the security checkpoint. Ivan whirled and gestured furiously for Atcho to go back to the car.

Atcho ran, jerked the driver's door open, and crammed behind the steering wheel. "We're in trouble," he called to Rafael, who was staring at the convoy. "I'll park behind a berm where we won't be so visible. Watch for Ivan."

* * *

Ivan's heart raced. He stepped inside the operations building. Daylight was hours away and the morning shift had not yet arrived. Someone must have alerted the night staff to the arrival of the convoy, because they seemed to struggle unwillingly to regain awareness despite the approaching end of their shift.

Ivan walked into a side room with a group of men seated around a table, and held up his KGB credentials. "Where is the Mriya pilot?"

They looked up, startled. One stood. "That's me. Who are you?"

"Colonel Chekov." Ivan handed over his ID. "You'll be flying the Mriya today?"

The officer nodded. "I'm Lieutenant-Colonel Stephan Zhukov." He looked tough, like someone not easily put off. After examining Ivan's credentials, he handed them back.

"I need to speak to you privately." Ivan turned to the others. "You will not speak of my presence among yourselves or anyone else. Is that understood?" He glared at them. They nodded.

When he was alone with Zhukov outside the lounge, Ivan grabbed the pilot by the arm. "We don't have much time. A convoy is coming through the gate now. It carries at least two generals, Kutuzov and Yermolov. One is under investigation."

Zhukov's eyes widened. "They are on our manifest."

"I'll be riding with you on your flight to Moscow," Ivan said. "Two more KGB colonels will accompany me. We're also here to make sure that terrorist threats against the aircraft don't succeed. You are to tell no one we're here, especially not those two generals."

Zhukov stepped closer. "Do you know of specific threats?"

"None that I can speak of, except to say that it could be tied in with my investigation. We're here as a precaution. Nothing can be allowed to happen to the Mriya. We won't take chances."

Zhukov leaned in, his face grave. "What do you need from me?"

"As you know, the flight schedule changed suddenly and with little notice."

Zhukov nodded.

"That was our tip-off. The other two colonels are waiting outside in a car. You need to get us aboard the aircraft unseen."

Zhukov grasped the urgency. "You can't drive onto the tarmac. You'll be exposed. Where are you parked?"

Ivan told him.

"There's an equipment shed near there. It's the only one. Put your car in there. I'll send the cargo chief. He has a van there with crew equipment to load onto the plane. He'll drive you down."

"That'll work. Make sure he understands secrecy."

"I can handle that. Hurry. The convoy must be moving through the gate by now."

Ivan walked swiftly outside. Rafael emerged from behind a low ridge and waved at him. "Let's go," Ivan barked when they reached the car. He spotted the shed, and Atcho drove inside. The crew van was parked there, just as Zhukov had said.

They watched from the shadows. The convoy had cleared the security gate, and its lead vehicle had closed almost a quarter of the distance. The motorcade disappeared behind a low rise.

The cargo chief arrived looking anxious. "We must hurry," was all he said as he climbed into the driver's seat of the van.

The lights of the oncoming convoy became visible again, about half a mile away. "We won't get to the plane before them," the cargo chief said. He shoved the gears and stepped on the accelerator. "Zhukov explained everything. I'll drop you in the shadows of the aircraft. Try to look like ground crew. Sleepy." He laughed, warming to the intrigue in which he found himself. "If anyone gets out of the vehicles, I'll distract."

Ivan nodded.

"Listen carefully," the chief continued as he sped out to the runway. "I'm on ground crew. I won't be flying with you. Use the crew door on the left side of the airplane. When you get in, go straight to an office near the bottom of the stairs on the opposite side near the front. It belongs to the loadmaster. He'll be flying, but he'll stay in a cabin upstairs for this flight. Zhukov will tell him. He won't mind. It's more comfortable. Do you understand?"

"Where will the generals be?"

"Upstairs in a cabin to the right of the loadmaster's."

Through the windshield, they saw the convoy emerge from behind the low hill and proceed to the apron. The cargo chief was right: they would arrive at the aircraft almost simultaneously. He drove to the side opposite the operations building and the convoy, and halted near the left-side landing gear. "Pretend you're inspecting the tires," he said. "I'll drive over to meet them."

Atcho's heart pounded as he led his small group onto the runway. They dispersed between the tires under the huge aircraft and stayed low, keeping to shadows as they made their way forward toward the crew door.

On the other side of the cargo plane, the convoy drew to a halt. The low fuselage limited Atcho's view, but he saw the bottom of the limousine as the back door opened and two sets of feet stepped out onto the tarmac. The cargo chief drove between the aircraft and the limousine, blocking the view.

Atcho signaled to Rafael and Ivan. Feigning tire inspections, they worked forward. The bottom of the crew door was head high, and it was closed. Standing below it, they were clear of the landing gear and far more exposed.

Atcho saw the van start to move again. "Get that door open," he muttered to Ivan, and then made his way to the front wheels. Clearance between the ground and the aircraft was higher there. He inhaled sharply. Generals Kutuzov and Yermolov stood conversing not more than seventy feet away. They looked over the plane while they talked, as if admiring it.

Yermolov's hand clutched an object that riveted Atcho's attention. He stared at it. From this distance, he could not be certain of what he saw, but was sure it must be the briefcase.

He squatted on the opposite side of the massive tires. By the crew door, Ivan and Rafael searched frantically for a latch or handle that would release the door. The only alternative was to go up the front ramp and through the gaping cargo hold. There, they would be illuminated by bright work lights.

Atcho returned his attention to Yermolov and Kutuzov. The pilot, Zhukov, approached them from their rear. They turned to greet him.

Another man in military uniform with KGB insignia left the operations building and called to them. As they turned toward him, Atcho hurried back to where his companions still fussed with the crew door.

"It'll be slightly open," he hissed. "Keeps air flowing." He shoved near its bottom, and it moved. He shoved again, found a handhold, and pulled until the door with its built-in stair-step unfolded to the ground. All three breathed a sigh of relief.

Shortly, they were ensconced in the loadmaster's office, bracing against the cold. Minutes later, they watched through the crack of the door as Zhukov led Yermolov and Kutuzov up the cargo ramp into the Mriya and disappeared on the stairs leading to the area of the cockpit. Yermolov still carried his briefcase.

Atcho tapped his companions on the shoulder. "That's it. I think that's the bomb."

They stared at it. Then, Atcho closed the door, and the three men rested as best they could in the cramped quarters. Soon, they heard the engines revving to operating power, and felt a jolt as the aircraft started to move.

* * *

Forty thousand feet in the air, and still two-hundred kilometers from its destination, the Sukhoi 35 began its descent, having already climbed down from its maximum altitude of fifty-nine thousand feet. It gradually slowed from its Mach 2.2 speed to just under six hundred nautical miles per hour. Curled up in the space behind the pilot's seat, Sofia had tried every position possible to ease her discomfort, but she was chilled to the bone, and her muscles ached.

"We'll be on the ground in about twenty minutes," the pilot called to her in Russian over the intercom.

"Thank you," Sofia called back. She did not relish the idea of commandeering a vehicle. *I hope my Russian accent is still good enough!*

Just then, the radio channel that fed directly to McFadden back in Moscow crackled in her ear. "Sukhoi 35, do you copy?"

"I hear you loud and clear," she replied. "Go ahead."

"Be advised that your target is already on the field. It is in the largest aircraft, and now preparing for takeoff. You must get aboard. Do you copy?"

Sofia inhaled sharply. "Good copy." She repeated her instructions. *How do I ask if both Yermolov and Atcho are on board?* "Are both the fox and the hound there?"

The channel was silent a moment, and then McFadden transmitted again. "Affirmative. The good shepherd tells us they are both present, and the aircraft is moving from parking position to runway."

"Roger. Out." Sofia assumed that the "good shepherd" referred to the priest at the Nevsky Cathedral, and that he had provided information on Atcho's whereabouts and the status of the aircraft.

She called to the pilot on the intercom. "There is a very large aircraft on the field now preparing to take off. You must delay it."

The pilot's annoyance was palpable. "The only way I can do that is to call an emergency and request immediate landing."

"Then do it. If I need to order you, I will." She hoped her bluff worked. The mission had been put together so rapidly that lines of authority had been all but ignored. The presence of the Soviet general at the aircraft just prior to takeoff should help.

"I'm low on fuel," the pilot called back. "I'll use that as an excuse." He flipped a switch. "Mayday. Mayday. Request immediate landing."

The fighter jet's nose lowered, and they descended rapidly. Then it leveled out as a column of lights pointed the way onto the field. Flying skillfully, the pilot lined up and prepared for final descent. At the near end of the runway, the largest airplane he had ever seen waited, and he recognized the Antonov 225 Mriya. He sucked in his breath.

Behind him, Sofia had scrunched around until she could just see over his shoulder, and she caught a glimpse of the massive orbiter shuttle. "Fly as low over it as you can," she ordered, "and stop short enough on the runway that it can't take off."

The pilot gave a quick nod.

* * *

Below, in the loadmaster's office of the Mriya, Atcho and the others felt the aircraft lurch to a halt. The engines wound back down to idle.

Upstairs in the cockpit, Zhukov watched the emergency landing of the Sukhoi unfold. He saw the two figures emerge from the cockpit. One ran to a rescue vehicle. Then, to his astonishment, that vehicle sped directly toward the left side of the Mriya.

Just as it moved out of sight below, Yermolov appeared in the cockpit behind Zhukov's seat. With an air of mild curiosity, he took in the events occurring beyond the windshield, asked a question, and then returned to his cabin.

A message in Zhukov's earphones from the tower informed him that someone was seeking entry through the crew door. "Everyone stay in place," he instructed his crew. "I'll see to this."

He hurried down into the cargo hold and opened the door. A woman in a Soviet uniform with KGB markings climbed up to meet him. "I must see Colonel Chekov," Sofia demanded in Russian, "by order of General Secretary Gorbachev." She produced a letter.

Obviously frustrated, Zhukov motioned for her to follow, and led her to the loadmaster's office across the cargo bay. "Will you be flying with us?" he asked.

"Yes," she replied, "but my presence—"

"I know," he interrupted, arching his brows, "top secret." He ushered her through the office door, and went to close the crew hatch. Then he made his way quickly back to the cockpit.

Inside the loadmaster's office, Atcho, Rafael, and Ivan heard the door open and close, and in the dim light saw the figure of a woman, and then heard a female voice call out in Russian. "Colonel Chekov, are you in here?"

Atcho's heart thudded. He recognized the voice. "Sofia? Is that you?" He crossed the small space rapidly and stood in front of her, his heart beating furiously. Anger, fear, relief, dread, and every emotion conceivable intruded between them. And then he reached forward and seized her in his arms.

"Are you crazy? What are you doing here? How did you get here?"

Sofia reached into her jacket. "The priest at the Nevsky Cathedral told us where you were," she said. "Gorbachev supplied a jet with pilot. I brought you this." She held in her hand a small box. On its side was the word *NukeX*. "You're going to need it."

* * *

McFadden walked into the office of the US Ambassador to the Soviet Union. "Sir, I have bad news," he said. "It's an emergency."

The ambassador stiffened, alert. "What is it?"

"There's a rogue Russian general on a plane bound for Moscow." McFadden raised his eyebrows. "He has a nuclear device."

The ambassador stared. "Does the Kremlin know?"

McFadden nodded. "We told them. We think the general intends to use the bomb to blackmail the Kremlin. Our eavesdroppers in France picked up on that, but we haven't been able to trace the source. The bomb-maker never surfaced."

"And the intel is credible?"

McFadden nodded. "Our analysts have been all over it."

"Why didn't Gorbachev order him arrested before he got on the plane?"

"It's complicated, but essentially, he could not be assured that the arrest order would be carried out."

The ambassador mulled that over. "Then why don't the Russians shoot the plane down before it gets here?"

"He's on the Mriya. I'm sure you know about that aircraft." The ambassador nodded. McFadden went on, "And unless they kill him immediately, he's lunatic enough to set the bomb off. We have a joint Russian-American team on board to seize him and the bomb."

"That's comforting." His tone was just shy of sarcastic. "What do we do meanwhile?"

"Right now, we have to get ready in case that nuke goes off near here. The general is a survivor, so I don't think he intends to detonate it, but his target is probably the Kremlin, and if he gets cornered..." His voice trailed away momentarily. "Our underground bunker is hardened against a direct hit," he continued, "but the Kremlin is only two miles away. If it goes off there—fallout."

The look on the ambassador's face showed that he took the threat seriously. "Are the Soviets doing anything about it?"

"I'm sure they are. It's too late to evacuate. It's a small bomb, a tenth of a kiloton. If it blows on the ground, the blast area will be about a mile wide. If it goes off in the air over Moscow or the airport?" He shook his head. "Anything can happen."

44

Colonel Dmitri Drygin strode through the halls at the Lubyanka, headquarters of the KGB. He always felt a mix of sensations when visiting this control center of the Soviet state.

Simultaneous with being a participant in the exercise of power, this organ of tyranny generated in him a sense of destiny. For better or worse, the future—his future—was shaped in these halls.

In his view, the supremacy of the state depended on terror of retribution, especially among those who used it to acquire and retain power. He smirked. *The strength of the system is that no one trusts anyone. The weakness of the system is that no one trusts anyone.*

Usually, when walking through this edifice, he felt privilege and resulting superiority. Today, uncertainty invaded the arrogance he had guarded against for his entire career. It sharpened his senses. He steeled himself to maintain a neutral countenance.

Within a day, the Soviet Union was scheduled for historic upheaval, and at the end of it a new national leader would dominate the Kremlin. He, Drygin, would participate in that, yet the prospective general secretary, Colonel General Borya Yermolov, regarded him with suspicion. In the culture of fear that had guided the Soviet polity for seven decades, that could be as good as a death warrant.

He shook his head at the irony. *I've always been a good soldier.* In his quest to avoid arrogance, he practiced erring on the side of doing what was right per Party doctrine, even when difficult and often when unpopular.

He remembered when Fierko, his once and current commander, had recruited him into the conspiracy by appealing to his sense of duty to the Party. Fierko had introduced him to KGB Chairman Nestor Murin early on. Concern over the damage Gorbachev's reforms were doing to the Party had been enough to convince Drygin that a change of regime was necessary.

The chairman had recognized Drygin's talent and had convinced him to go into deep cover with his current alias, and to act as liaison with Yermolov during last year's failed conspiracy. Murin had further directed Drygin's actions personally in shaping Yermolov's return to Moscow. Drygin chuckled. *Fierko wouldn't be happy if he knew that.*

Drygin had thrown himself into all assignments with professional enthusiasm and attention to detail. He had worked diligently during the planning of the assassination, and not one single element had gone awry until plan execution. *The plot failed because Yermolov selected Atcho to be the primary assassin.*

A further irony was that, on arrival in Moscow yesterday, he had reported immediately to Chairman Murin, who put him in charge of checking security arrangements for Yermolov's arrival in Moscow. *I'm supposed to ensure the safety of the man who wants to put me away.* A faint smile formed on his otherwise implacable face.

He arrived at the chairman's suite of offices. Murin was sitting at his desk when Drygin entered. "You asked me to report back when I'd checked all preparations."

"Are we ready?"

"Yes. The aircraft will park away from any terminal or regular cargo area as always when security risks are anticipated. Given that the Mriya is arriving to be commissioned, that's easily explained."

He briefed that a limousine would draw up to the aircraft as soon as it landed. It would bring General Fierko and his guest directly to the Lubyanka. They would come through a basement entrance, and take secured elevators and halls to Murin's office.

The route from the airport would be secured with the normal contingent for a visiting colonel general, and would be augmented by unmarked vehicles and plainclothes KGB officers. Several security teams would be on hand to board and inspect as soon as the aircraft landed. Drygin would be there to hold them back until Fierko and Yermolov were safely away from the airport.

"Good!" Murin dropped his chin into his hands in thought. "We'll use similar procedures to take Yermolov to the Kremlin tomorrow. I'd like for you to be present when we visit Comrade Gorbachev."

More ironies. "As you wish. Now I should go. The Mriya will be on the ground within the hour."

45

In the loadmaster's office near the stairwell of the huge cargo plane, Atcho stared at the NukeX in his hand. It had an irregular oval shape, was flat on the bottom, and had a contoured back, textured to allow it to fit snugly in his hand without slipping. On one end were three buttons.

The cabin was closed off from the cargo bay and had soundproofing, but the roar of engines, the rush of wind on the skin of the jet, and the typical creaking and groaning of a cargo plane nevertheless made talking difficult. Sofia and Ivan crowded around Atcho. Rafael was checking his gear in another corner.

"It's simple to use," Sofia said. She took the NukeX and demonstrated. "This red button powers it up. This yellow one tests it without turning on the heat, and this black one does the job. After you power it up, you put it flush against the bomb's trigger area, and hold the black button down.

"It takes fifteen seconds to reach maximum heat, and about thirty seconds to do its job. If you're not blown up, it worked." She smiled grimly, and handed the NukeX to Atcho, who stuffed it in his jacket. "So, what's the plan?"

Atcho and Ivan stared at her. "We hadn't really discussed one," Atcho said awkwardly.

Sofia glanced at him reproachfully. "Doing things the Atcho way?" she kidded.

"We should plan what we are going to do when we get on the ground," Ivan interjected.

"What do you think we should do?" Atcho asked him.

Ivan straightened with a questioning look. "We don't know what kind of reception there'll be in Moscow. We can stay on board until the crew leaves and go with them. Any security teams sent to inspect the plane should have left by then."

Rafael joined them. Atcho acknowledged him and faced Ivan. "I have a different idea."

Ivan drew up sharply. The tone in Atcho's voice invited wariness. "What?"

"The priority now has to be to seize control of that bomb, preferably before Yermolov arms it. Then we have to deliver him into custody." He stared straight into Ivan's face. "This aircraft can travel over nine thousand miles on a full tank. We took off with a full tank."

As understanding dawned, Ivan glowered. He drew close again. "I'm not a traitor," he bellowed. "I will not let you steal this airplane."

Atcho stood. "We're not going to steal your airplane." He grasped Ivan's shoulder. "Your job now is to make sure Yermolov fails—that's what your general secretary expects." He pulled back and studied Ivan's face to see if he understood. Satisfied, he went on. "If we land in Moscow, anything could happen. We can't even guarantee that we can get off the airplane safely, much less that we can stop Yermolov, and we could lose that bomb."

"I'm listening." Ivan's chin jutted out in defiance. "But we will not land on American or NATO soil. I won't allow it." He was silent a moment as another thought entered his mind. "If that was your plan, why didn't we take over the plane shortly after takeoff? Doing it then would have been a lot less dangerous."

"Maybe," Atcho replied, "but we had a lot of ground to cover before we would be out of Soviet airspace, with the crew to control, and the whole Soviet air force alerted. This way, we're much closer to international waters. By the time they can react on the ground, we'll be almost clear of the Soviet border and in international airspace."

Ivan mulled that a moment.

"Don't worry," Atcho continued. "There's a place where the US military has landing privileges. It has a runway that will handle this aircraft. The Soviet Union and its allies also landed there. I know because Cuba used it as a way station when they sent troops to Angola."

Understanding dawned on Ivan's face. His angst receded a bit. "I know where you mean, but I'm not convinced."

"We don't have time to powwow. If you have a better suggestion, let's hear it."

Ivan grimaced, then gestured consent. "I'll hold you to your word." Atcho gave him a thumbs-up.

Sensing that a meeting of the minds had taken place, Sofia and Rafael crowded in. Atcho went over his plan.

46

A slight change in the engines' pitch and an increase in the pressure against his ears informed Yermolov and Fierko that the big jet had begun its initial descent. Yermolov stood.

"I'm going to the latrine before they tell us to strap in," he said. "It's been a good flight." He indicated his briefcase. "I want to freshen up a bit." He stepped out and strode past the stairs to the restroom, taking his briefcase with him.

A few minutes later, he left the latrine, closed the door with an audible click, and mounted the two stairs in front of the flight cabin. He entered and walked its short length, and stood behind the pilot's seat. "We're circling now, sir," Zhukov told him. "We'll start our final descent shortly. Now is a good time to buckle up."

Yermolov nodded. He retraced his steps past the flight crew, and walked down the two stairs to the crosswalk.

* * *

Atcho also felt the change in flight attitude as the Mriya began its descent. The rest of the group had noted it too. He signaled to them. "Weapons ready?" he called. They nodded and stood up.

With Atcho in the lead, they stole into the cavernous cargo hold. Dim lights outlined its massive dimensions, stretching far into darkness. They crept to the center of the aircraft and then toward the stairwell that led up to the crew level and the cockpit.

"Let me lead," Ivan called into Atcho's ear, "in case we run into Russian speakers."

Atcho stepped back and let Ivan proceed ahead of him. They came to the stairs. It was a steep, two-tier set extending up in opposite directions with a landing between them.

Ivan went up the first set and stopped on the landing. Atcho followed, with Rafael and Sofia close behind. Ivan started up the second flight. He peered over the top onto the crosswalk, and then heard a loud click to his right. A foot and then a leg appeared out of the shadows. Ivan pulled his head down and shrank into darkness. The others froze.

Peering through subdued light, Ivan saw the tall figure of Yermolov loom with his back to the stairs. The general had just left the latrine, took the two steps leading into the flight cabin, and disappeared into its interior.

Ivan turned and moved silently back down the stairs. "Yermolov went into the flight compartment," he told Atcho, who nodded and looked at his watch. As the plane continued its descent, air pressure increased. Ivan moved back to his position on the stairs.

Moments later, Yermolov left the crew compartment. He descended the two steps to the walkway, and had turned to go to his cabin when movement in the stairwell leading down to the cargo bay caught his attention. He leaned to take a closer look. In the shadow, he saw a dark mass, and then the face of a man.

He pulled back. He was too late.

Ivan reached up, locked his hand around the general's ankle, and yanked. Yermolov fell backward and tried to clutch anything that would support his balance. There was nothing. Ivan braced a foot against one of the stairs and wrenched.

Atcho appeared next to him. He grabbed Yermolov's other foot, and together they dragged him down.

Yermolov almost fell on top of them. Atcho and Ivan tugged on his legs again and dragged him down to the cargo level. Yermolov landed in a heap. He howled, but his voice was lost in the bowels of a behemoth in flight.

Rafael jumped to assist. Atcho waved him away. "Go take care of the other general," he yelled. He turned to Sofia. "Go with him and find that bomb!" They nodded and rushed toward the stairs. Yermolov reached up to grab Rafael, who kicked his hands away. He and Sofia drew their pistols and disappeared up the stairs.

Yermolov flailed at his still unknown assailants. "I'll kill you."

Ivan let go of Yermolov's leg, stepped alongside him, and kicked his chin. The general lay still.

"Go help them!" Atcho told Ivan. "I'll be there as soon as I tie down this son-of-a-bitch. Don't let the plane land. Get to the crew compartment. Take control." Ivan gave him a thumbs-up, drew his pistol, and headed up the stairs.

Meanwhile, Rafael and Sofia reached the upper level. They crept along the short crosswalk by the crew compartment. Ahead were the two cabins that the cargo chief had mentioned. He had said the one for the generals was on the right.

Holding his pistol at shoulder height, Rafael eased in front of the door. He reached down and turned the doorknob. Pushing gently, he peered through the crack. The couch to his right was empty.

Rafael shoved the door open and hurtled across to his left. Fierko sat there reading. He barely had time to look up before Rafael knocked him against the aircraft's outer wall. When their motion stopped, Rafael was on top of him with a pistol at his head.

"You move, I shoot," Rafael roared. "Do you understand?"

Sofia appeared in the door and shouted a translation.

Fierko's eyes flashed with rage, but he nodded and gave no resistance. Rafael's gestures added implicit emphasis.

"Where's the bomb?" Sofia demanded in Russian. Seeing Fierko's eyes widen in confused surprise, she yelled, "The briefcase. Where is Yermolov's briefcase?"

Fierko was bewildered. "His briefcase? He took it with him, to the latrine." Sofia bolted for the door.

Rafael motioned for the general to lie on his stomach. Then he bound Fierko's hands and feet with cargo straps.

* * *

In the next compartment, the loadmaster heard the thud of Rafael landing on Fierko, but did not know the cause. He had turned off the lights in the cabin an hour earlier, but was sleeping lightly when he heard the disturbance. He sat up and peered around in the dark. Then he went to his entrance and stepped through. The generals' compartment door was ajar, but the crosswalk was quiet.

He withdrew into his cabin, but just then, one of the ceiling lights cast the shadow of a man moving on the crosswalk. Thinking he might catch sight of one of the generals, the loadmaster stayed and watched through the crack. Then he froze. He saw Ivan creeping cautiously toward the generals' open door. In his right hand, he carried a pistol at the ready, and entered the cabin. Thinking furiously, the loadmaster backed into darkness and closed his door.

In the generals' compartment, Ivan looked over Rafael's shoulder and saw that he had tied Fierko's hands, and was lashing his feet. "You got him?"

Rafael signaled to confirm. "There's no bomb," he called.

"What?"

"The bomb. The briefcase. It's not here. Sofia went to look for it in the latrine."

Ivan grimaced. He kneeled next to Fierko's head. "Where is the briefcase?" he yelled in Russian.

Fierko stared, unblinking.

"Where's the briefcase?" Ivan roared. "It's a bomb, a nuclear bomb."

Fierko's eyes widened with a hint of terror. "I told the woman. Yermolov took it with him. He went to the latrine."

Ivan translated for Rafael. "Tell that to Atcho, when he comes. I'm going to the flight cabin."

In the next compartment, the loadmaster cracked his door open. He saw Ivan re-emerge, halt, and speak to someone inside.

Ivan returned his pistol to his belt. He walked to the crew cabin, mounted the two stairs, entered, and closed the door.

The loadmaster cursed. His Makarov was locked away in his office on the cargo level. He stepped quietly onto the crosswalk. It was empty. The door to the adjacent cabin was ajar, but he could not see inside. He kept his back close to the wall as he crept past it, reached the stairs, and climbed down.

* * *

Atcho knew that Yermolov would not be out long. The general had been stunned by Ivan's kick to his chin, but he was already stirring. Atcho rolled the man onto his stomach and pulled his arms behind him. Then he took a cargo strap from his pocket, and looped one snugly around Yermolov's left wrist.

Atcho had just cinched the cargo strap and looped it around the right wrist, but had not yet tightened it. He sensed movement behind him and turned his head slightly. From the corner of his eye, he saw the loadmaster hurtling through the air toward him. He dropped his head and rolled to his right.

The loadmaster clipped Atcho's shoulder, accelerating Atcho's roll. He continued to careen forward, but was thrown to his left and landed in a heap, banging his head on the cold steel floor. His waist covered Yermolov's face. All three men lay stunned.

Yermolov was the first to stir. The movement on his back had jarred him awake. He became aware of a mass falling to his right, and was infuriated when more weight landed across his head. His jaw ached where Ivan had kicked him.

When he tried to move, he found that a strap had been looped around both wrists. Frantic, he pulled against them. The one on his right wrist fell away. Working both arms forward under the weight of his body and that of the loadmaster, he struggled against throbbing aches, but managed to roll onto his right side, and found another person there. He pushed the loadmaster off his head. In the faint light, he saw Atcho's face.

Pain forgotten, rage surged through Yermolov. "You bastard!" he thundered. "I'll kill you!"

The aircraft creaked while banking to its left. Yermolov lurched, and found himself sitting with his legs stretched downhill. Atcho rolled into him. The loadmaster lay still.

Atcho had been only slightly stunned, and when he rolled, he opened his eyes. In the half-light of the cargo bay, Yermolov's face was in shadows with dark pits where his eyes should be, the image of a devil in flight.

The aircraft banked steeper. Atcho's left shoulder was pinned against Yermolov. Through shooting pain, he pulled both arms under him and shoved off so that he rolled across Yermolov's legs. He kept himself rolling on the downhill side.

Yermolov jerked his right arm free from under the loadmaster. As Atcho rolled past, he slammed his fist down on Atcho's head.

Atcho reeled under the blow, but kept moving. He struggled to his feet, glaring at Yermolov. "You're mine," he roared above the din.

The jet straightened out, its momentum throwing Atcho into Yermolov's chest, flattening both. Seconds later, its nose dipped further into its descent.

Atcho tried to roll to his right, but was held back by the upward angle of the floor. He forced his legs to a crouch.

Yermolov rolled down in the opposite direction over the limp figure of the loadmaster and struggled to one knee. He panted hard and looked across at Atcho with a malicious grin. "You really are a pain in the ass, you know that, Atcho? You never learned when to stop."

Atcho fought to catch his breath. Between them the loadmaster stirred, now downhill from Atcho. Without hesitation, Atcho stepped over and kicked the man's head. He fell back into unconsciousness. Using momentum, Atcho swung around and faced Yermolov. Ten empty feet lay between them.

"You're so cruel," Yermolov crooned. He wiped the back of his hand across his mouth.

"You're done."

Yermolov looked amused. "Seriously? Do you know where you are?"

Atcho glared, irony conveyed in his expression. "Not where you think we are. We won't land in Moscow. My friends will see to that."

Yermolov's face contorted into shocked realization. Atcho reached for his pistol. It was not in its holster. Reading his gesture, Yermolov chortled, "You lost your gun?" He reached for his own, but found his holster empty too. He dropped his glance to check for it.

Atcho lunged, attacking downhill, but his motion was dulled by tossing and bumping as the big plane descended through turbulent clouds. Metal screeched on metal. With the roar of engines, the smell of fuel and hydraulic fluid, and the sound of wind on steel skin, only the scream of demons in flaming hell could be more raucous.

Atcho caught Yermolov mid-chest with both feet. The general stumbled backwards on the downhill slant and landed on his buttocks in a sitting position.

The jet lurched upward. Atcho fell hard, slamming his right temple into the rough steel floor. Consciousness waned.

When he looked up again, Yermolov stood over him. He punched the side of Atcho's face, pounding his head into the floor. Atcho lay almost prone on his right side.

Yermolov dug his right knee into Atcho's stomach. He pulled his fist back to deliver another punishing blow to Atcho's face.

Atcho saw it coming and jerked his head aside. Yermolov's fist slammed into the steel floor. He howled in agony and let go.

Atcho rolled away and struggled to his feet. Every wound screamed in pain. Yermolov watched him, wild-eyed. He put his good hand on the floor and started to push himself up.

With a roar, Atcho attacked. He stepped toward Yermolov, spun on the ball of his foot, ducked his upper body, and delivered a powerful kick to the jaw. Yermolov went down and did not move.

Atcho looked around. The loadmaster had begun to stir again. As Atcho glanced in that direction, he saw his pistol on the floor nearby. Breathing heavily, he staggered over, picked it up, and then found Yermolov's pistol lying two feet away. He picked it up too.

The loadmaster sat up, shaking his head, and leaned on his arms behind him. His eyes locked on Atcho.

Panting heavily, Atcho pointed his pistol. The man lay back down.

A few feet away Yermolov lifted his anguished face. Atcho waved the pistol at him. "Stay where you are!"

Yermolov grinned with malevolence, despite his pain. "Or what? You aren't going to shoot me." He looked around. "You might miss, and hit something vital."

Atcho pulled the slider on his Glock. "Where's the bomb, Yermolov?"

Yermolov raised doleful eyes in surprise. "Is there anything you don't know?" He laughed in satanic staccato. "Find it." He grinned again, his eyes burning with evil. He looked straight into Atcho's eyes, and rose onto one knee. Then, before Atcho could stop him, he reached into his pocket and pulled out a small object, and jabbed a button with his finger. "You've got twelve minutes."

In horror, Atcho realized that Yermolov had just armed the bomb via remote control. Setting his jaw, he closed the distance between them. The general braced for another skirmish. Atcho lowered his pistol to Yermolov's lower right thigh. "I don't have time for games." He pulled the trigger. The pistol jumped in his hand.

Yermolov screamed. A dark pool of blood spread along the floor, rippling with the vibration of the aircraft.

Atcho turned to check the loadmaster, whose eyes were wide with fear. With flicks of his wrist, Atcho signaled for the man to turn Yermolov onto his back and tie him to a cargo rail. "Hurry!" he yelled without knowing if the man understood. "Bomb!"

The loadmaster seemed to grasp the word "bomb." He suddenly moved frantically, and secured Yermolov to a cargo rail in short order. When he was done, Atcho tied him up and checked Yermolov's bindings. Then he put his mouth close to Yermolov's ear.

"I'm putting a tourniquet on your leg. Lie still, or you'll bleed out." He grabbed Yermolov's jaw and wrenched it around to look full into his face. "Reagan wants you alive. I don't care either way, and it's my call."

47

Atcho rushed upstairs and found Rafael keeping watch over Fierko. "Where's the briefcase?"

"Yermolov took it to the latrine. Sofia's searching for it." He stared at Atcho's bloodstained clothes, torn and dripping with sweat.

Atcho gestured toward Fierko. "Is he secure?"

"He's not going anywhere."

"Make sure, and then go help Sofia find the briefcase. The bomb is already active. Yermolov set it by remote. I'm going to the flight cabin."

Sofia had found the latrine, and now searched frantically for the briefcase by the dim light on the wall. It was not on the floor, or behind the commode. She opened a cabinet door, but it too was empty. She looked along the wall for an opening, and on the ceiling, but found nothing. She looked again at the commode, but the opening at the bottom was too small for a briefcase.

Rafael showed up behind her in the door. Her look told him her effort so far had been futile. He looked over the latrine just as she had, but saw nothing different.

Sofia looked up at the ceiling again. "What about up there?" she suggested. "Maybe that ceiling raises." It was beyond her reach, but when Rafael stood on the commode he could push up on it slightly, and found that it raised. He tried to reach around beyond the ceiling tile, but found nothing, and in any event, could not reach far.

"Here, I'll lift you," he told Sofia. She moved out of his way while he positioned himself. Then he put his hands together with fingers interlocked, and leaned down. She stepped into them, he hoisted her as far as he could, and she grappled around in the dark space beyond the opening, out to arm's length.

Just as Rafael thought he would drop her, Sofia's hand hit a boxlike object. At that moment, a high pitch electronic sound blared from inside the opening. Her heart dropped. "I think I've found it," she called.

Rafael struggled for better position, and Sofia tugged at the object until she found a handle and could grasp it securely. As Rafael's strength gave out, she held on to it firmly, and when they went down, the object fell with them. It was a briefcase, and the electronic sound came from inside it.

"Get to the flight cabin," Sofia yelled. "Let Atcho know we've got it. It sounds like it's been armed."

Rafael struggled back up and bounded out the door, while Sofia examined the briefcase. It looked ordinary, brown, with a hard surface and a regular latch. She turned it over and examined the other side, but could find no indication of where a trigger mechanism might be.

Gingerly, she pressed the latch release, and held the spring-lock so that it opened gently. Inside, she saw the metal sheet that covered the contents, but nothing that indicated a trigger mechanism. As she held it, the high-toned noise continued, jarring her nerves, and then a control panel popped up. It had a counter, and immediately started counting down. Sofia's blood froze, and she felt suffocated. The counter crossed the three-minute mark.

* * *

The airplane had flown straight and level for a while, but started to bank left again. Soon it would begin its final descent.

When Atcho had entered the crew compartment a few minutes earlier,

Ivan stood behind the pilot's seat. He wore a headset, and he looked relieved to see Atcho.

The crewmembers stared at him, taking in his battered appearance. Gun in hand, he pushed past them to the cockpit.

Lieutenant-Colonel Zhukov and the copilot concentrated on gauges and switches, and the sky. Each had a hand on three of the six throttle controls between them. The aircraft rocketed toward the ground. In a few minutes, they would flare for touchdown.

Atcho tapped the pilot on the shoulder. Zhukov's shock on seeing Atcho's bloodied clothes registered on his face. He shifted his eyes and locked them on Ivan. "This is one of your KGB colonels?" he demanded. Ivan confirmed with a slight nod. Zhukov scoffed, and returned his attention to flying the aircraft.

Atcho grabbed a headset from behind the pilot's seat. "Do you speak English?" he asked Zhukov.

The pilot turned to him in surprise and nodded, but quickly returned to his controls. "I'm busy."

"Listen carefully. Don't land this airplane."

Zhukov whirled. He stared at Atcho and then glared at Ivan. His expression became grim. The copilot overheard the conversation. He turned and saw Atcho and his pistol. The blood drained from his face. Pilot and copilot returned to their task of landing the airplane.

It straightened into final descent on its glide path. Within minutes, it would experience turbulence under the wing as it approached the ground and flared. A miscalculation could be catastrophic.

"Zhukov," Atcho said, and as he did, he brought the pistol to the side of the pilot's head. "You cannot land. People will die."

Zhukov swore. "We'll sort this out on the ground," he growled. "Step back."

"There's a bomb on board. Increase power and take this plane back up!"

"I don't believe you."

Atcho glanced out the windshield. In the distance, lights indicating the glide path flashed at him in rapid sequence. Already he could make out the near end of the runway. He jabbed the pistol against Zhukov's cheek. "Take it up. Now!"

Ivan crouched at Atcho's back. He had pulled his pistol, and pointed it at the crew. The navigator and one of the engineers were on their feet. They appeared to be calculating a rush. Their expressions registered both dread and resolve.

The door at the rear of the compartment burst open. Rafael entered and sized up the situation. He pulled his pistol and gestured to the crewmen to sit down. "Do your jobs," he ordered. "Do you understand?" Deflated fury flashed from their eyes, but they sat down. Then Rafael looked at Atcho. "She found it," he called. Atcho wheeled slightly and returned his grim stare.

On the right side of the cockpit the co-pilot pushed the throttles for more power. Zhukov reacted angrily. "I'm the pilot," he shouted. "Do as I say."

Atcho whirled back around, holstered his pistol, and wrapped his arm around Zhukov's neck in a chokehold. The man struggled against Atcho's grip. Atcho held firm, and lifted him so that his flailing arms and legs did not collide with flight controls. Twenty seconds later, Zhukov slumped in his seat.

"Help me!" Atcho called to Ivan. They pulled the sagging figure backward onto the floor.

At that moment, Sofia entered. Atcho was shocked by her appearance. Her face was drained of color, and perspiration streamed down her neck. She leaned against the doorframe. In her arms, she carried the open briefcase.

Sofia staggered to Atcho. Inside the briefcase, he saw the flat metal panel that covered the interior, including the etched shape that resembled a small rocket. The digital counter centered at the top flashed past the two-minute mark.

"I think I tripped a fail-safe when I tried to grab it," Sofia said, her eyes wide in uncharacteristic panic.

Atcho stared. "No, you didn't. Yermolov set it off by remote." He saw faint, brief relief cross Sofia's face. Then he looked over his shoulder at the empty pilot's seat. "Can you fly?"

Sofia shook her head. "You know I can't."

"Then you'll have to disarm the bomb." He pulled the NukeX from his jacket and shoved it at her. "Here! You know what to do. I've got to help fly this plane."

Sofia gaped, indicating the bomb. "Where's the trigger?"

Atcho stared at it. "Use your judgment. Think like the bomb-maker. It's not large. It has to be at one end or the other of the briefcase." He climbed into the pilot's seat and put on the headset.

Sofia staggered to the back of the cabin, with the bomb and the NukeX.

"I've never flown a jet this big," Atcho called to the copilot. "I don't know Russian markings. Tell me what to do."

Despite his terror, the copilot functioned competently. He pulled on the yoke, rotating the Mriya's nose skyward to begin its flare preliminary to touching down. "Keep pressure on the throttle," he shouted, panic in his voice. "Keep the yoke steady. I'm resetting switches." Seconds later, he called over the radio to Moscow's control tower. "Landing abort! Landing abort!" The aircraft continued to settle toward the ground.

"Lower the nose," he told Atcho. "We have power. We need airspeed!" He glanced over nervously. "We're going to touch the ground. Just for a moment. We're off center. If the wheels land on soft earth..." He shook his head.

Looking out the windshield, Atcho saw that they had veered right of the runway's centerline. He felt pressure on the yoke, and followed the copilot's movement.

They felt a thump as the landing gear touched down. The Mriya began to yaw. Ivan and the crew were tossed to one side. They grabbed for handholds, their eyes terrified.

At the back of the cabin, Sofia went to her knees, the briefcase wide open in front of her. *Was the bomb-maker right-handed or left-handed?* She guessed right-handed, and turned the briefcase so that the lid was to her left. That would seem to put the trigger mechanism at the opposite end in the left corner, within the etching, where working on it would be easier. She pressed the NukeX down on the bomb there, and pressed the red button.

The device hummed. She pressed the yellow button, and a light indicated that it functioned properly. Then, she pressed the black button, and felt heat rise from around the edge of the device. The counter crossed the 60-second mark.

Sweat poured from Sofia's brow and dripped from her chin onto her already damp shirt as she watched the numbers counting down to 35 seconds. Smoke poured from inside the briefcase, setting off blaring overhead alarms. The stench of melting plastic and metal filled the cabin.

A thought struck Sofia. *What if the bomb-maker is left-handed, or the trigger is in the middle?* Swallowing panic, she slid the NukeX slowly along the length of the etching to its bottom end, and held it there as the countdown continued.

Meanwhile, the copilot fed power into the right-hand engines and adjusted the flaps. The plane straightened out. It rolled along the ground, with the right landing gear half on, half off the tarmac. Then, it lumbered back into the air. As it did, it yawed right. He fed more power to the right engines. The plane straightened and climbed smoothly.

Ivan stayed crouched behind Atcho, still covering the crew with his pistol. Relief spread across the crewmen's faces. He felt it too. Then he looked at Sofia.

Sweat soaked her clothes. She hunched directly over the bomb, applying all the strength and weight of her upper body. Her arms trembled. She watched the counter with fascination. It moved past the 15-second mark, then the 10 second mark. Sooner than she could believe, it was on final countdown. Three, two, one...zero. Sofia closed her eyes, her whole body clenched, and she said final prayers. Then, nothing.

She looked up, shaking. Ivan and the crew stared at her. She looked back down at the NukeX and released the button. Then she clambered to her feet and leaned against the back wall, exhausted. Gradually, the ventilation system cleared the smoke.

In the cockpit, Atcho glanced at the copilot. He had smelled the smoke and heard the alarms behind him. His eyes showed grim determination. "You're doing great," Atcho called to him. "Climb to cruising altitude and head west." He exhaled.

* * *

In the cargo bay, the loadmaster struggled against his bindings, in vain. He gave up. A few yards away, pain seared through Yermolov's leg with each bump and jolt. When the aircraft touched ground, he screamed in agony. No one heard him, not even the loadmaster. The erstwhile general dared not move his wounded leg for fear of loosening the tourniquet. Mercifully, he swooned into unconsciousness.

48

Drygin sat in a staff car near the runway. He had seen the Mriya bank into final approach, amazed that such a large machine could look and perform so gracefully, even majestically. It followed its glide path smoothly, and when it flared, it began to settle as gently as a swan on a lake.

As he observed, he thought he saw it take an unexpected leap skyward. Then it veered to the right of the centerline.

Drygin watched, horrified as it dropped rapidly. He heard the engines spinning back up to greater power. Despite his normally cool composure, his breath caught.

The jet touched down directly in front of him, with the right side of the landing gear rolling over the edge of the runway. The hot wind of jet engines nearly blew him off his feet as the nose fell. The smell of fuel exhaust assaulted his nostrils. His jaw dropped.

He heard power to the engines increase. The plane swung to the right, straightened, raised its nose, and rose back into the air. Then, it started a steady climb into the heavens.

Drygin stared. Catching himself, he radioed KGB headquarters. "Patch me through to the chairman," he shouted, "and don't go through all that authentication bullshit. He'll take my call." Moments later, Chairman Murin's voice came over the radio. "The Mriya didn't land," Drygin roared.

"What do you mean? Did it arrive from—?"

"Yes," Drygin interrupted, "but it aborted and took off again." For a few seconds, he heard only Murin's breathing over the phone.

"Go straight to the Kremlin," Murin ordered. "I'll meet you there."

* * *

Atcho looked back at Ivan. "How's the pilot?"

"He's coming to. He'll be mad as hell."

"He'll live. Give the radio operator that special phone number you have."

The copilot looked over questioningly. "You aren't terrorists?"

Atcho ignored the question. "Tell your radio operator that I want to speak to the man who answers that number, on a secure channel. You'll be able to hear the conversation."

The copilot relayed the message. Then he told Atcho, "The tower wants to know what we're doing." The plane continued to climb, headed for cruising altitude.

"Tell them we'll fly due west until we speak with the man who answers that phone. We flew out on a full tank, right?"

The copilot nodded. A few minutes later, Atcho saw motion out the left windshield. A MiG pulled alongside. Another appeared on the opposite side. Both pilots scrutinized the Mriya.

"Copilot, when are we going to get our phone call?"

"It's coming in now."

"Good. Set it up so that the entire crew can hear the conversation." He heard crackling in his ear, and then a voice.

"This is Mikhail Gorbachev. Who is this?" Atcho glanced over to the copilot again, saw him blanch and his eyes grow large.

"This is Atcho. Can you hear me, sir?"

"I hear you." Gorbachev was clearly irritated. "What are you doing?"

"Exactly what you asked me to do. As they say in Texas, Yermolov is hogtied and ready for roasting. We're on the Mriya."

There was silence on the other end of the line. When Gorbachev spoke again, his tone had softened. "I'm glad that you have Yermolov, but what are your plans for my airplane?"

"I'll return it. If we had landed in Moscow, your Mriya might be safe, but your government would not be."

More silence. "What will you do now?"

"Take a ride to the Azores, sir."

"I see." He was quiet a moment. "And you need me to clear the airspace ahead of you?"

"Exactly. I'm sure Mr. Reagan will help. It would shorten flight time if we could turn south, and fly over Europe."

In his office at the Kremlin, Gorbachev paced with his phone to his ear. He had been seated at his desk when the call came in. He heard a knock on his door. Nestor Murin opened it and peered inside. Gorbachev indicated for Murin to wait outside.

The Mriya cruised on autopilot. Atcho stood and glanced at the copilot. The man regarded him with awe. Zhukov recovered and rose slowly to his feet.

Intending to move out of the way so that Zhukov could reclaim his seat, Atcho swung around. Seven sets of eyes stared at him. Ivan's expression changed to relief. Sofia still leaned against the back wall, sweat soaked, looking beleaguered. She shot Atcho a weak grin and a thumbs-up.

Ivan and Rafael put their weapons away. Zhukov took his seat with a disgruntled, no-nonsense attitude, but made no protest.

Gorbachev's voice came back over the radio. "What are you doing with Borya Yermolov?"

Atcho looked back and forth between Rafael and Ivan. "Following orders. President Reagan wants Yermolov delivered to him."

"That's my airplane," Gorbachev protested angrily. He managed to sound both exasperated and dignified.

"I understand, sir. I have orders."

Gorbachev was momentarily silent. "There'll be repercussions."

Ivan and Rafael wore blank expressions. Atcho glanced at the crew. They appeared anxious. "Sorry, sir. That's above my pay grade. Unless you want to shoot us out of the sky, we're going to the Azores. You can take it up with Mr. Reagan."

Gorbachev was silent again for several seconds. "Take care of my airplane," he snapped, and the phone clicked off.

* * *

After Gorbachev hung up, he dialed another number and issued orders. Then he opened the door for Murin. A colonel he did not know accompanied him. They crossed to the conference area. Before they had taken their seats, Murin faced him.

"Sir, we have two urgent matters to discuss. The first concerns the Mriya. As you know, it was scheduled to arrive today."

Gorbachev regarded him with a cold stare. "Yes. There's been a problem. I just spoke with the flight crew."

Murin's surprise showed. "Can you fill me in?"

"It's resolved." Gorbachev's voice was like ice.

Murin studied the general secretary, finding him curiously resolute. He indicated the colonel who accompanied him and chose his words carefully. "This is Colonel Drygin of the KGB Border Troops in Novosibirsk," he said. "He is a direct report to Lieutenant-General Fierko, the commanding general."

Gorbachev regarded Drygin coolly. "Why is he here?"

"This could take a while," Murin replied. "May we sit down?"

Twenty minutes later, Gorbachev summarized. "I understand," he told Murin in clipped tones. "Yermolov intended to execute a coup. Fierko coordinated the activity, is that correct?" Murin nodded. "Colonel Drygin uncovered the conspiracy, and brought it to you?"

"Yes, Comrade. Yermolov and Fierko are both on the Mriya. Fierko had set up a security mechanism to provide safe passage from the aircraft directly to the Lubyanka."

"And what was to happen to you?"

Murin shrugged. "You know how these things go."

Gorbachev scrutinized both men. "We owe Colonel Drygin our gratitude," he said perfunctorily. He stood and shook Drygin's hand. "With Fierko's departure, opportunities for officers loyal to the Soviet Union and the Party will open up. Was there something else?"

Murin also rose to his feet. "No. I need to attend to the Mriya."

"That situation is taken care of," Gorbachev replied. His mouth smiled, but his eyes did not. His voice was steely. "You take care of rounding up conspirators." His eyes glinted. "Bring Fierko to me. You'll find him in the Azores."

"The Azores?" Murin asked, startled. "What about Yermolov?"

"That's not your concern. Show yourselves out."

49

Collins pressed a button on the television remote to see what might be on that he could watch for more than five seconds. Finding nothing interesting, he rose from the couch and plodded into the kitchen. He was about to pull another beer from the refrigerator when he heard a knock on the door, and Ronald Reagan strode in. Burly followed close behind, but maintained a neutral expression.

"Sorry to barge in. I've got news you might like to hear."

"I'm honored. What's the news?"

Reagan tossed his head. "We got him, Tony. Your gambit worked. We got him."

* * *

Zane McFadden found the ambassador in a corner of the crowded bunker. "It's over, sir. We can return to normal routine." He grinned. "The rogue general is all trussed up, the bomb's burnt to a crisp, and they're on their way to the Azores."

The ambassador clambered off the floor. "Thank you."

* * *

When the Mriya touched down at Lajes Air Base in the Azores, two Soviet officers were there to arrest Fierko. They stripped him of rank, and led him off the Mriya in handcuffs. The loadmaster rejoined his crew.

A US Marine general took Yermolov into custody. Four stout MPs lifted him onto a gurney, and a medic field-treated his wounds. They wheeled him past Atcho and his companions as they stood on the tarmac.

Yermolov was conscious. As he looked about with eyes dulled by morphine, his glance landed on Sofia. "Ms. Stahl," he crooned. "Not quite the party we had last time we met." He laughed uncontrollably. His view shifted to Atcho, and his eyes filled with fury. Then he relaxed into an air of futility. "This isn't finished," he chortled in the throes of delirium. "I promise, it's not finished."

Ivan leaned over Yermolov. "Just like you told me last year?" His contempt was visceral. "Don't ever threaten me or my family again. Where I'm going, I'll own my own gun, and so will my wife and son."

"Get him out of here," Atcho told the MPs. He turned to the Marine general. "Where are you taking him?"

"Where he won't see the light of day."

The MPs wheeled Yermolov to a waiting Seahawk helicopter. Soon, they disappeared over the horizon of the blue Atlantic.

* * *

After a day and night of military travel, a helicopter brought the four companions to the White House. Ivan had been quiet for most of the trip. At first Atcho had attributed his silence to exhaustion, but each time Atcho or Sofia looked at him, they saw that the Russian stared into nothing.

"It'll be OK," Atcho told him. "We take care of our own."

"Speak for yourself," Rafael jibed, jabbing Ivan in his side. "I still don't like you."

Ivan smiled wanly. "You're not my shot of vodka either," he retorted, and punched Rafael's knee. Then he stared once again into the distance.

On arrival, a Marine led them through a maze of halls. A boy lounged far down a corridor. He was blond and slender, and he looked athletic. He glanced up when he heard the approaching group. His eyes widened, and he ran toward them. *"Papa!"* he yelled. *"Mama, eto Papa!"*

Next to Atcho, Ivan lifted his head. "Kirill?" he called. "Lara?"

Lara burst into the hall. She stared at them. Then she ran headlong, threw her arms around Ivan's neck, and wept.

Atcho and Sofia stood to one side with Rafael to give the family space. Atcho felt a tap on his shoulder. Burly stood there, grinning. "You still mad?"

Atcho bear-hugged his big friend. "I'll get over it," he said. Then, Burly pointed down the hall. Ronald Reagan strode toward them with his entourage.

Sofia tugged on Atcho's sleeve. "Hey, mister," she said. "You need to know something before things get exciting again." She paused to be sure she had his full attention, her eyes gleaming with mischief. "If you ever try to get away from me again, you're dead." He spun around to take her into his arms.

50

Murin rose from his chair to greet Drygin. "Congratulations on your promotion to major general." He poured two glasses of vodka.

"Thank you. This comes as a surprise."

"It's well deserved. We'll need a replacement for the commander of KGB Border Troops in Novosibirsk." He did not mention Fierko. Drygin left the subject untouched.

Murin turned on a television. "This report might interest you."

Drygin nodded absently as the screen blinked on. Two reporters faced into the camera. Drygin read the English subscripts.

"Our guest this evening is Tony Collins, investigative reporter for the *Washington Herald*." The female news anchor turned to face Collins. "You scooped us all. That was quite a headline." She held up a copy of the current edition. "MAJOR SHAKEUP IN SOVIET UNION."

"This article is incredible. You talk of purging key figures, including the commanding general of the KGB Border Troops and the ambassador to Cuba. Even the Soviet Army's top commander was replaced by..." She looked at her notes. "...Colonel General Kutuzov, and he will be promoted to the highest rank." She stopped and looked at him. "How did you get this story?"

Collins leaned back with a wan smile. "We have good people."

The news anchor pressed on. "A few days ago, your articles about Rasputin seemed like human-interest stories, so their appearance on the front pages of Soviet newspapers caused a sensation. Did they have anything to do with today's news?"

Collins grinned like a Cheshire cat. "Ah, Rasputin. Who knew what chaos an obscure Siberian mystic would unleash on humanity?" His grin disappeared. "Lucky for us, tough people risk life and limb to keep the rest of us safe." He looked steadily into the camera. "We owe you our thanks."

The news anchor picked up again. "In other Soviet news, Russian Orthodox Church leaders celebrated Mr. Gorbachev's loosening of religious freedoms; and Moscow hailed the goodwill flight across Europe of its new Antonov 225 Mriya heavy-lift cargo jet as a success. All that amidst rumors of a nuclear scare. Stay tuned."

Murin turned off the television. "What did you think of that?"

Drygin swirled his drink while taking time to formulate a response. "It's difficult to know what to think. What did you think?"

Murin peered at him over his glasses. "You're always an enigma," he said. He swirled his drink. "As a dry run, the entire exercise was worthwhile. We learned many lessons."

"A dry run?" Drygin's face showed rare astonishment.

Murin nodded. "The old days are gone. A coup in today's Soviet Union requires a dress rehearsal. It's such a complex operation. Friends and foes have to be identified, authorities compromised, nuclear protocols tested, world reaction gauged..."

"Do you mean that Yermolov—"

Murin scoffed. "He was never in the cards. Who was going to listen to a man who claimed joint ancestry of both the last tsar and that pop star mystic?" His disdain showed. "To run a superpower? Besides, he lived outside the country all those years. Who could trust him? I needed you here to arrest him when he tried to execute the coup."

Drygin hid his astonishment. "And then who would have been the general secretary?"

Murin smiled inscrutably. "I guess we'll never know."

Drygin swirled his drink slowly as he contemplated. "What about the nuclear device? How did Yermolov get it? If Atcho had not had that NukeX—"

"Ah, Atcho," Murin muttered. "We keep underestimating that man. He gave Yermolov a run for his money, and he nearly cost us an airplane." He scanned Drygin's puzzled face. "We don't know how Yermolov got the bomb."

Drygin stared. "We don't know? Do we have any idea at all?"

Murin shook his head. "No," he said grimly. "That's an open question and maybe an open danger. We're still working on it."

"What was Yermolov going to do with it?"

"Blackmail, I'm sure. As the Americans say, it was his ace in the hole against me. I have to admit, I didn't see it coming."

"What about the ancestry documents. Were they real?"

Murin shrugged. "He always had them. I don't know where he got them. He left them for me to deliver if he ever needed to escape."

Drygin contemplated that. "So, is it possible that they were real?"

"I suppose anything is possible."

Drygin let that sink in, and then asked his next question cautiously. "Will Gorbachev retaliate against you?"

Murin arched his eyebrows. "I'm sure he received reports that I was involved," he said dryly. "He has no way to confirm them. The fact that he didn't inform me that Yermolov was on the Mriya with the bomb is significant. Fierko gave a full confession without implicating anyone above himself. He knows he would be better off dead than giving me up. Besides, he expects me to rescue him. Jeloudov too.

"If Gorbachev comes after me, his precious election will be out the window." He squinted at Drygin. "Never rule out the unthinkable, that he knew about the conspiracy from the start. What better way to lure a megalomaniac into a trap than open the doors for his ambition?"

Drygin's expression showed atypical puzzlement. "Are we still talking about Gorbachev?"

Murin chuckled. He studied Drygin's discomfiture. "The real benefit was identifying Yermolov's support. Otherwise, we could have taken him in Cuba.

"In any event, elevating Kutuzov to command the army will insulate both of us. No one will take on both the KGB and the Soviet military at the same time. Gorbachev was weakened by the situation, and won't dare question Kutuzov. And, the Politburo affirmed my innocence. Having friends on the inside always helps." He took another swallow of his drink. "But, you can never know for sure what the future holds." His tone was one of finality, as if shelving the subject. He smiled broadly and held up an outstretched hand.

Drygin kept his seat. "Sir, just two more questions?"

Murin looked impatient, but retracted his hand. "Just two."

"What about my men? What will happen to them?"

Murin stared at him without expression. "Ah, yes. *Your* men." He swirled his drink. "They were very loyal to you, weren't they?" Without waiting for an answer, he sniffed and replied, "No worries about them. They will be disbanded and returned to regular units. What's your other question?"

Drygin chose not to press the issue, and changed to his last subject. "Would Yermolov's tenets work: restoring military strength, clamping down on political dissent, and loosening economic freedom?"

To Drygin's surprise, Murin threw his head back and laughed, almost uncontrollably. "Ha, ha! That was the funniest part of the whole episode." He took a breath to control his mirth. "Yermolov and I dreamed those up in a bar one night when we were both drunk." Still red-faced from laughing, he faced Drygin. "No one in his right mind would believe those 'tenets.'" He spat out the word. "Only a certain kind of man could make them work." He lifted his glass in the air. "We'd need another Rasputin!"

Drygin took in Murin's response without emotion. Then he rose, and the two men shook hands. "Now, General," Murin said, "it's time for you to come out of deep cover."

Drygin looked at him sharply. "I don't know what you mean."

"You know very well what I mean. You've operated in the shadows long enough. As of this moment, you will take on your own name, Comrade Vladimir Putin."

EPILOGUE

December 1991 – A village outside of Paris, France

Collins studied the man sitting across from him. He seemed eerily familiar, but Collins was sure they had never met before. The man was small and nervous, and he eyed the reporter with a sheepish countenance mixed with guilt. Then, he looked around at his companions, who bore similar expressions. They concentrated their worried stares on Collins.

"This is dangerous for us," the man said. "We could still be killed."

"Don't be afraid of me," Collins replied. "It's been three years since all that happened. No one knows I'm here. I want to understand why you produced that bomb? What did you hope to accomplish?"

Collins had spent many months investigating gaps in the Atcho/Rasputin episode. Sources were sometimes willing, sometimes reluctant to cooperate, but with cajoling, patience, and being an irreverent pest, he extracted the entire story. This was the last unknown detail.

He had returned to Paris months ago and sought out the tavern where the unfortunate CIA officer had first spotted Yermolov. With much patience, he identified and met the Rasputin followers that had been there with him that fateful night—all except the one who made and delivered the bomb.

After many evenings and pitchers of beer, he gained their trust and learned the name of the bomb-maker. After many more nights and more beer, he convinced them to bring him to the tavern.

Obviously reluctant to speak, the man sat quietly. The heavy smell of fish soup hung in the air. "You're familiar with the legend of Rasputin and the beginning of the Soviet empire?" he asked at last.

Collins nodded. "I've learned a lot in the past three years."

"You know my background? I am a retired nuclear physicist."

"Your friends told me. They said that at first you refused to make the bomb. What made you change your mind?"

The man nodded. "I was a refugee in this country, as were my companions." He took a draught of his beer and looked around at his circle of friends in the booth. "We all came from Russia, and most of our parents knew Rasputin in Moscow. Our families fled during the Russian Revolution." He seemed to hesitate before going on. "My family went to the Ukraine. My parents were executed right in front of me during Stalin's purges. Shot through the head. I escaped and came here as a boy."

The pain of remembrance was plain on the man's face. As Collins watched him, he again sensed that strange familiarity. "Were you seeking revenge?"

The man smiled wanly. "I suppose that's partly true, but keep in mind that I could have built the bomb at any time. The request came from General Yermolov." He scanned the anxious faces of his friends. "We are not ignorant peasants seeking the return of a legend," he said abruptly, and leaned forward. "Did you ever meet the general?"

Collins nodded. "A few times, many years ago while he was living in the United States. I interviewed him, and of course I've seen many photos of him."

"Then look at me."

Startled, Collins stared at the man. "Excuse me?"

"Look at me." When Collins returned only a bewildered gaze, the man went on. "Rasputin's sexual escapades were well known. He left children behind."

Understanding dawned. Collins peered closer—and saw in a flash an older, altered version of General Paul Clary's face, of Borya Yermolov's face.

Now he peered intently at the man. "Are you saying that you are descended from Rasputin, and so is Yermolov? That you're cousins?"

The man nodded. "Distant cousins. I guess it's to my shame that I built the bomb." He burned rebellious eyes into Collins. "I'll tell you honestly, I hoped for him to succeed. I even hoped he might blow up the Kremlin." He glared in defiance. "I don't apologize for that hope. The bomb, maybe; but not the hope." He sank back in his seat.

They sat there a while longer, staring into their beers, Collins and this group of Rasputin followers, including their nuclear bomb-maker. Then, they stirred as if to depart. The retired physicist started to rise.

"One more question, if you don't mind," Collins said.

The man settled back again into his seat. "Go ahead."

"Where did you get the materials to make the bomb?"

The old man smiled slightly, and raised tired eyes to meet Collins'. "Maybe another time." With that, he rose to his feet, and left the tavern.

VORTEX: BERLIN

During the final days of a crumbling Soviet empire, Atcho discovers a dark conspiracy.

Behind the scenes, powerful men have set plans in motion. Pulling strings to keep the Iron Curtain intact.

Even if it means setting off a nuclear weapon.

But as Atcho fights through an onslaught of attacks, he learns something shocking about the conspirators...

His own wife might be one of them.

Get your copy today at
severnriverbooks.com

AUTHOR'S NOTE

The story you have just read is historical fiction based on some actual events. What follows below is fact.

Mikhail Gorbachev, General Secretary of the Soviet Union, left Moscow to enjoy a vacation at his dacha on the Black Sea in Crimea on August 4, 1991. At the time, he faced increasing opposition from hardline communist leaders to his policies of *glasnost* and *perestroika*. He claimed that those policies would bring about political and economic restructuring, and greater transparency and accountability in government.

Gorbachev had signed an agreement with Soviet republics that decentralized national government and allowed them more autonomy. Hardliners feared that the agreement would lead to the dissolution of the Soviet Union. The chairman of the KGB formed a "Gang of Eight" consisting of highly placed Soviet officials, and on August 17, he flew to Crimea to meet with Gorbachev.

The KGB chairman's objective was to require the general secretary to either sign documents establishing a state of emergency during which "order" would be restored, or to resign. When Gorbachev refused both alternatives, he was placed under house arrest. The KGB cut his communication lines, the state press reported that he was sick, and an emergency government was announced.

Gorbachev defeated the coup attempt, but it so weakened the Soviet government that on Christmas Day 1991, Gorbachev resigned as general secretary. The next day, the Soviet Union was voted out of existence. Another casualty of those events was the KGB itself, which officially ceased to exist.

ACKNOWLEDGMENTS

There are so many people to thank, beginning with my
5th through 7th grade teacher, Irene Fisk (RIP), who forced academic excellence on me despite my most egregious attempts to avoid it. Then my
beloved wife, Barbara, and our great kids, who suffered through keeping
noise down in a cramped apartment while I eked out my first novel.

For *Rasputin's Legacy,* special mention needs to be made of the following
people for their wonderful contributions: Carmine Zozzora, Bill Thompson, Anita Paulsen, Margee Harwell, Bob Jackson, John Shephard, Joe
Galloway, Benghazi hero Kris "Tanto" Paronto, Lieutenant General
(Retired) Rick Lynch, West Virginia Secretary of State Mac Warner, a friend
who must remain anonymous, Christian Jackson, Tom Mitchell, Angela
Beck, Barbara Hall, Bobby Hall, Rich Trotter, Larry Acker, Rand Ballard,
Sam Stolzoff, Jim Vaughn, Candy Silcott, Ralph Masi, John Dinnell, Lance
Gatling, Stuart Stirrat, Mandy Walkden-Brown, and Dr. Osama Shams.

My sincere gratitude goes out to these wonderful people who participated
in one form or another to bringing *Rasputin's Legacy* into publication.

ABOUT THE AUTHOR

Lee Jackson is the Wall Street Journal bestselling author of The Reluctant Assassin series and the After Dunkirk series. He graduated from West Point and is a former Infantry Officer of the US Army. Lee deployed to Iraq and Afghanistan, splitting 38 months between them as a senior intelligence supervisor for the Department of the Army. Lee lives and works with his wife in Texas, and his novels are enjoyed by readers around the world.

Sign up for Lee Jackson's newsletter at
severnriverbooks.com
LeeJackson@SevernRiverBooks.com

Printed in the United States
by Baker & Taylor Publisher Services